Notes on Love

Seven Deadly Sinclairs: #1

Naaz Spencer

Cover design by _Books and Moods_
Interior formatting by _AJ Wolf Graphics_
Editing by _Heart Full of Reads Editing Services_

Published by Naaz Spencer

Trigger Warning

This book contains topics that some may find triggering. These include discussion of loss, grief, suicide, infertility, mature language and sexually explicit scenes.
If you are uncomfortable reading these situations, then Notes on Love may not be for you.
Reader discretion is advised.

Dedication

Ellie – you are a superwoman and inspired this story more than you'll ever know. Never let anyone make you believe otherwise.

Author's Note

The Seven Deadly Sinclairs series is about seven brothers each representing a sin and their journey to find love. The books are a series of interconnected standalones and can be read in any order but for the best understanding should be read in numbered order.

Seth Sinclair – Wrath
Aiden Sinclair – Lust
Noah Sinclair – Gluttony
Ethan Sinclair – Greed
Warren Sinclair – Pride
Mason Sinclair – Sloth
Zane Sinclair – Envy

Chapter One

- Seth

When I stormed out of the office six months ago, blinded by white hot rage, I never intended to return. I was sick of everything in my life. The job. The people. Myself. But half a year away, flitting from country to country and screwing whatever woman caught my eye had not cured the fury that ricocheted through the chambers of my heart.

Despite what the headlines reported, I was miserable. The expensive dinners and playboy lifestyle couldn't paper over the fact that I was thirty-two and my life had fallen apart in the most public fashion. The coverage had been relentless and suffocating, but no matter how many miles away I was from London, it continued to follow me.

Eventually, I decided I was better back in the city. Back in the office, buried under paperwork and meetings. At least it was more fulfilling than whatever the fuck I had been attempting the last few months.

No amount of alcohol and pussy had healed the deep wounds that Anna left. Nothing had tipped the scales of my mood out of vitriolic and towards something more palatable.

Early Friday morning, an hour before the official workday began, I slipped into the building that housed Sinclair Technologies and savoured the peace of the empty space. The electronic buzz echoed through the foyer as I swiped my access card and took the lift to the top floor.

This was the calm before the storm. A chance for me to settle in and find my bearings again. Dad had continued to run the business during my absence and informed me that there was a stack of minutes from meetings from the past few months for me to familiarise myself with. They needed to be addressed before I could step comfortably back into my position, priming myself to takeover. Without anything to distract me, I could let work become my sole focus. At least the business wouldn't humiliate me and leave a gaping hole in my life.

As I stepped onto the floor, I caught sight of Kirsty. My personal assistant was a middle-aged woman with a nervous disposition who always came across as hesitant to speak to me. She kept out of my way and most communication happened primarily via email. The arrangement suited us both. Ten years of working together and there was yet to be a murder.

It surprised me to see that she was in the office so early, especially when she didn't know I was planning to stop by today. It had been a last-minute decision. Dad probably kept her busy with some tasks.

"Mr Sinclair," she said, seeing me. Her blue eyes grew wider as I approached. "I didn't expect you to be in today."

I spent the past four days at home, building up the patience to walk out the door and back into the office after my spectacular exit. There would be questions and photographs and…

The vein in my temple pulsed at the thought.

"I didn't realise I had to run it past you, Kirsty," I snarled.

Her face fell. "No. Of course you don't. Sorry."

I strode past her, craving the sanctuary of my office, but something made me stop.

In all the years I'd worked here, the doors to every office on the top floor remained closed. None of the company owners we took under our wing liked to be disturbed. But the door opposite my room was wide open and the potent scent of patchouli wafted out of the space and into the corridor.

Stepping into the doorway of the room, the sight horrified me. The standard issued cream walls had been painted a shockingly obnoxious tangerine and an alarming number of sticky notes covered the space behind the desk. An incense burner stood next to the monitor, and a stick dropped ash into the tray below as tendrils of smoke drifted lazily into the air. On the other side of the monitor was a large vase of sunflowers in full bloom.

"Kirsty!" I yelled, stepping out of the room. "What the fuck is this?"

Kirsty hurried around her desk, brushing her hair out of her face, and stood in the glass doorway that separated the assistants' desks from the offices. "It's Kiran's office, Mr Sinclair," she answered nervously.

Kieran. Dad had briefly filled me in on the latest addition to the business. He had been following the name Kieran Jeffrey because his interest was piqued by artificial intelligence. The AI pie was something he had been passionate about for some time, but I was yet to stick my fingers into it. However, it looked like Dad had made his move while I was away. Business didn't stop for anyone. Not even a Sinclair in meltdown mode.

Glancing back into the office, I grimaced. I would have been excited for an introduction to Kieran, but if he was as obnoxious as the room, I highly doubted that we would get along.

Who the fuck painted an office orange?

"Morning, Kiran!" Kirsty said brightly.

Stepping out into the corridor again, my gaze fell on a petite woman who made me double take and my mouth ran dry. She was dressed in a pair of yoga pants that hugged her thighs and hips, and the brown skin of her torso peeked out from the space beneath her cropped shirt. When she turned her head to look at me, I noticed full dark lips and a gold nose ring on the left side of her nose.

My cock twitched happily behind the zipper of my trousers as she walked down the corridor towards me with confidence, long black ponytail swinging. She adjusted the duffle bag on her shoulder, accidentally hitching her shirt up higher and revealing more skin.

"Are you looking for something?" I asked when she came closer.

"No," she replied, flashing me a smile that lifted her features.

"Then how can I help you?"

"By moving so I can get into my office."

"This is Kieran's office," I informed her.

"No," she said, smile not faltering. "It's *Kiran's* office. K-i- r-a- n. I'm Kiran. Nice to meet you."

Kiran stuck out a hand, gold bangle dangling off her wrist. I stared at it for a moment before looking back at her face.

"Kiran," I repeated, feeling a modicum of embarrassment for messing up something so simple.

It quickly morphed into anger as I realised this woman was the owner of the bright office behind me. She owned the company that specialised in AI that we had absorbed with a hefty investment. But how was that possible? She looked like the furthest thing from a business professional.

"Are you planning on introducing yourself?" she asked, but there was no hostility behind the question. "Although, I think I could wager a guess. Seth, right? You look a lot like your father. Younger, obviously." Kiran laughed. It was a light, melodic sound that flooded the corridor.

"It's Mr Sinclair," I corrected her, feeling the irritation prickle in my throat.

She shook her head, raven ponytail swaying with the movement. "I don't like formalities," she said, shooing me with her hand. "Plus, we're equals here."

I stumbled out of the way, and she breezed into her office, taking a deep breath and exhaling. She dropped the bag by the desk and sank into her chair.

"We're not equals," I said, following her into her office against my instincts. "You work for me."

"Correct," she said, shaking her mouse. "But you also need me and my team. Partnerships work best when we can be on an even footing. I don't expect you to call me Miss Jafri. I certainly don't call your father Mr Sinclair. I think Seth will do fine. And again, it's Kiran. K-i-r-a-n. Not Kieran. K-i-e-r-a-n. You're not the first to mix that up, so don't worry about apologising."

There was a kind smile on her face as she continued to correct my earlier mistake. I was about to snap at her when there was a knock on the door.

"Good morning, Arthur," Kiran said.

"Dad," I greeted him.

Arthur Sinclair was the mastermind behind Sinclair Technologies. With a voracious appetite for tech and a keen eye for trends, Dad had landed on Forbes billionaires list for the past three decades. Even as he crept towards his mid-sixties, he showed no signs of slowing down. Dad would never sit back on a yacht and relax. He was still brimming with ideas. Still watching the market and sending daily emails. It came as no surprise that we'd acquired a new company while I was on leave.

"Nice to have you back," he said to me. "I see you've both met. Has he played nice, Kiran?"

"A credit to you and your wife, Arthur," she replied.

Dad huffed a laugh. "I know that's a lie. How was yoga this morning?"

"I was late and caught the last half of the session. Left hip is still tight, but that's my fault."

"Still looser than mine," he said, rubbing the spot.

"I told you, come along with me."

"Celeste would never let me live it down if I tried to get in trousers that tight. And I am not made to bend like that."

"Not yet."

"Dad," I cut across the conversation sharply. "Can we have a word? In private."

"Would you mind, Kiran?" Dad asked her.

"Carry on," she said, waving us off with a polite smile. "I need to get changed."

As we walked out of the room, Kiran shut her door then closed the blinds as we walked across the corridor into my office. The shattered glass had been replaced and a brand-new computer sat on the desk. The hole in the wall had been patched up and painted over in the standard cream colour that didn't make my eyes want to bleed.

"What is she?" I asked once the door clicked shut.

"I'm sorry?" Dad asked, taking a seat without hesitation and crossing his ankle over his knee.

"Kiran."

"I think you'll like her," he said, eyes bright. "She's got a lot of ideas, and I'm excited about her future with the company."

"What's her worth?" I asked.

Dad raised an eyebrow. "I feel that may fall into the same bracket as asking a woman her age."

"I want to know more about what we've invested into. There's nothing wrong with that."

"It's in the paperwork," Dad replied. "Or why don't you set up a meeting with her and ask her yourself?"

Because I felt I might throw up if I had to sit in her office with its luminescent walls.

"You hired her. I trust she's not a complete psychopath," I said.

"Time will tell."

"And I have enough on my plate."

He nodded at me. "Yes, you do." Rising from the chair, he said, "Are you sure you're ready to be back?"

Dad wasn't on about the office, but the country. He wanted to know that I was stable enough to be on the same island as Anna without losing my shit again. The statements that Tiffy, who handled my press releases, sent out would have been signed off by Dad in the wake of all the destruction I caused before fleeing.

"Yes," I told him firmly.

He clapped a hand on my shoulder. "Take it slow. Ease yourself back into it."

"I'm perfectly capable of getting back up to speed."

"I know you are." Dad tapped twice on my chest. "But heartbreak sometimes catches you off guard. Show yourself some kindness, son."

Dad left my room, whistling to himself and forgetting to close the door behind him. Grumbling to myself, I walked over to it and prepared to slam it shut when the door opposite opened.

Kiran had changed out of her gym clothes and into a deep green dress. She bent at the waist, sticking a stopper in the gap under her door to keep it open and drawing my eyes to her pert ass. For the second time that morning, my dick stirred. My mind dived into the gutter with minimal encouragement.

If Kiran wasn't working here, she would be exactly the type of woman I would take home to satisfy my every craving and curiosity. I'd destroy her purely because I wanted to, and I could. Her laughter earlier had been sweet, but there was more that could tumble from those lips if you knew how to coax it out of her.

She straightened up and brushed her loose hair behind her left ear. The flash of gold stood out on her ring finger, and I bit the insides of my cheeks. The fact she was married irritated me more than the paint or the assumption that I would apologise over getting her name wrong. She had succeeded in an area I failed, and it stung worse than expected.

The smile she offered me was the last straw.

"I hope you don't burn that all the time," I snapped, gesturing past her to the incense.

She glanced over her shoulder and then back at me. "No. Sometimes it's lavender. It's a calming scent. I'm sure it'll help your ass from bouncing off the walls."

What did she just say?

Without another word, I slammed the door to my office shut with such force that the frame shook.

Fuck her and her lavender.

Chapter Two

- Kiran

"I'm around the corner from the building. I'll be five more minutes," I said.

The phone was wedged between my shoulder and my ear. One of my hands precariously balanced a coffee holder with two takeaway cups, and with the other hand, I searched around for my access card. I was already running late, and apparently punctuality was something Seth Sinclair appreciated.

"Hurry," Kirsty mumbled down the line.

Cutting the call, I stuffed my phone into my coat pocket and picked up the pace. As I burst through the doors to the building, I almost dropped the coffee, and my heart fell to my stomach. Thankfully, luck was on my side, and I avoided the accident.

Once the doors to the lift closed, I leant against the wall and let out a deep breath. I hated rushing in the morning because it set the tone for the day.

The bell in the lift chimed, and I pushed myself away from the wall and stepped out onto the floor. Kirsty shot me a look of urgency from her seat behind her desk while the other assistants on the floor continued with their work.

"Where is he?" I asked, coming up to her.

"In his office. He has another meeting at nine-thirty," Kirsty told me.

I pulled a face before jogging down the corridor. "Thank you, Kirsty," I called over my shoulder.

Deciding against stopping in my room, I knocked hard on Seth's door.

"Come in!" he barked.

When I pushed open the door, Seth was at his desk with a crease in his brow.

It had been a week since he'd returned to the office and he had a permanent scowl plastered on his face. He barely graced the floor with his presence, and I assumed it might be because he was catching up after his sabbatical.

"You're late," he said, looking up from his screen.

The first thing I noticed about my new boss, other than his intimidatingly towering form, was his eyes. They were a shocking blue colour that reminded me of the arctic. Completely void and without a hint of warmth. They pinned me to the spot, and I offered him a smile.

"I brought coffee as an apology," I said, holding up the cups. Walking over to his desk, I popped it out of the holder and placed it in front of him. "Americano. No sugar. No milk. Kirsty told me that's what you usually get."

Stubble lined his jaw and there were shadows under his eyes. I wanted to ask if he was okay, but we were yet to foster that type of relationship. Unlike everyone else I'd met since moving here, Seth was icy, and I didn't know how to thaw him.

He eyed the cup on the table as I dropped into the chair, unbuttoning my coat and shrugging it off. My heart continued to pound, and I took in a deep breath, trying to find my calm again.

"You had time to stop for coffee?" he asked.

12

"I put in a mobile order before I leave the house, so I just have to collect it. I had a few things that needed to be sorted this morning and —"

"A lay in?"

"Sorry?"

"Or another gym class?"

"I wish," I muttered, kicking off my heels and pulling my feet up onto the chair.

Seth blinked as I shifted to sit cross-legged. "What are you doing?" he asked.

"Getting comfortable," I answered. "You called this meeting and I understand that I'm late. I'm sorry about that, but what did you want to discuss?"

"I know nothing about you," he replied.

"Not true. I asked Kirsty to give you the company portfolio."

"I got that. I'm not on about the company. I don't know *you*."

My brow furrowed. "What is it you want to know?"

"That you have no intentions of trying to screw my family over."

"You realise your dad hunted me down, right? I didn't turn to him with cap in hand. We were running fine without the Sinclair empire."

"Then why did you agree to be bought?" Seth set his elbows on the table and steepled his fingers.

He was beautiful with his angular cheekbones and sharp jawline. His skin was still bronzed from his time away and the entire look, wrapped up in a designer suit, made my heart hurry its pace. But the coolness was off-putting. Seth's personal ice palace made him less appealing the moment he opened his mouth.

"Partially bought. Because I'm not an idiot," I explained. "I know a good deal when I see one. Seth, with all due respect, I don't feel the need to explain myself to you."

"You don't?" He cocked an eyebrow.

"No. Arthur and I had a lot of discussions before any of this was finalised. Me and my team have been here almost a month with no issue, and now that you're back, you're questioning my integrity."

I always knew the transition would be hard. Overnight, I went from working for myself to having someone sit at the table with me, but I couldn't refuse Arthur Sinclair and the opportunity to work with Sinclair Technologies. They were known for taking small businesses and putting them on the map.

"I think I have every right to do that when you're working with my family," Seth said.

"Well, fuck," I replied, snapping my fingers. "Guess my plans to seduce Arthur and steal his billions are ruined now."

"This isn't funny."

"Good, because I don't find it amusing either." I drank from my cup, needing the caffeine. "Seth, I'm not a gold digger."

"Murderer?"

My heart stopped in my chest at the word and the walls closed in. I knew today was going to be a bad day.

"Intentions for blackmail?" Seth pushed.

In through the nose for four.

Hold for seven.

Out for eight.

He could rant all he wanted if it meant I could breathe.

"He built this company from the ground up. We've had issues with employees before so I'm less trusting than my old man."

Maybe there was a heart in that chest after all.

I knew little about Seth or the rest of the Sinclair brood, aside from the glimpses I caught on magazine covers in the supermarket. I'd wiped myself from social media years ago and Googling people felt dirty and wrong. Everyone should be afforded some privacy in their lives.

Everything I knew about Seth came from conversations around the office. He left after a violent outburst, destroying his office and bellowing at his dad. Half of the company liked him and his no nonsense approach to work, while the other half preferred to keep out of his way.

"Seth," I said, once the world was steady again. "I appreciate you're looking out for your family, but I have no ill intentions towards them. I'm here to work. To learn. To offer advice on an area you're not familiar with. Calling me into an early morning meeting to question my integrity is a colossal waste of time."

"For you —"

"For both of us." I flipped over my wrist and checked my watch. "Kirsty said you have a meeting at nine-thirty. Finish your coffee, sharpen your teeth, and go for them instead of me, Tin Man. If you're interested in getting to know me properly or what I do," I said, uncrossing my legs and slipping my heels back on, "my office door is always open. You don't need to book a meeting."

I stood up, gathering my coat and bag.

"I would rather it be officially on the calendar," he said icily.

"As you wish. Talk to Kirsty and she'll fit you into my schedule."

"Excuse me?"

Seth stood up from behind his desk and strode towards me. He easily towered over me by more than a foot, meaning he surpassed the six-feet mark. For the first time, I breathed in his scent. It was woody and earthy. Sweet and spicy. Agarwood. Seth smelled like home.

"Why would Kirsty know about your schedule?" he asked, folding his arms across his chest.

The white material of his shirt strained against the muscles of his arms, and I tipped my head up to look him in the eye.

"She's been my assistant while you were away. Arthur thought it would be better for her to keep busy."

A muscle in his jaw flexed, and he took another step towards me. Seth was used to intimidation tactics, but he didn't scare me. This brief interaction with him left me curious about what went on in his head.

"She's my employee. If you need an assistant, I suggest you hire one yourself," Seth gritted out through his teeth.

"Sure," I replied breezily. "I'll speak to human resources about putting an ad out this afternoon."

I'd never had a personal assistant until I moved to London, but what a godsend it had been. For the first time in years, I didn't feel like I was spreading myself thin to the point I might disappear.

I thought my response might make him smile. That might have been a stretch. Seth hadn't smiled once since he'd come back to work. But I was complying with his wishes and I expected him to relax. He could see I wasn't trying to pick a fight with him, but he remained stoic.

"Is that all?" I asked.

"Yes."

"Okay. Well, have a good day."

Turning away from him, I walked out of the room and across the corridor to my office. I searched for my access card again, carefully juggling my belongings, trying not to spill coffee and make my morning even worse.

The heat of a body radiated behind me, and a familiar scent invaded my nostrils again. I looked up to see an arm reach past me, unlocking my door. Glancing over my shoulder, Seth stared down at me, irritation colouring his features, but I noticed he held the coffee I gave him in his hand.

"Thank you," I said, struggling to find the door handle while still looking at him.

He found it first and pushed the door open. I stepped back, wanting to put some distance between us.

"Tin Man?" he asked suddenly.

I thought I'd get away with the comment.

"Figure it out," I said.

"Mr Sinclair," Kirsty called down the corridor.

"On my way!" he barked in return.

Seth gave me one last curious look before striding down the corridor. I watched him go, appreciating the view, before ducking into my office and praying the rest of the day would run smoothly.

Chapter Three

- Seth

I hissed a curse as my little toe made contact with the cardboard box in the corner of my room. The apartment I shared with Anna had been sold and the money was split before I moved into a house. An impulse purchase and much bigger than what a single person needed, but it was for show. I didn't want anyone thinking that I was wallowing in misery in another flat. No, I was moving onwards and upwards.

Tiffy had furnished most of the place. Tables, chairs, sofa. I let her decorate as I moved everything in. Unfortunately, I hadn't unpacked before taking my sabbatical, and I was yet to find the will to since I arrived back home.

Standing in front of the mirror and ignoring the dull throb in my toe, I dressed for the day. I buttoned up the white shirt and tucked it into the navy trousers, assessing myself for any creases or wrinkles.

A thought fleeted through my mind. What colour would Kiran be in today? So far, she had graced the office in yellow, purple, and green. The usual muted, monotone colours that made up work attire had escaped her and instead she chose to cycle through the rainbow.

If I thought my meeting with her might have popped a pin in her positive attitude, I was sorely mistaken.

Not only was she a walking rainbow that I couldn't help but stare at, but she laughed loud and often. The moment she stepped out of her office, she was rarely alone. Someone always appeared at her side. It pissed me off that this woman couldn't fall into line and be fucking miserable like everyone else. That was how life worked. We were all part of the machine, and she had no right to be so *happy* right under my nose.

With that thought in mind, I knotted my tie a little more vigorously and secured it in the centre of my collar.

My phone vibrated on the bed and I picked it up to see Aiden's name across the screen.

The second eldest Sinclair brother, Aiden, was the only one who had been immune to Anna's icy personality. He had the thickest skin out of all of us, and Aiden was only too happy to welcome me back home.

"What do you want?" I asked, answering the call.

"I thought you were coming to the gym this morning," he said.

"Why would you think that?"

"Because you —" Aiden sighed. "Anyone ever told you you've got a little anger issue?"

"I don't know why you'd think such a thing," I deadpanned.

"Seth, this would be a much better way to work it out than knocking someone out in the office."

"I'm not going to pick a fight with anyone."

Most people irritated me, but that didn't mean that I would resort to physical violence.

Another flurry of thoughts flickered through my mind. Paul draped himself against Kiran's door every lunch break without fail. When she went to grab tea from the kitchen, he trailed her into the room.

Okay. There might be one person I would swing for. He was behaving in an unprofessional manner, and if she lodged a complaint, then it would be more paperwork and a migraine for me.

"I want to make sure you're alright," he said.

"Are you talking as my brother or as a doctor?"

Wedging the phone between my ear and shoulder, I manoeuvred my suit jacket on and took one last look in the mirror before exiting the room.

"Both," Aiden answered. "I'm all for dipping dick into as many women as possible, but you looked so goddamn miserable in every photograph on the internet."

"My life fell apart. Did you expect me to be jumping for joy?"

"No, but amidst beautiful women and sandy beaches, you still looked like a bulldog who chewed a wasp."

"Don't you have a clinic to get to?" I snapped.

"Tell me you're going to start coming to the gym with me."

"No."

"I'm going to turn up at the office."

"I'm going to tell security to blacklist you."

"There's not a single person who hasn't succumbed to my charms yet," he said, cocksure of himself as usual.

It was a low blow, but I wanted to knock him off his pedestal, so I said, "What about Tiffy?"

"Fuck you," Aiden said, still sounding cheery. "I haven't directed my charms at Tiffy."

"Keep them away from her. We can't afford to lose her because no one else will deal with you."

"Love you too, bro."

I hung up on him, done with the conversation for now.

Walking down the stairs, I grabbed my keys and skipped out on breakfast. As I stepped out of the door, I caught sight of them with ease. Not that they tried to conceal themselves.

At the end of the drive, two people waited with cameras in hand. Large lenses were attached to the body, and the moment I closed the door, they raised and flashed. Ducking my head, I hurried to the car and my knuckles turned white as I pulled away from home.

Press might have been part of the job, but I didn't appreciate them encroaching on my home. I would need to call Tiffy and tell her to deal with it. My property was off limits.

By the time I made it to the building, I'd pulled out my phone to send a voice note to Tiffy.

"Tiffy, I need you to —"

"Hold the doors!"

My foot barely stepped over the threshold of the lift when I glanced over my shoulder to see Kiran running through the lobby. Her hair fanned out behind her and she held a coffee cup in her hand. I pressed myself against the wall to stop from being run over.

"Thanks," Kiran panted, jabbing at the button for our floor.

The doors closed, and there was a faint floral scent that was soon overtaken by the smell of synthetic sugar.

"What the hell do you drink?" I asked, eyeing the cup in her hand.

The mouth of the cup had her lipstick stain around it, dark brown and a perfectly plump imprint. I couldn't help but glance at her lips and suddenly felt the urge to loosen the knot in my tie.

"It's a cappuccino," she said, not looking at me.

She ran her tongue between her lips, and it took all my strength not to press her against the wall, stop the lift, and repeat the action myself.

"That does not smell like a cappuccino," I gritted out through my teeth.

"It has a few pumps of caramel syrup."

"What do you classify as a few?"

"More than two, but less than five," she said, looking up at me with a wry smile.

Great. She probably tasted as sweet as her personality.

The lift stopped, and she pulled her attention away from me, but I couldn't take my eyes off her. I watched her features light up as a man with thick-rimmed glasses joined us in the cramped space. He instantly pulled her into a hug that she returned, and the vein in my neck pulsed.

"I thought I was going to beat you. I was looking forward to dinner on you," he said, squeezing her and then pulling away.

"I almost didn't make it." Kiran laughed, pulling his tie playfully.

I cleared my throat, gaining their attention. It was uncomfortable to stand in a space with two people who were so familiar with each other. I didn't maintain a relationship like that with anyone in this building. And then my mind whirred, wondering if this man was her husband, and I straightened up, taking him in.

He was nothing special. Not when he was standing next to Kiran. Gangly, floppy blonde hair, and a scruff of stubble around his chin. How had this man landed a woman like her?

"Sorry," Kiran said, taking a quick swig of her coffee. "Seth, this is my second-in-command, Michael Perry. Mike, this is Seth Sinclair."

"Second in command. That's all I get from you?" Mike asked, looking offended.

I waited for the confirmation.

"I'm not introducing you as my best friend —" Kiran started.

"Of ten years," Mike interrupted her.

"— to the big boss man."

Mike shrugged and held his hand out towards me. I shook it less aggressively than I had contemplated a minute ago. Best friend. That made a lot more sense.

"Big boss man," I muttered after I let go of his hand.

But Kiran and Mike lapsed into conversation, and as we reached the top floor, they both took off together without sparing me another glance. I echoed her footsteps the whole way down the corridor, a mixture of sugar and flowery scents drifting through the air.

"Have a good meeting," I said, wanting to get a foot back into the conversation.

Kiran stood in her doorway, holding the door open and looking at me.

"Thank you, Seth," she said, smiling.

Something burnt in my chest, and I rubbed my palm across my heart.

"Have a good day," Kiran said before closing the door on me.

Chapter Four

- Kiran

A little after four in the afternoon and I could feel my energy levels had dipped to next to nothing. I spent most of the week running up and down from the office to the third floor, where my employees were situated. I'd never been the type of boss to sit back and dictate, but sometimes that meant feeling like I was running on empty.

Despite the fact that it was a Friday afternoon, I had a few hours of work left, and so I decided that tea would be a good pick-me-up.

Venturing out of my office, I walked down to the kitchen and pulled my mug out of the cupboard. It was a neon green colour and made me grin the moment I clapped eyes on it. The tea I'd brought into the kitchen was slowly dwindling, and I was glad to see that people were taking an interest in it. I popped open the box of green tea and boiled the kettle before pouring it into the mug.

"I think you're ruining the health benefits when you add in that much sugar," a deep voice said from behind me.

His words startled me and sent the spoon flying from my mug and into the air. I did my best to catch it, the warm metal burning the skin of my palm.

"Shit!" I hissed and dropped it, letting it clatter noisily to the ground.

"Shit," Seth echoed, striding across the space. He switched on the cold tap, letting the water run. "Come here."

I followed his orders, cradling my hand and looking at the bright red patch on the pale skin of my palm. When I reached the sink, I expected Seth to move out of the way, but he took my wrist and held it under the running water.

The feel of his fingers on my bare skin made my cheeks flush. I couldn't ignore that my neighbour across the corridor was devastatingly handsome. I wasn't avoiding him, but it helped to stay out of his way other than the typical hello, because Seth had some sort of wizardry that made my brain short circuit. It was a shame his personality could rival Scrooge.

"Are you okay?" he asked gruffly, eyes on my palm.

"I'll live," I replied. "It wasn't that warm."

He didn't look convinced. "What were you doing?"

"Making green tea. Do you want a cup?"

Seth's eyes flicked up to my face. Blue and ringed with black. They reminded me of an icy tundra that was framed by long, dark lashes.

"Not if you're shovelling sugar into it," he answered.

If possible, my cheeks grew warmer. "It tastes bitter otherwise."

"I think that's the point."

"I don't like it."

"Then don't drink it."

"It's meant to be good for you."

"Kiran." There was a warning in the way he said my name. "This is a circular argument."

"I won't add any sugar to yours," I told him brightly.

28

He sighed and let go of my wrist, switching off the tap. I pulled my hand away and grabbed some tissue to dry off before examining my palm.

"Do you need the first-aid kit?" Seth asked.

"No," I replied, turning my hand in the light. "Looks fine." Skirting around him, I pulled open the cupboards and looked at the range of mugs. "Which one is yours?"

The heat of his body was behind me, just like it was when he opened the door to my office after our meeting. It made my mouth run dry and my muscles tense.

"This one," he said, reaching past me and pulling down a plain white mug. When he set it on the counter, I pulled a face. "What?" Seth snapped.

"It's white," I said, picking it up.

"It's a mug, Kiran. It holds liquid."

"I know. But it's so plain."

He picked up mine and scrunched his nose. The expression made him look less like the billionaire tech mogul he was and more like the child he could have been.

"I'd rather it be plain than have this abomination," he explained.

My jaw dropped open, and I reached for my mug, but he held it out of reach. With a 'hmph', I made his tea.

"I'd rather have an abomination than be boring, Tin Man," I shot back.

"We'll have to agree to disagree."

"Seems to be our thing," I muttered, holding his mug out to him.

He regarded it for a second before turning his nose up and walking out of the kitchen with my neon abomination in his hands.

"Hey!" I called, following him out with his mug. "That's mine, and this is yours."

Seth shrugged before coming to a stop in his doorway. I almost bumped into his perfect peach but managed to stop myself. He turned on me slowly, looking down with his icy eyes, and I held his mug out to him again.

"I think I'll keep this one," he said. "It'll do you good to cut some sugar out of your life."

Seth stepped back into his office and closed the door in my face. After the shock, I balled my free hand and hammered on the door. And that fucker actually laughed. He laughed!

"Tin Man! I want my mug!" I yelled.

"Kiran, is there a problem?" Arthur asked, peeking his head out of the door to his room.

I flushed all the way from the roots of my hair to the tips of my toes. "No," I blurted.

"Are you sure?" he asked. "Has Seth done something?"

"No, no! Um, it's nothing. Thank you."

I scurried into my office with the plain white mug and prayed that I would be left alone for the rest of the evening with my bitter tea in the boring cup.

Chapter Five

- Seth

This month turned into hell. News of my return had hit the press and I couldn't avoid reporters. They appeared as I ran errands, prolonging simple tasks and aggravating me. "No comment" had become the words that I parroted just to get some peace. I hadn't seen Anna, and I had no intention of seeing her, but no one seemed to understand that.

In a bid to avoid the flock of reporters, I came into the office even earlier and left as late as I could manage.

Surely there was another Sinclair they could bother. Another brother that could give them column inches. Where was Aiden when you needed him?

Returning from lunch, a photographer whose flashbulb incessantly went off in my face had followed me back to the building. My hands balled into fists, and I felt the anger coil in my chest until I wanted to pull it back and land it across his cheek.

Thankfully, for him, the building was in sight and I slipped through the door that behaved like a barrier.

The pain radiated through my jaw as I clenched my teeth and took the lift straight up to the top floor. When the doors opened, I was greeted by the sight of three strangers standing nervously near the assistants' desks. One of them was an elderly gentleman who rested his walking stick on his lap, another was a girl with neon pink hair, a septum piercing and multiple tattoos, and the last was a man dressed sharply in a suit and clutching a folder.

"Kirsty," I asked, ignoring the three of them.

The bowl that sat on her desk momentarily distracted me. Brightly coloured lollipops filled the container, and I imagined that this had to do with the ray of sunshine we'd recently adopted into the company.

"Yes, Mr Sinclair," she asked, breaking me out of my thoughts.

"Why are there people on my floor?"

"Kiran's interviewing for a PA this afternoon."

It was difficult to ignore the frown Kirsty wore. She probably found it easier to work with Kiran than myself.

Kiran had sprinkled her pixie dust everywhere. The kitchen held a selection of herbal teas instead of just coffee, the floor always smelled of something spiced, and someone was mostly in the doorway of her office, trying to catch her attention. That last one irritated me more than I liked to admit. Paul, the owner of a healthcare analytics business, continued to stand at her door, eliciting laughs from her, forcing me to schedule an update meeting with him at the end of the month. That put the fucker back in his office.

"Where is she?" I asked.

"One of the boardrooms. She told me to send the first one down to her in ten minutes."

"If anyone looks for me, I'll be with her."

Kirsty didn't stop me as I walked away, throwing one last cursory glance at the three applicants.

Two floors below sat multiple rooms that were used for meetings, presentations, and interviews. It didn't take long for me to spot Kiran through the glass front of one of them. Her long hair was twisted up into a bun and she wore a bright yellow dress that swayed around her knees. She looked like one of the sunflowers she kept in her room. Kiran easily made herself the most colourful person in the building every single fucking day. There was no avoiding her. She was not made to blend in.

Rising from the chair, she stuck her hand out before shaking thin air. What the fuck was she playing at? I watched carefully as her mouth moved and then as she turned, I noticed a bright orange sticky note stuck to her ass.

God help me.

I walked into the room without warning, and she jumped, letting out a squeak.

"Kiran," I said. "What are you doing in here?"

Her cheeks were pink. "I was preparing for the interviews."

"By talking to yourself?"

"Would you believe one candidate is actually a spirit with excellent credentials?"

"With you? Yes."

She laughed.

Kiran did that a lot. The sound often drifted across the corridor, loud enough to be heard through my closed door. There was more than one occasion where I'd left the desk, wanting to know what or who amused her, but stopped myself from venturing out of the room.

"I get nervous," she explained. "I thought I would practise so I don't mess it up when they come down here."

After the office incident, I thought Kiran might be cautious around me or treat me with indifference, as was the case for most of the staff. But she continued to smile if she caught me in the corridor, even if I didn't have the heart to return it.

"It might help if you aren't decorated in stationery," I told her.

Without thinking, I reached out around her, aiming for the sticky note. A sharp pain radiated in my stomach as her fist met my abs with surprising force.

"What are you doing?" she hissed.

Doubled over, I held up the tiny square of paper. "You must have sat on this," I mumbled. "I'm not sure how well that would have gone down during interviews."

"Shit!" Her eyes grew wide. "I'm so sorry, Seth. I thought… You don't know who's a creep these days."

I sucked in a deep breath and straightened up slowly. "Are you sure you only take yoga?"

"I took a few self-defence classes last year. Are you okay?"

The concern was written all over her face and it made something deep inside me stir. I hadn't seen someone look at me like that in such a long time. Like they actually cared how I might feel.

"I'm fine," I told her. "I think it was the shock of the assault."

"Assault seems a little harsh," she argued. "What are you doing down here?"

"I came to find you. Have you seen your candidates?"

"Mhm," she said, pinching the note from my fingers and going back to the file on the table. "Spotted them earlier."

"They were the top applicants?"

"They were the applicants that I thought would work best with me."

"Kiran, those are two very different specifications."

"I know," she said airily.

"Who's on your panel?"

"Gareth is coming up from human resources. Just the two of us."

"I think I should sit in as well."

She turned back to face me. "I don't think that's necessary. Aren't you busy this afternoon?"

There were a few spreadsheets that needed looking at before the quarterly meeting, but it could wait. My growing concern was that Kiran would employ someone that would waste her time and leave her looking for another assistant in a few weeks.

"There's nothing pressing," I lied.

Kiran pushed herself up so that she sat on the edge of the table. Her dress slid a few inches higher and my gaze ran over her thighs. A flurry of thoughts ran rampant in my mind, none of which would make her believe I'd pulled the note from her dress out of kindness.

"You're not happy with my choices, are you?" Kiran said, cocking her head to the side.

"I didn't see their applications."

"Exactly. But I did. And I spoke to each of them informally."

"What?"

"I like to speak to people before I interview them. All the formalities make people nervous, so you never get who they really are. A video chat before can give you a better idea. It's how I've always hired my staff."

"Do you do anything traditionally?"

"I put my knickers on one leg at a time."

It was meant to be a joke. It was a comment to make me laugh. But all it did was make my mind wonder about what she wore beneath that dress. If she was just as colourful or if she leant towards something tamer. Thoughts that were wholly inappropriate for me to be having about an employee. I clenched my teeth and thought about the football scores to stop all the blood rushing south.

"I'm sure you do," I muttered.

"This isn't my first rodeo, Tin Man. I know what I'm doing."

Tin Man. It hadn't taken long to figure out what she meant by it. Kiran believed I didn't have a heart, and she wasn't wrong. There was no doubt in my mind that she'd dug up everything she could about me. The breakdown of my relationship and my subsequent handling of it was available for anyone with an internet connection.

"I just caught you interviewing thin air. Forgive me if I'm a little sceptical," I said, feeling irritated by her.

Having Kiran in the vicinity gave me emotional whiplash. Her sunny disposition and approach to business grated on my nerves, but if I found myself looking at her for too long, my inner teenage boy rose to the surface.

"If it makes you feel better, you can sit in," she said, sliding off the table and standing in front of me. "But you're not allowed to interrupt. This isn't about your company. This is for me."

"Fine," I said, even though I disagreed.

Gareth from HR joined us, and I took a seat beside Kiran as the interviews began. She had a talent for making people feel at ease, assuring them it was a chat. I wanted to remind her she was running a business that turned over a hundred thousand pounds in profit last year and was projected to do even better this annum. She needed a competent assistant who could handle pressure. But I promised her silence, and I was a man of my word.

Sitting back in the chair, I noted things about Kiran. She talked with her hands, gesturing wildly. When she found something amusing, she scrunched her nose. And she listened to every wild tangent without a care for the time.

Three interviews took nearly two hours, but she was still smiling by the end. As Gareth disappeared back to his floor, she shifted in her chair and turned her attention to me.

"Who did you like best?" she asked.

Glancing at her folder, there was clearly one candidate who stood out. I tapped the name 'Astra Bishop' on the piece of paper before her. The page was decorated in Kiran's looping cursive from the notes she'd taken.

Kiran's hand suddenly shot out and covered mine. Her palm was soft against my skin and she lifted my hand gently from the table.

"What happened?" she asked softly.

Her gaze was on the fingers of my left hand and I curled them into a fist, hiding them from her.

"Sorry," she apologised, letting go of my hand. "That was so rude of me. I shouldn't have —"

"It's okay," I said, clearing my throat.

Flexing my fingers, I showed her again. My middle finger was half the height it should have been.

"My brother slammed my hand in a car door and broke my fingers. Damage was worse on that one and they couldn't save it," I explained.

"Why did he do that?"

The corner of my mouth twitched at the memory. At the time, it wasn't funny. I swore I would kill Aiden, but the older we got, the more ridiculous the story was.

"I was thirteen, and he was eleven," I told her. "And he just found out I erased his progress on *Pokémon* blue."

Kiran stared at me before she let out a nervous giggle. "You can't be serious."

"Very serious. He thought he was going to leave home and become a master."

"Did he?"

"No. He's a doctor."

"Both are noble causes," Kiran said gravely.

"I guess. I'm still disappointed he never brought an Articuno home."

"Maybe he felt he already had one," she said, closing her folder.

Momentarily, her warmth had caught me off guard, and I revealed a small piece of myself to her. But she suddenly wrapped it in a layer of caution as if she realised who she was talking to. It made me sit up straight and put up my walls again.

"Is that what you think of me?" I asked. "I'm an ice monster?"

Kiran looked up, setting her dark brown eyes on me. They flickered with emotion as she said, "Not at all."

Curiosity gripped me hard and fast. "What do you think of me?"

She smiled, getting up from her seat. "We don't have time to delve into that now. I need to phone Astra and let her know she got the job."

Chapter Six
- Seth

I shared the lift with Astra as we left the office at five-thirty on Friday. Her bright pink hair was split into two buns and she wore shocking green eyeshadow. Yet another rainbow assault to my eyes — courtesy of Kiran and her decisions.

"How did you find your first day?" I asked, wanting to eliminate the awkward silence.

She shifted her gaze to me. "You talk?"

"I… yes."

"You didn't say a word during the interview."

"I was under strict instruction not to."

Astra snorted and then answered my question, "I like Kiran. She seems nice, but I'm nervous about messing up."

From the notes on her file, Astra had been the youngest applicant. Twenty-one and looking for her first job after university. Despite her lack of experience, she'd been most competent during the interview, and it was easy to see how she and Kiran gelled together. An explosion of colour that left a trail of sticky notes around the floor.

Reassurance, outside of my brothers, was not something I handed out freely. It wasn't my job to bolster the confidence of others. If she felt unprepared, then she shouldn't have applied. I bit back on giving a response and stared at the number above the doors as we descended through the building.

"You know," Astra said after popping the bubble of gum she blew. "I was gutted when the news of Anna's cheating broke."

My fists balled at my side and an acidic burning crawled from the pit of my stomach up through my oesophagus. It soured my tastebuds and spots blurred my vision.

"I really hope you both work it out," she continued. The doors to the lift opened and she stepped out. "You were a gorgeous couple," Astra called over her shoulder.

I slowed my pace, letting her jet through the foyer and out the door, not wanting to hear any more of her opinions about Anna. The brief mention of my ex tainted my mood and rather than meet with Aiden for a catch up, I wanted to head home and mindlessly binge through a boxset.

Digging into my jacket pocket, I searched for my phone when something hit my legs, followed by a gentle 'oof'.

When I turned around, a small boy looked up at me with large brown eyes that held a familiarity. He had a mop of black hair that fell in curls around his ears and across his forehead.

"Sorry," he panted, moving his hands.

Slowly, I kneeled, so I was at his level. "Are you lost?"

He shook his head vigorously so that his curls bounced with the movement. "I'm hiding."

"From?"

I was alarmed that a little kid was running through the foyer of our building, but even more concerned that he was using the place as refuge.

"My brother." The grin that spread across his face spelled mischief.

"I'm not sure that's a very smart plan," I said. "Where is he?"

The boy pointed towards the other end of the foyer, where a corridor led off to toilets and storage rooms.

"How about we find him?" I suggested. "We don't want him to worry."

But he looked past me and grinned, showing off the gap where he'd lost a tooth.

"Ma!" he yelled, and shot past me, shoes squeaking against the flooring.

Swivelling on the spot, I saw him run across the foyer and straight at Kiran. He knocked into her legs, failing to skid to a stop, and she stumbled backwards. I stood up, knees cracking, and walked towards the pair.

"Maaz?" Kiran asked the boy. "Where's Shah? Did you run off again?"

As she spoke to him, she used her hands in a series of gestures. Standing behind Maaz, I saw the devices partially hidden under his hair behind his ears. They weren't random gestures. Kiran was using sign language.

"It's a game, Ma," he told her in an exasperated tone.

"I found him when he bumped into me," I explained.

Kiran looked up and sighed. "I am so sorry." She pulled her son into her gently and ruffled his hair. "This one is an absolute nightmare when he wants to be. Which is most of the time."

"Am not!" Maaz argued, pushing her hand away and earning an eye roll from his mum.

"Ma?" another voice called out in the foyer.

"I have him!" Kiran said in return.

A boy, much older than Maaz, approached us. He dived straight at his brother, who squealed as he was dangled upside down.

"Next time Ma leaves you with me, dippy, I'm going to throw you in a skip and let them take you away," he threatened.

"No! Ma! Ma!" Maaz said, laughing wildly.

"Put him down, Shah," Kiran scolded. "You're not putting my baby in a skip."

Shah did as he was told and set his brother back on the ground. Straightening up, he stood taller than his mum and when he clocked me, his dark eyes narrowed.

"Who are you?" he asked abruptly.

"Shahzad," Kiran said sternly. "Be polite. This is Seth — Arthur's son. Seth, these are my boys, Maaz and Shahzad."

It surprised me to see that Kiran had a son who must have been a teenager. Shah had to be sixteen or seventeen, judging by the stubble he sported.

"It's nice to meet you both," I said, formally.

"Why don't you two go to the car and I'll join you there?" Kiran suggested.

She handed her keys over to Shah. He took them from her before putting his little brother in a headlock and practically dragging him out of the foyer. A flurry of memories flickered in my mind of growing up with all my brothers and the relationship we once shared.

"Boys," Kiran laughed weakly, looking at me. Her voice broke through the nostalgia. "They're a handful most days."

"Just the two of them?" I asked.

"Two was more than enough."

"How old are they?"

We fell into step, walking out of the building and towards the carpark together.

"Maaz is five, and Shah just turned sixteen." There was a silence between us before Kiran bumped her shoulder against my arm. "You can say what you're thinking. I must have had him young."

"It's not my business," I muttered, vaguely embarrassed that she'd realised the obvious line of thought.

"You told me about your finger when I asked, so I guess it would make us even."

"It's not quite the same."

She shrugged. "I am a teen pregnancy statistic. Had him just before I turned sixteen."

"You must have been terrified."

I tried to imagine Kiran at fifteen, with a bulging stomach and the impending prospect of motherhood on the horizon. At that age, I was in a blazer and boater hat, studying for exams and wrestling with my brothers. The difference in our situations should have horrified me, but it made me curious to how she'd built herself to managing a successful company.

"I cried nearly every day," she admitted quietly. "But I couldn't bring myself to any other option but to keep him."

We stopped by my car and she looked over to the boys who were still fighting by her Range Rover. Shah wrestled his brother into the backseat and their laughter echoed through the empty carpark.

"You think you know what love is," she said, eyes glued on them. "But then you have children, and you realise there's nothing that could ever be greater than that."

For a second time that night, bile rose up my throat.

"I need to get going," I said shortly.

Kiran turned her head to me. "Have a good night," she said. "And thanks for finding Maaz."

Her heels clicked as she walked towards her car, and I slammed the door shut as I slid into the driver's seat of mine. My mind raced as I drove through the streets of London.

Kiran had a perfect little family. I don't know why it never occurred to me. A husband and two sons. It made sense that she would always be smiling. Always be in a good mood. She'd struck gold in life. What could she possibly be upset about?

Twenty minutes of tying myself in knots and I ended up outside of Sugarworks. The building was pristine white, and the lighting was a dim pink in the autumn evening. I couldn't help but think my brother's pastry restaurant was somewhere Kiran would like. Bright and sweet. It was the embodiment of who she was.

Walking into the building, I saw Aiden at a table. He was content as he demolished a slice of cheesecake that sat before him.

"I thought you stood me up," he explained when I joined him. "Again. I was five minutes out from calling Tiffy and asking her to join me."

"Why don't you grow some balls and ask her on a date?" I asked, taking the seat opposite him.

He gave me the middle finger. "It's not like that and you know it. Plus, look how well commitment worked out for you."

"This was a mistake," I grumbled, getting out of the seat.

Aiden kicked me under the table and made me sit down again. "What's wrong with you?" he asked.

"Everything," I told him.

"Too broad." He waved the fork in large circles that slowly got smaller. "Be more specific."

"Everyone wants to know about Anna. If I've seen her. If I'm going to see her. If I'm getting back together with her."

"Are you?"

"No. I can't forgive her for what happened. For what she said."

"You shouldn't," Aiden replied, stuffing another bite of cheesecake into his mouth.

He was two years younger than me and the polar opposite of his twin, Noah. The clash of personalities often led us into fights over the years. He was flighty and loved the finer things in life. The only time he was serious was when it came down to his job as a fertility doctor. And he was the only one I trusted when things weren't going the way they should have.

"Do you think it's ever going to happen?" I asked him, ignoring the itch in my throat that grew painful.

"Bro." Aiden put the fork down and looked at me. The same blue eyes stared back into mine. "It's hard to tell with unexplained infertility. Difficult to treat something when you don't know the cause."

Aiden had gone through this with me before. We sat in his office two years ago as he broke down the results after months of tests by his colleagues. I couldn't understand how Aiden had no definitive answer. Years of studying and the best he could give me was 'we're not sure.' I punched him. Hard.

"There are other avenues to having children," he said. "I know so many couples where IVF didn't work, so they chose adoption or surrogacy."

"Do you think it feels the same? Having a child that isn't biologically yours?"

"I'm the wrong person to ask," he answered. "I deal with the biological aspect. Not the psychology behind it. What's brought this up? Have you found someone new and haven't told us yet?"

I scoffed. "Nothing like that. I met my colleague's kids today and watching them had me thinking about what life could have been."

"It still could be like that. Reduce the stress, find a girl, make her a Sinclair, and we go from there."

"Because it's that easy?"

"Sounds like it to me."

"You have to be the dumbest doctor I know."

"If I'm so dumb, would I suggest we should go out and get drunk?"

Deep down, I knew I shouldn't. Aid would suggest it because he didn't have a shift tomorrow. Yet, getting drunk, blotting out all the anger and sadness, was exactly what I needed.

"Should we wait for Noah to close up?" I asked, giving in easily.

A grin spread across Aiden's face. "Yes! It's going to be a good night."

Chapter Seven

- Kiran

Paul's presentation was taking painfully long. I sat at the back of the room with Mike by my side, taking notes, but my eyes kept flitting to the clock, and I stifled a yawn. The room was warm, and my eyes were heavy with fatigue.

"Questions?" Paul asked, looking out at the crowd of directors and colleagues.

Mike started to raise his hand, and I grabbed his elbow and yanked it back down.

"Do *not* make this any longer than it needs to be," I told him. "Email him the questions. I'm begging you."

Mike pushed his glasses up his nose and sighed. "And if he doesn't respond?"

"I'll make sure he does."

The only person who asked questions was Seth. He sat at the front of the room, back pin straight, and directed Paul to move through the slides before dissecting everything slowly. By the time we were allowed to leave the room, I was tripping over my feet, taking the stairs back to the floor where my office was.

My gaze shifted to the clock in the screen's corner as I rapidly typed out an email. The clacking of the keys made my head pulse, and I almost dismissed the knock at my office door as a part of the headache until I heard a voice.

"Kiran?"

I looked up to see Seth standing in the doorway. It was rare for him to make an appearance. He preferred to sit in his room with the door shut when he was in the building.

"Can I come in?" he asked.

"Of course," I said, nodding to the chair opposite my desk. "Is there a problem?"

He sat down and covered his eyes with one of his hands. "Has anyone ever told you that your office is unusually bright?"

Seth had looked in pain all day, and I was surprised at how vigorously he'd shot questions at Paul.

As I went back to the email, I asked, "How much did you drink last night if you're still suffering?"

"More than my liver is happy with," he groaned.

I laughed under my breath. "You're not a young one anymore, Tin Man. All that grey is trying to tell you something."

Seth's dark hair was littered with silver strands that shone when the light hit them at a certain angle. He made no effort to cover them up, but I liked how they looked, and it fit with the nickname I'd bestowed on him.

"Remind me why I came in here," he said, uncovering his eyes.

"I wish I could, but I don't even know the answer to that mystery." I hit send on the email and then cursed. "Shit."

"What's wrong?"

"I forgot to add an attachment," I mumbled.

Instantly, I opened up a new email again and apologised before adding the attachment this time.

"How's everything going?" he asked casually.

"Busy," I admitted, trying to stay calm. I'd just watched him rip into Paul and didn't want to be next on his list. "There's a project I've been discussing for almost a year and we're finally putting the grant application together," I rambled.

"Grant application? Is it a research project?"

"Yes," I replied.

"Is that a smart investment?"

"We'll have to wait and see," I told him.

"Working with another company or?"

"University."

"Who has a good AI programme here?"

"It's not here. A professor at MIT reached out and we've been emailing ideas back and forth, trying to get something concrete. We've both got an interest in brain-inspired artificial intelligence, so that's the route we're heading down. I don't want to say too much. Nothing's set in stone."

Even talking about it set butterflies rampant in my stomach. It had been a long time since I'd been this excited over a project, and when Professor Dan Hargreaves reached out to me, I wasn't ashamed to admit I fangirled a little.

"There must be a lot of ethics attached to that," Seth said, leaning forward.

I hummed in agreement. "Lots of red tape and hoops to jump through, but we've both done it before."

"Would you be moving there?" he asked.

I peered past the monitor to see he'd narrowed his icy blue eyes and watched me carefully.

"No," I assured him firmly. "We just moved to London. Shah starts A levels next year and I don't want to put Maaz through any more upheaval. He needs some stability in his life. When we moved here, I made a promise that it was permanent." Looking at the clock again, I closed out of my emails. "Speaking of my troublesome two, I need to get going," I muttered.

"Now?"

"Shah has a parents' evening. They want to talk about progress before he sits mock exams. GCSEs have a numbered system now instead of letters. I'm not sure why they changed it, but there we go."

"The day isn't over," Seth said as I shut down the computer.

"Sorry?" I asked, pushing my chair back and away from the desk.

"A workday is nine to five."

The glimmer of warmth that he'd walked into my office with had well and truly vanished. In place was the Seth I was accustomed to, sitting, looking at me sternly. The steely gaze made the panic swell in my chest before I forced it away.

"A traditional workday might be, but when you run a business, you afford yourself a level of flexibility," I told him gently.

Seth shook his head and pushed himself out of his chair. "You want to assess your commitment to your company."

"I am fully committed to my company," I shot back.

"Leaving whenever you feel like it doesn't make it seem that way."

There was a hot flash of anger that exploded in my chest. Seth didn't know about my life. He didn't know about what I went through to pull this company up to where it was today. There were sleepless nights and lost weekends. Why was he throwing a fit over me leaving an extra hour early? We started before nine o'clock most days. I couldn't be accused of slacking and yet that was exactly what was happening.

"If you're not careful, you're going to sink it before you get a chance to submit that grant," he said coldly.

"What would you know?" I snapped. "Didn't you walk out for months?"

"We're a well-established company with a proven track record."

"I don't have to listen to this." I got out of my chair, refusing to waste any more time on a pointless argument.

"You have a husband," he said. "Why don't you get him to pull some of the weight?"

My heart slammed violently against my chest, and I felt the sting of tears in my eyes.

"What is it, Kiran? Perfect marriage not so great behind closed doors?" Seth sneered.

I tried to remind myself that Seth wasn't mad at me. He was a man with walls that reached up to the heavens. Everyone in the building knew that he had a temper and something must have made him deeply unhappy to lash out like this. It wasn't a personal attack.

But it was.

He'd proven he wanted to protect his family, but felt it was his right to attack mine. That made my blood boil, and I refused to let him get away with it.

"Listen here, you pompous prick," I said, pointing an index finger at him. "My boys come before anything else. The company could sink to the bottom of the fucking ocean and I wouldn't care, because Shah and Maaz needed me. Don't you *ever* make it sound like it's an option to leave them and stay at work."

"You —"

"You know what, Seth," I said, grabbing my bag from the floor. "It wouldn't kill you to be kind for once. Wouldn't hurt to remind yourself that you aren't the centre of the universe. People have lives that don't revolve around you. They have their own issues and sometimes they need some understanding. It must be a lonely life being a complete and utter asshole."

I stormed past him and left the office, not regretting a single word I'd said.

Chapter Eight

- Seth

There was a chill in the air that had nothing to do with the November weather.

That afternoon, when I knocked on Kiran's door, the effects of the hangover still lingered in my system. My brain and liver were one shot away from being pickled, and it took all my focus to listen to Paul as he droned on in a stuffy room.

I needed something to take away the pain. A personal ray of sunshine to pull me out of the pit I'd thrown myself into.

Kiran told me I didn't need a meeting and so I waltzed into her office, prepared for whatever she would throw at me. A dig about my hair and my age made me wonder if I should start dyeing it again. Anna would book appointments with the hairdresser the moment I hinted at turning grey. She refused to be seen with me unless I was immaculate.

I hadn't expected Kiran to mention America or grants. The thought of her disappearing from the office, from my life, put me on edge, and I wasn't sure why. And that set the tone for the rest of the conversation.

Here was this perfect woman with her perfect life, and I wanted to chip away at it. I wanted her to be miserable like I was because it bothered me that she could be so happy. It grated on me as she had everything I wanted. So I found a crack, and I dug my fingers in and pulled with all my might, wanting to wipe the smile from her face. But Kiran had come back swinging, and when she left the office, I was filled with a deep sense of shame that I couldn't get rid of.

That was two weeks ago. Kiran's office door remained shut ever since. She walked out of the kitchen if I entered and Astra refused to book me a meeting. A better man would have walked across the corridor, knocked on her door, and apologised for being an asshole. A better man wouldn't have said those things to her.

I still heard her laugh and smelled the lavender that crept out from under her door. But Kiran became a spirit in my life. No matter how much I felt her presence, I rarely saw her.

"You look miserable, Mr Sinclair," Kirsty said, shrugging on her coat. "Did your meeting not go well?"

"Kiran wasn't in today," I blurted out.

No strange scents. No light in the office. Not a single note of laughter. It had driven me to distraction all day.

"Yes, she was," Kirsty said.

"She wasn't in her office all day."

Kirsty suddenly looked nervous.

"What's she said to you?" I asked.

"She said she doesn't want to talk to you. She didn't say why, but she told Astra to make sure her schedule couldn't fit you in."

Kirsty confirmed what I already knew. Kiran was doing her best to avoid me.

"Mr Sinclair," Kirsty said quietly. "She's down on the third floor. Been there all day. She's been working on something with Mike."

"Is she still there?"

"I'm not sure, but if you're looking for her, I would start there."

Nodding, I jogged towards the lift and jabbed the button, letting it take me down to the floor Kiran had been hiding on. It was seven-thirty and there was a chance she wasn't here anymore, but I needed to check.

I stepped out onto the floor. The space was filled with desks cluttered with monitors and there was a faint glow at the end of the room. Kiran sat at a desk, pulling at her hair as she stared at the screen.

"Mike, please don't stress over it," Kiran said. "How many times have we done this?"

"More than I can count," Mike said from her phone on the desk. "It's part of the process. I owed you anyway."

"Cleaning data should be classified as another circle of hell. Right above debugging code."

Kiran laughed, tipping her head back, and my heart flip-flopped in my chest at the sound. Like it set my world back on its axis. The moment her eyes landed on me, her face fell.

"Mike, I need to go," she said. "I'll text you any updates, but don't hold your breath." Then she cut the call. "What do you want?"

"You're here late," I commented, stuffing my hands in my pockets.

"Making up the hours," she said. "Don't want anyone to think I'm slacking."

"No one thinks that."

"Even so."

"How was Shah's parents' evening?"

Kiran fixed me with a stare so cold I felt it in my soul. I was used to this woman's warmth and glow, but my temper had wiped it away.

"I'd rather not discuss my family with you," she said.

"Okay." I could respect that decision. "Is there anything I can do to help?"

"No," she said shortly. Then she added quietly, "I'm used to doing things on my own. It'll be quicker if you just leave me to it."

"Right." I'd been dismissed. "I guess I'll leave."

She raised a hand, but her eyes were already back on the screen.

Throughout my life and my time with Anna, I'd upset various people and never really cared. Burnt so many bridges, turned my back on people, and still slept peacefully. But this argument with Kiran made me uncomfortable in my skin, and yet, I couldn't bring myself to apologise.

Driving home, I couldn't leave it like that. She was sitting in the building, working on God knows what until God knows when. Kiran had a family waiting for her at home, whereas I had nothing. But she was 'making up the hours.'

I stopped at the supermarket and then a restaurant that made the best Chinese food I'd tasted before going back to the building.

When I walked back onto the third floor, it was an hour later and Kiran was standing by the window, staring out at the city. In the few months I'd been back at work, quiet was not a word I would use to describe her. She was always talking to someone and if she didn't have company, then she was muttering to herself like a madwoman. It was as if silence made her uncomfortable, so she did everything in her power to fill it.

"The view was one reason Dad picked the building," I said.

She jumped and whirled around to look at me. In the dim glow given off by the screens, her eyes looked glassy.

"What are you doing back here?" Kiran asked. "I thought you'd left."

"I did, but I wasn't sure if you'd eaten, so I brought you some food." I lifted the bag in my hand and she eyed it. "It's all vegetarian because I didn't know if you ate meat or not."

Her stomach growled, and she looked at the floor, embarrassed. "You shouldn't have."

Kiran left the window, walking towards me. I handed her the bag, and we stood there quietly. She couldn't bring herself to say thank you, and I couldn't bring myself to say sorry.

"You should stay," she said. "I can't eat all this alone."

"I don't want to interrupt your workflow," I lied.

With every day that passed, I felt like I was treading a thin line with Kiran that could send me spiralling into complete disaster. I never took a specific interest in the people that worked for me, but Kiran was turning into a professional obsession. She was completely off limits and I kept Paul away from her with that in mind, but I struggled to follow my own rules.

"Okay," Kiran replied. "Be kind to your liver, Tin Man."

She shuffled back towards the desk and I watched her, wishing I could stay in her company.

"You were right," I said, causing her to look up at me. "It is a lonely life as an asshole."

Chapter Nine
- Kiran

The guilt chewed away at me and robbed me of sleep. I never should have called him an asshole and especially avoided saying he had a lonely life. Seth proved himself to be a prick but also picked up some good food. He had moments where I glimpsed past the walls, but then he fortified his armour and resorted back to being a miserable git.

I lit the lavender incense stick and let it burn before the scent filled the office. We could all use some calm today.

Instead of avoiding Seth, I would stop by his room and we could talk. Maybe I would figure out what made him explode at me like that. Two weeks of keeping my office door shut and walking out of any room he entered had drained me. This wasn't how I treated people, but I wanted to protect myself. I needed the time to reset and keep my mouth in check. We didn't need another blowout.

Tea. I needed some tea to clear my head and focus on work. Seth hadn't come into the office yet and I didn't know if he would be in today. I could ask Kirsty, but after my quiet instruction to not let

Seth anywhere near my calendar, I couldn't guarantee he hadn't returned the favour. It wouldn't surprise me to find that Seth was petty.

As I walked down the corridor, I witnessed an accident that made me laugh before I ran towards the doors. The partition between the offices and where all the assistants sat was clear glass and a handsome man walked straight into it without realising. A thin trickle of blood dripped from his nose.

I wrenched the glass door open and grimaced.

"It's not the first time," he said, pinching the bridge of his nose.

"Come with me," I said, guiding him towards the kitchen. "Sit."

"Yes, ma'am."

He dropped into a chair without argument. Wadding up some paper towels, I handed them over to him and he pressed them to his nose, stemming the blood.

"Are you going to be okay?" I asked, perching myself on the edge of the table.

"I'll live," he replied, pulling the tissue from his nose and then placing it back again. "It's been a while since I've stopped by the office. Told Dad the whole glass building was a pile of shit. I'm Aiden Sinclair."

He may have been platinum blonde, but there was no denying that this man was a Sinclair. He had the same eyes and cheekbones. The hair must have been inherited from his mother.

"Seth's brother," I pointed out.

"Ah, he's mentioned me." Aiden removed the tissue from his face and shot me a grin. His cheeks dimpled and his eyes crinkled at the corners.

It was strange to see a Sinclair so openly happy when Seth seemed unfamiliar with the emotion.

"Did he tell you I was sexy and smart?" Aiden asked, looking up at me earnestly.

I stopped myself from snorting. "Sweetheart," I said, cupping his cheek, "you just walked into a glass door and admitted it wasn't the first time."

"Did he mention I'm a doctor?" he asked, puffing out his chest.

"He did mention you're the reason he has half a middle finger."

"I was training up a Magikarp! Do you know how much time and patience went into that game?"

I laughed and hoped that Shah and Maaz would continue to grow close as they grew older. If the Sinclair brothers could remain on talking terms after a missing digit, then I had reason to believe the age gap between my sons wouldn't tear them apart.

"How are you finding working with my big brother?" Aiden asked.

"He's…" I trailed off, wanting to be polite.

"A prick, right?"

"He has his moments," I admitted timidly.

So far, Seth was proving to be in a league of his own. Arthur Sinclair, the patriarch, was a patient man who had a spine of steel. He knew how to talk people around without talking down to them. And Aiden was showing himself to be a loveable dork.

"I think I would as well if I got publicly humiliated," Aiden commented, dabbing the end of his nose and looking relieved that the bleeding had stopped.

"I'm sorry. Publicly humiliated?"

Aiden shot me a look. "Yeah. You know what happened with Anna."

"Anna?"

"Anna Lindberg." When I didn't respond, he said, "Do you live under a rock?"

"I don't really care about pop culture," I admitted.

"You're a weird one," he said cautiously. "Gorgeous but weird." Aiden laughed as I blushed at his assessment. "Anna was Seth's fiancée. She got caught fucking some guy in the back of a car and the pictures were posted everywhere online."

My heart sank to my feet. Being cheated on was a heartbreaking event, but to have it posted for the world to see must have been soul destroying. Was it any wonder that Seth spat out the word husband?

And I'd been calling him Tin Man while he dealt with picking up the debris from his shattered relationship.

"I had no idea," I muttered.

"He's always been a hothead, but understandably, he's been worse for the past few months." Aiden shrugged. "How about you give me your number and if he gets too much to handle, you can call me? Or you could just call me?"

"Did he come back for her?" I asked.

Seth had returned after months away and I wondered if his mood swings were because he was trying to patch things up with his ex. His head must be all over the place.

"I'm trying to flirt with you," Aiden whined. "And you seem more interested in my big brother."

"Maybe you need to work on your game," I told him.

"Let me take you out and I'll show you how wrong you are."

"What the fuck are you doing?" Seth's voice joined us.

My head snapped towards the door where he stood, looking pissed.

"Shamelessly flirting with your staff," Aiden answered proudly.

Seth's jaw tightened as he looked at us. "Kiran's married."

"Kiran," Aiden said my name. "Beautiful name for a beautiful creature."

"Move!" Seth barked.

Aiden laughed as he rose to his feet. "See you soon, gorgeous," he said, kissing my cheek. "Thanks for the help and if you ever get bored with your husband…" He winked.

"Now!" Seth yelled.

Aiden tossed the paper towels in the bin and walked past Seth, who gave him a rough shove down the corridor.

I made myself a cup of tea and returned to my office, closing the door behind me.

Googling people was wrong. It was an invasion of privacy and you couldn't believe everything you read online. But Aiden had opened a can of worms and I typed Seth's name into the search bar.

Pages of results presented themselves before me. The first few articles were about his heavy night out a few weeks ago. Seth with Aiden and another man who must have been Aiden's twin, all stumbling down the street. One thing was for certain — the Sinclair family had attractive genes.

Scrolling through, the articles focused on a fundraiser the family attended and then to Seth's arrival back in the UK. Inflammatory headlines that speculated he was seeing his ex again, two fist fights he had on the streets of London, and finally I stumbled onto the pictures of Anna in the car.

Nausea hit me hard. The betrayal was posted for everyone to see with no worry about the man affected. Seth woke up every day knowing that the woman he planned to marry had cheated and that everyone on this island had an opinion about it.

I fell down the rabbit hole, clicking through every article and reading reports. Before the incident, the column inches were flattering. The photographs of them together left a prominent ache in the centre of my chest. Seth and Anna were a real-life Barbie and Ken. Red carpet events, gorgeous white sands, front row of fashion shows; no matter where they were, your eye was drawn to them. It hurt to look because they embodied perfection.

Even after I closed out of the browser and pulled up my work for the day, Seth stayed in my mind.

Why would she do this to him? They had the world at their feet and she'd thrown it away for a fumble in the backseat. If I had someone like Seth... I put a pin in that thought immediately.

"Come in," I called when someone knocked on the door.

I expected to see Mike, who had been sporadically emailing about the data clean up throughout the morning, but Seth walked into the room. He was missing his jacket and the sleeves of his shirt were rolled up to his elbows, making my face heat.

"Hi," I mumbled.

"I wanted to apologise for my brother's behaviour," he said curtly. "Aiden lacks a filter between his brain and his mouth around attractive women."

I blushed again and shook my head. "It's fine. I witnessed him walk into a glass door and yell at me about a Magikarp. No line he fed me was going to work after that."

"He should know better."

"There was no harm done."

Seth walked towards the desk and placed his hand on the surface. When he removed it, a crisp twenty-pound note sat in front of me.

"You don't have to pay me back for the food," he told me. "I'm practicing kindness. You'd be undoing your work if you tried to pay me."

"Seth," I said, biting my bottom lip. "What I said —"

"You had every right."

"No, I didn't."

"You did. Sometimes, I'm not a very nice person. But I'll try to work on that."

"Let me know if you need help," I mumbled.

Seth nodded and left my office. As the door closed, I let out a shuddering sigh. I needed to make a list. I needed some order back in my life. This man was tipping my world off its axis, and I needed to focus.

Pulling open the drawer with all my sticky notes, my jaw dropped. Yesterday, there had been a single pad of orange notes in there that I was working my way through. Today, it was stacked to the brim with neon stationery, neatly packed in their cellophane wrappers.

I ripped off an orange note and scribbled a quick list on there before swinging my chair around to the wall.

There was a note that escaped my attention this morning, but it stood out among my lists and reminders. Composed of big broad strokes, the writing was scruffy, but I could read it clearly.

I'm still trying to find my heart – Tin Man.

Chapter Ten
- Seth

"Would you at least think about it?" Tiffy asked through the video call.

"No, and Tiffy, I told you to only call me if it was life or death. A celebrity dance competition is not life or death."

She rolled her green eyes and sighed. "It might be good for you. Cute dance partner. Positive publicity."

"I said no," I gritted out.

"You're such a grump."

"Ask Aiden."

"He doesn't have time."

"And you thought I did?"

Tiffy shrugged and wound her red hair around a finger. "So you want me to tell them no?"

"That's exactly what I want you to tell them."

"You're going to be breaking a lot of hearts."

"How?"

"Plenty of people would love to see you in lycra, rolling those hips."

"I think I need to talk to your father about the way you're treating us as clients," I said, narrowing my eyes.

"I never said I was one of those people that wanted to see it. You can keep your hips to yourself." Tiffy snorted.

She had known us her entire life and worked with us for years. Tiffy was a ball breaker who didn't fall at our feet like most of the women we came across. The majority of her time was spent with Aiden, but even he had failed to make his move on this formidable woman.

There was a knock on my office door and I ignored it until it became more rapid and louder.

"I have to go," I mumbled. "Tell them no."

"Yeah, I heard you the first time," she replied, and cut the call.

"Come in!" I barked, balling my hands into fists.

Kiran pushed open the door moments later with a smile on her face, and immediately, some of my anger dissipated away.

"Most people knock once," I told her.

"I don't do things like most people."

"Don't I know it?" I muttered under my breath. "Can I help you with something?"

"Yes, you can." She walked into the room properly, and I noticed a gift bag in her hand. "I was wondering if you could hand this to Aiden for me, please?"

"Aiden?" I asked, sitting up in my chair. "As in, my brother?"

"The one and only."

My jaw tightened, molars grinding together. The temperature in the room rose as a fresh flood of anger washed over me. Aiden, with his brash and cocky attitude, had caught her attention. When I asked him what they spoke about in the kitchen, he acted coy, and I was seconds away from knocking the smug look off his face. He was only saved because Dad walked in and it felt wrong to make the old man play referee.

"What is it?" I asked. It was meant to come across as friendly, but it was cold.

The smile stretched on her lips, and she took the seat in front of me without invitation. Placing the gift bag on the floor, she pulled out the contents. In her hands, she held a bright red Gyarados plushie.

"He's still really upset about the *Pokémon* incident. I didn't like the thought of him feeling like he missed out on some childhood dream, so I looked around online and found this little guy."

She placed it on her lap and beamed. When she smiled like that, full and bright, her eyes crinkled at the corners and there was a vague dimple in her left cheek. It made my chest ache with want and there was a need to reach out and pull her to me.

My hands balled tighter, short fingernails pressing into the flesh of my palms.

"Shah said the red one was better than the blue," she continued.

"It's a shiny," I replied curtly.

Her smile dropped and her eyebrows rose. "I'm not sure I understand."

"It doesn't matter," I said, shaking my head.

"You'll give it to him?" she asked me.

Fuck no.

There was no inch of me that wanted to take the stupid cuddly toy from Kiran and gift it to Aiden. He would never let me live it down. Aiden would find a way to worm into her life and that wasn't his right. She was mine.

What the fuck was I thinking? She wasn't mine. She was a married woman with a family, and here I was behaving like a teenager with a crush.

I would never make a play for a married woman, but she was my personal speck of sunshine, and I didn't feel like sharing her with any of my brothers. It was bad enough the rest of the floor took up so much of her time.

"I would have asked for his number or address, but I get the feeling you don't trust me that much yet," Kiran said quietly.

She was not getting his address, but that had nothing to do with me not trusting her. If she turned up on Aiden's doorstep, then there was no way this family wasn't going to have to dig us out of yet another scandal. He was too dumb for his own good.

"I'll give it to him," I said, holding a hand out for the damn plushie.

Kiran flashed her megawatt grin again and got up from her seat. She rounded the desk and handed it over to me.

"You're a star!" she exclaimed. "I really hope he likes it."

"I'm sure he will," I muttered bitterly. "Was there anything else?"

She blinked at me a few times before shaking her head. "No. I'll let you get back to work."

There was a moment of hesitation before she turned on her heel and left, closing the door behind her.

I let out a deep breath and set the stuffed animal down on my desk. What the hell had Aiden said to her that warranted Kiran wanting to fulfil his childhood dream? I needed to minimise any more contact they had before she was swayed towards fulfilling any of his adult dreams. Aiden's moral compass was known to go missing the moment he saw a pretty face.

The dark beady eyes of the plushie stared back at me from the desk and the familiar sensation of bubbling erupted in my chest.

Everyone always got along with Aiden. Golden boy with the gift of sweet talking. The family sunshine. Of course, he and Kiran would hit it off.

Without taking too much time to think about it, I opened the bottom drawer of my desk and stuffed the stupid thing in there, slamming it shut afterwards.

No.

Aiden wasn't getting the missing piece of his dreams.

Chapter Eleven
- Seth

The trip to Manchester had not been on my calendar. Dad had been eager to accompany Kiran on this particular business trip, and I was content to hear the cliff notes when he returned, but he pulled out last minute, and Kirsty rearranged my schedule so that I could take his spot. I wanted to say no. I wanted to dig my heels in and tell him Kiran was fine to go on her own, but I'd put him through enough over the past few months.

At four in the morning, in the pouring rain, I pulled up outside Kiran's address and texted her. Five minutes later, she spilled out of the door and ran towards the car. Part of me hoped to catch sight of her husband, the last piece in the puzzle of her life. It was the urge to rub salt in the wound. I wanted to sneak a glimpse of the man who Kiran had chosen to spend her entire life with. But she was alone.

Kiran opened the back door and tossed in her duffle bag before jumping into the passenger seat, shivering and wet.

"I hate winter. I hate the rain. I hate early mornings," she grumbled, clipping her seatbelt and rubbing her hands along her thighs.

I turned up the heat and pulled off before saying, "You strike me as more of a summer person."

"Why would you think that?"

I shrugged, not wanting to give her a slice of my thoughts. Kiran's laughter and warmth reminded me of summer. She encouraged people around her to grow and blossom. When she started to slip away, you tried to hold on to her for a little longer. That last point might just be me. Every time a conversation with her came to an end, I hated that I couldn't find an excuse, against my better instincts, to keep it going.

"I don't think I've ever seen you out of a suit," she commented.

Four o'clock was too early for me to slip into a shirt and tie. It was more comfortable to drive in jeans and a jumper. The plan was to stop at a service station before Manchester and get changed.

"Don't worry," I said. "I won't embarrass you. I brought my best tie."

She laughed and dropped her head back against the seat. Kicking off her shoes, she pulled her feet up and sat cross-legged.

"Thanks for agreeing to come up with me. I know you probably had better things to do than trail me for the day," she said.

"Don't worry about it," I assured her. "How many universities do you work with?"

"Just Manchester. It felt good to give back after they gave me the tools to start the business."

"Kiran."

The sound of the wipers furiously waving back and forth matched my heartbeat. For the last few years, I had little interest in the people around me, but when it came to Kiran, I was full of questions. My curiosity grew until it pushed against my skeleton, begging to be released.

"How did you do it all?" I asked.

"What do you mean?"

"I found university difficult, and I didn't have a baby to look after."

Kiran turned her head to look at me. The staggered streetlights illuminated her face periodically, highlighting the slope of her nose and long, dark eyelashes that brushed against her cheek when she blinked. Clenching my jaw, I stared out at the road ahead of us.

"I nearly didn't make it," she said eventually. "I was such a mess after Shah was born. Before he was born. My parents kicked me out when I told them I was pregnant. Claimed I brought shame to the family by having a child out of wedlock. But Jamal's parents let me stay with them. They weren't happy about it, but I was carrying their grandson after all."

"They didn't like you?"

"Who was going to like the girl who led their son astray?" she asked in return. "Took a year off, trying to sort my head out. Fought with Jamal like it was a full-time job. That scared me enough that I started studying again."

"Did you split up?"

She shook her head. "Stayed together. Moved out of his parents' place when we were eighteen. Those years were a blur, if I'm honest. I was going to classes and then coming back to the flat for Shah. Staying up to finish assignments and look after him. Jamal and I got married when we were twenty. It's like I've been on autopilot for years, just trying to figure out what's next."

"Have you ever slowed down?" I asked curiously.

She stared out ahead of her. "Around the time Maaz was born, I guess."

"I imagine having children makes you stop and reassess."

"Having kids changes your life in ways you couldn't imagine," Kiran said quietly.

The conversation lulled before Kiran asked about Aiden. It irked me that my shitty little brother had left a lasting impression on her, but it was typical. Aiden was the most outgoing of all of us, and even when he was in trouble, people couldn't help but love him. I shouldn't care that Kiran might have a favourite Sinclair, but it irritated me that Aiden slipped into the spot above me.

We stopped at a service station just as the sun started to peek weakly over the horizon. I pulled her duffle bag from the back seat and turned to hand it to her. In the early morning light, I noticed Kiran wasn't wearing makeup. A dusting of light brown freckles laid across the bridge of her nose, but something on her cheek caught my attention.

"What happened?" I asked.

My fingers reached up and touched the scar beneath her right eye. She pulled away from me and rubbed the blemish with her hand.

"Old accident," she replied rapidly. "You'll learn I'm a little clumsy. I'll meet you back here."

Kiran hoisted the bag onto her shoulder and walked towards the building. Something knotted in the pit of my stomach, settling there like lead. She brushed it off so quickly, which made me think it wasn't a simple accident.

My fingers flexed as I locked the car, and my mind raced with awful thoughts. She mentioned she and Jamal used to fight, and I hadn't seen him around either, which made me curious if he had anything to do with the scar. The thought made my blood boil, but I knew better than to storm in with an accusation that barely had any basis other than an unhealthy dose of jealousy behind it.

We made it to the university where Kiran was hugged tightly by two staff members who lectured her years ago. She'd agreed to partner with them and offer postgraduate students industry experience.

Ignoring the stares that were thrown my way, I watched her obsessively as she spoke to students, listening with genuine interest while they described their projects. And I found myself joining in, asking about their progress and what they planned to do after they finished.

The more I was around Kiran, the more my patience grew. I took her lead and allowed myself to take an interest in other people. It was difficult to continue being an asshole in her presence.

"Do you want me to drive?" Kiran asked as we walked back to the car after dinner.

We had sat for food with one of her lecturers and I reverted to my silent ways. Kiran said I was free to go, and she could take a train back home, but I didn't want to leave. I was still collecting strands of summer that could be called on when she wasn't around.

"You've been networking all day," I replied. "Relax. I'll drive."

We'd thankfully missed the traffic coming out of Manchester and hit the motorway, heading for home.

"Would you mind if I call the boys?" Kiran asked.

"No, carry on."

She dug around in her bag, pulling out her phone, and a few seconds later, she beamed at the screen.

"Ma!" Maaz screeched.

I stopped myself from laughing at how excited he sounded to see her.

There was the sound of fighting before Shah's voice floated in the car. "Everything okay?" he asked.

"Yes, darling. I just wanted to let you know we're on the way home. Have you both had dinner?"

"Burgers!" Maaz yelled, but it sounded distant.

"I fed dippy, don't worry," Shah said. "How's the prick?"

My head snapped towards Kiran to see she'd flushed red.

"Shah," she said through gritted teeth. "No earphones."

"Fuck."

"Language. I'll speak to you when I get home."

Kiran cut the call, and I stared out at the road, grinding my molars together. The silence blanketed over us so heavily we were at risk of suffocating.

I knew I was a prick. Kiran had told me what she thought, but I didn't realise she would share those thoughts with her family.

"He didn't mean it," Kiran said. "I'm sorry."

"You've made it perfectly clear what you think of me, and you're entitled to your opinion," I snapped.

"I am, but sometimes I get it wrong."

A muffled ringing started in the car and Kiran fished my phone out of my jacket that was draped across her legs.

"It's Tiffy with a mermaid emoji," Kiran said.

"She put that emoji there," I replied. "Can you answer it and tell her I'm driving?"

"Sure." Kiran lifted the phone to her ear. "Hi! Personal secretary to Seth Sinclair. He's unavailable to take your call."

I could hear Tiffy on the other end of the line. "Who the fuck are you?"

Kiran chuckled, and I shook my head, feeling the anger drain away slightly.

"Put it on speaker. You're a liability, Jafri," I told her. She hit the speaker button, and I spoke to Tiffy, "What do you want? I'm driving."

"Driving or screwing?"

"Driving," I snapped. "Kiran works with us."

"As if that's stopped any of you before. You and Aiden are the worst for it."

"Don't paint me with the same brush as Aiden," I told her, looking at Kiran, who had covered her mouth to stifle her laughter. "What do you want, Tiff?"

"To let you know Anna turned up at my office."

My grip on the steering wheel tightened. "Why?"

"She wants to see you."

"And what did you say?"

"Over my dead body."

Tiffy had never been a fan of Anna and had barely hidden her distaste, but she dropped the vague ruse of professionalism the moment Anna's infidelity came to light.

"But," Tiffy continued, "that woman's a law unto herself, so I'm letting you know before she decides to show up at your building unannounced. Plenty of people are still asking if you two are getting back together."

"Thanks, Tiff. I'll let security know tomorrow morning."

"Already done."

"Thank you."

She hung up, and Kiran quietly placed it back inside my jacket pocket.

"Maybe you should talk to her," Kiran said, breaking through the awkward silence that settled between us again. "You must have loved her once if you were going to marry her."

The vein in my neck throbbed painfully. "You went looking for stories about me?" I hissed.

"No," Kiran said. "Aiden mentioned what happened."

Of course, my brother couldn't keep his mouth shut. He was trying to impress her, even if it meant throwing me under the bus. Especially if it meant throwing me under the bus.

"You looked very happy together," Kiran said. "I'm not saying forgive her but talking might help."

"How?"

"I don't know, but —"

"No. You don't know. You don't know anything about my life, Kiran. Not everyone has some magical fairy-tale where it all works out in the end," I snapped. "You've read things and you've spoken to my brother, but you don't have any idea how it felt to have it plastered across the internet. To have people wanting you to relive it. Everyone has a fucking opinion because it isn't their life."

"You're right," she mumbled. "No one knows how you feel. But try letting people in instead of pushing them away, Tin Man, and then maybe someone might understand your side of it."

Chapter Twelve
- Kiran

"You're going to burn out if you don't stop," Mike said, handing me a glass as I continued to type an email on my phone.

He dropped onto the sofa beside me, causing my body to shift and bump into his side while a sticky note drifted to the floor from the nearby wall.

"Kind of expected at this point," I muttered in response.

I managed to hit send before Mike snatched the phone out of my hand and tossed it to the other end of the sofa.

"Okay!" I said. "You have my undivided attention, you needy human being."

"Lies. I know you're still thinking about the grant."

I took a deep drink from the wineglass filled with orange juice. "I can't help it. It's going to be such an amazing opportunity if we get it."

"What do the Sinclairs think?"

"Arthur's excited to see where it goes. I think he's got his fingers crossed as tightly as we do," I said.

"And Dreamy Sinclair?"

"His name is Seth."

"I'm aware," Mike said, lips pulling into a smirk.

"You are terrible. You can't fancy the boss."

"Have you told yourself the same?"

The apples of my cheeks grew warm, and I looked into the glass. "I don't fancy Seth," I whispered, worried the boys might hear even though they were up in bed.

"Then you have to be blind. That man is perfection, wrapped in a designer suit."

I let out a deep breath and leant back against the cushions.

"You have thought about it," Mike said, mirroring my movements and nudging me gently.

"Like you said, I'd have to be blind."

"Was he impressed with your big brain project?"

"It's *our* big brain project, and I don't know. When we spoke about it, it ended in an argument."

"What?" Mike's brow furrowed, and he turned his body to me. "You don't argue with people."

"Apparently, I do. Seth… I don't know. He has a way of getting under my skin sometimes. There are times when he's so sweet and then it's like he gets in a foul mood and takes it out on me, and I can't help but snap at him."

A silence settled over us and I twitched uncomfortably in my seat.

"That might not be such a bad thing," Mike said eventually.

"It's awful," I replied instantly. "I've been calling him Tin Man, and I didn't realise his ex cheated on him and he found out through the internet."

"Tin Man?" Mike asked and then the realisation dawned on him before he chuckled. "Oh, you always were sharp with nicknames."

"It's not funny. I'm an idiot, and I never should have called him that."

"He's a big boy, Kiran. I'm sure he'll live." He quickly realised what he said. "I didn't mean —"

I held up a hand. "I know you didn't."

"I stand by what I said. It's a good thing."

"How?"

"Kiran, somewhere along the way, you lost yourself. I love you. You're my best friend. But you can't go through life trying to keep every single person happy."

"Why not?"

"Because you're a human being. Sometimes you get pissed off at the hot guy who doesn't have a filter and that's okay."

I shook my head and sighed. "I probably looked like the most insensitive cow."

"You are way too hard on yourself. Has he said anything to you?"

Seth had said plenty. In small pockets of vulnerability, he told me about his missing finger, and that he was still looking for his heart. He could be funny and gentle. But our most recent interaction had proven that there were parts of his life he was still trying to heal from. Part that forced him to cage his heart in barbed wire, refusing to let people in.

"We had a fight on the way back from Manchester," I admitted quietly.

"Over what? He doesn't want students in the building?"

"Nothing like that. He actually seemed really interested in the partnership we have with the university."

"Then what was the problem?"

I almost didn't want to admit it to Mike because there were bound to be more questions, and I didn't know if I had answers for him.

"Kiran?" he pressed.

"His PR lady phoned while we were in the car and brought up his ex. Said she wanted to see him and I made a comment about how maybe it would be a good idea for them to sit and speak. He snapped. Told me I didn't know anything, and that I was living a fairy-tale life."

Mike's expression hardened. "Is he fucking serious? A fairy-tale!"

I looked at my friend and placed a gentle hand on his arm. "He doesn't know. I haven't told him."

Mike sighed and took my hand, lacing our fingers together and squeezing tight. "You should have."

"It's not about point scoring," I reminded him gently. "He can think what he wants about me and my life. I just wanted to help him. He's so…" I trailed off.

"Why do you want to help him, Kiran?" Mike asked, sipping his wine. "If all he does is get under your skin, why do you even want to talk to him? I've heard he's always been like that, but if he's upsetting you, then I will book a meeting with him."

"Listen here, Mr Man, I don't need you fighting my battles for me," I teased.

"Who else is going to do it?" he asked, slinging an arm around me. "Let me look after you now and then."

"Isn't that what you've been doing for the past five years?"

He pressed a kiss against my temple, and I felt the lump grow in my throat. I couldn't cry. How many times had I fallen apart in front of Mike? He was going to be sick of me if I kept going.

"But seriously," he continued. "Maybe write him off as a lost cause. I don't want you getting hurt because he can't practice what he preaches. Telling you that you have no clue about his life when he doesn't know the first thing about yours."

"I can't," I said, picking at the lint on my trousers.

When Mike didn't reply after a few moments, I looked up to find him staring at me.

"You like him, don't you?" he said.

"No," I replied, completely panicked.

"You do."

"No," I said firmly. "But I think everyone deserves a chance to work through their demons, and he's figuring out how to get over the mess that happened in his life."

"How much time do you spend with him?"

The room heated. "We work on the same floor. His office is opposite mine."

"And that's it?"

"Mike, I'm not going there. Not with Seth. Not with anyone. It's strictly professional."

It was a surprise to me that my trousers hadn't spontaneously combusted with all the lies I was telling him.

Strictly professional? It felt that way, but there were times when the lines became blurry. When he stood a little too close, or went to brush my scar, or left a mountain of sticky notes in my drawer as an apology. Every single time Seth showed uncharacteristic softness, my heart betrayed me and yearned to see more.

"Have you thought anymore about —"

"No."

"Kiran," he said, drawing out my name. "I thought moving down here was a fresh start."

"For the business."

"For you and the boys."

"It is."

"You've barely done anything but work or spend time with Shah and Maaz."

"I'm finding a balance."

"No, you're not. You're doing exactly what you used to, but in a new city."

"You're starting to sound like Shah."

"Your son speaks a lot of sense. We worry about you." Mike whispered the next words, "I want my old Kiran back."

I leant against his side and shut my eyes tight. We wanted the same thing, but I wasn't sure it was for the best. I was certain she didn't exist anymore.

Until Seth.

Chapter Thirteen

- Seth

Productivity in the offices was in steep decline. Glittery tinsel covered every available surface, the trees were dotted around the floors, and everyone was in high holiday spirits.

Everyone apart from me.

Kiran's words still knocked around my skull. When I laid in bed and closed my eyes, it was her face that I saw in the darkness. Big, brown eyes staring at me and clouded with disappointment.

When I first set my eyes on her, all I wanted was her body. I wanted a taste and a rush of the tiny, petite woman who glowed when she smiled. But Kiran had managed to get stuck on a loop inside my head. She got under my skin. All the kindness and positivity made me itch. And the worst thing was, I knew why.

I didn't deserve the effort she made with me.

Time alone in my house, away from cameras and family, gave me ample time to think. No one, other than my parents, rushed to my aid when the news broke. Anna wasn't the only venomous one that existed. My bite was just as bad, and I bore witness to all the damage it caused.

Kiran was the first person in a long time who offered me kindness without an agenda. She overshared and unapologetically did things her way. And every time I thought about pulling her in even closer, drowning myself in all the warmth she radiated, something happened and I fucked it up.

I fucked it up because I knew it was pointless. If anything remained in my chest, it would never be received by her. She had her happily ever after, and I was asking to be crushed for a second time if I continued to seek her out.

And yet, that was exactly what I did in my own way.

I wasted an entire day locked up in my office, trying to find information on Kiran Jafri. Google came up with very little. There was information about her company and the deal she struck with Dad, but that was it. No personal pages. No interviews or soundbites. It was like she didn't exist.

An Instagram link for Shahzad Jafri appeared, and I clicked it to find an open profile. Her son's feed was a mess of photographs with his friends, but Maaz and Kiran sometimes made an appearance. I stopped on a photograph of the three of them together. Kiran pressed her face against Maaz, who poked his tongue out at the camera. Shah wrapped his arms around both from behind. The sun hit their faces and there was genuine joy radiating out of the photograph.

"Seth!" Astra called, and I clicked off the tab like I'd been caught watching porn.

"What?" I snapped, aggravated that my sleuthing had been interrupted.

Astra's hair had changed from vibrant pink to a deep teal colour.

"Sign Kiran's card," she said, waving a large card and pen at me.

"What for?"

"It's her birthday today."

I could cross international spy off my list. How had I missed out on that simple piece of information?

"Sure."

She walked into the room and slid the card and pen across my desk before bouncing on the balls of her feet as she waited.

Opening up the card, I looked at all the signatures inside. Dad's scrawl sat large in the centre of the page. Kirsty. Astra. A million fucking more until there was barely any space left. I squeezed my signature in and handed it back to Astra. She let out a squeal as she snatched the card back and exited my office.

I blew out a deep breath and rolled my chair away from the desk.

It was her birthday.

Picking myself out of my chair, I noticed Kiran's door was open, and I crossed the corridor before I could talk myself out of it. Standing at her door, she wasn't inside, and I stepped into the space.

Three bouquets of flowers lined the wall, and there was a cluster of small gift bags. If there was an office collection, no one had bothered to inform me of it.

I walked behind her desk and pulled out the drawer where she kept her sticky notes. She had finished the orange pad and moved onto hot pink. Pulling a fresh note from the top, I scrawled across it.

Happy birthday, Kiran. I hope this year brings you everything you wish for and more – Tin Man x

Sticking it to her monitor, I got up from the desk to see Kiran in her doorway. I had to stop my jaw from hitting the floor.

The Kiran I saw daily was always decked out in bright colours and prints. She had abandoned those today for a black shirt dress, cinched at her waist by a belt and displaying her legs. The satin material shone under the office lights and I looked away from her body to her face. Kiran's lips were painted bright red and a pair of gold hoops hung from her ears. I was staring at a goddess and if she asked me, I would have dropped to my knees and worshipped her there and then.

"I brought you some cake," she said, holding up both her hands that had paper plates. "Your office was shut. I... Did you need something?"

"No," I said, getting up from her chair. "I was looking for you to wish you a happy birthday."

"All this fuss," she mumbled, blushing vividly. "You must think it's so silly."

"There's nothing silly about people wanting to celebrate your existence."

That made her look up, and I rubbed the back of my neck.

"How about I shut the door and we can enjoy this cake?" she suggested.

I nodded and watched as she bumped the door shut with her ass, dress grazing up her thigh with the motion. I groaned internally, committing myself to hell for lusting after a married woman. Frozen to the spot, Kiran came towards me and I could hear whatever blood hadn't rushed to my dick pounding in my ears.

"Seth," she muttered. "My desk. You're in the way."

"Sorry," I grumbled, taking a step away.

She squeezed past me and put the plates on the desk before sitting down. I took the seat on the other side of her desk and grabbed a slice of cake.

"Red velvet?" I said.

"It's my favourite."

"Same."

She smiled at that. "Astra ordered it from Sugarworks. It's the best thing I've eaten."

"I'll be sure to let Noah know." I laughed.

"Noah? Oh! Sugarworks is your brother's place? Yes! Please tell him I'll marry him in a heartbeat."

Jealousy ran hot through my veins and I pushed it down forcefully.

"I wanted to say sorry for snapping the other day in the car." I stabbed my plastic fork into the cake. "It's a raw topic and I haven't really wanted to discuss it with anyone."

"It's okay. I shouldn't offer advice on a situation I know nothing about. Can we draw a line under it? I don't enjoy arguing with you."

"Classify it as your birthday gift from me."

"You've already given me more than enough. The sunflowers…" She nodded to the bunch at the wall. "And the necklace." Kiran pulled the chain from around her neck to reveal a golden compass pendant. "I love it, but you and Kirsty shouldn't have."

"As long as you like it," I said, praying I had a poker face. "How's your day been?"

"Maaz almost burnt the kitchen down this morning trying to make pancakes and then smothered me in bed."

I let out a hearty laugh. "That's the usual, right?"

"Happens more than I would like to admit," she said, rolling her eyes. "Work's been good and I'm going for dinner with the team. Hence the dress. We're heading out straight after work."

"You look stunning," I said, unable to help myself.

Kiran dropped her eyes to the cake and scrunched her nose. "I look ridiculous, but I'm under strict orders."

Whoever had told her the dress code for the evening was a selfish fuck who wanted to see more of her.

We ate the cake between Kiran chatting about her grant application, and when I left her office, she called after me.

"Seth! I hope you know that I'll always be willing to listen whenever you're ready to talk."

It took me a moment before I nodded. "Thanks."

Instead of walking into my room, I headed towards my assistant. Kirsty was sucking on a lollipop from the bowl on her desk and had tinsel wrapped around her bun as she bobbed along to Christmas music. When I slammed my palms on her desk, she jumped out of her skin and the sweet fell from her mouth.

"Mr Sinclair!" she said, clutching her chest. "Is everything okay?"

I leant in. "Everything is fine. I just want to know how we ended up gifting Kiran flowers and a necklace?"

Kirsty went red across her cheeks, the heat spreading down her neck. "I… I…"

"Out with it."

93

"I thought you might want to get her something, but you haven't been yourself, so I went ahead. I'm so sorry, Mr Sinclair. I should have asked, but I made a call. Please, don't fire me." The last sentence came out as a whisper.

"I'm not going to fire you," I said, realising I had been exceptionally harsh to my assistant when she looked out for me more than some of my friends. "Thank you, Kirsty. She loved them both. Send me the receipts and I'll pay you back."

"Oh, of course. I'll have them on your desk by the end of the day, Mr Sinclair."

"You can call me Seth."

Her eyes widened, but she tried it out. "Okay… Seth." She giggled immediately afterwards. "It's strange."

"You'll get used to it."

A wolf whistle made me straighten up. I was ready to swing for whoever looked at Kiran and thought that was an appropriate response. But I turned around to see Astra grinning at me. My leaning over Kirsty's desk had given her a front-row seat to my ass.

"Eyes back in your head," I told her, walking away to my office.

"You're spoiling my fun!" she called after me.

I swung into Kiran's room and she looked up at me, eyes large and curious.

"Tell your assistant to stop objectifying me. I'm not the office eye candy," I informed her.

Kiran leant back in her seat, eyes travelling from my feet up to my face. "I'm not so sure about that." She winked.

I gave her the middle finger and finally walked back into my office, closing the door behind me.

I was well and truly up shit creek without a paddle.

Chapter Fourteen

- Kiran

Birthdays were just another day on the calendar for me. I never wanted to celebrate another year around the sun, but everyone around me seemed to ignore my requests and go full throttle. Mike insisted I come to dinner with the team and once dessert was polished off, he directed the both of us to an upscale bar to finish the night with drinks.

I wasn't some young, working professional who fell neatly into the London nightlife. I was a mum of two who was permanently exhausted and always five pounds away from her goal weight.

Fiddling with my nose ring, I wondered how quickly I could make my escape.

"Are you sure I can't convince you to come clubbing tonight?" Mike asked. "Birthday shots and grinding against some gorgeous strangers."

"Sounds amazing," I deadpanned. "But it's not really my thing. I think I'm going to head home. You should enjoy the night."

"Kiran," he said, cupping my face in both his hands. "When are you going to live your life again?"

Mike's eyes were hidden behind thick-rimmed glasses, and his blonde hair fell across his forehead. I brushed some of it away before placing my hands over his.

"I am living it," I answered softly.

He shot me a sceptical look before pressing a kiss to my head. "Want me to wait for you to finish your drink?"

"No," I said, waving him off. "Go find some sexy stranger, but stay safe."

"You're such a mother." He laughed and grabbed his jacket, kissing my cheek as he left.

I wanted to rip my heels from my feet and soak them in warm water. Maybe I could pick up a large pizza for the boys on the way home and we could cuddle up with a horror film. It would probably piss off Shah that I didn't stay out and enjoy my birthday, but he had his own ideas about how I should lead my life.

Finishing the last of the non-alcoholic champagne, I put the glass on the bar top and shrugged on my jacket. The sound of shattering glass pulled my attention towards the door and I caught sight of a familiar figure. Seth pushed himself out of his seat with his arms spread wide. His shirt was soaked, and a woman stood in front of him, looking furious.

Anna. There was no denying it was his ex with her blonde hair and to-die-for figure.

"I'm not sure how we lasted as long as we did!" she yelled viciously.

I didn't register my feet moving until I joined them.

"Seth," I said.

They both looked at me and Seth's brow crumpled in confusion. He trembled with anger and the vein at the side of his neck pulsed beneath the skin.

"Kiran?" he said, narrowing his eyes.

"Who are you?" Anna demanded.

I looked at her and smiled. "Kiran Jafri. I work with Seth."

"I can only imagine what business you handle with him dressed like that."

My cheeks flamed with embarrassment.

"Don't you dare insult her!" Seth spat.

I placed a hand on his arm and shook my head. "Don't worry. We need to go. You're attracting a lot of attention."

"We're not done here," Anna said forcefully.

"I think you are. Respect his boundaries and leave him alone," I said sharply before finally pulling Seth away and out the door. "Can you drive?"

"Yeah," he said.

We slipped into his car, and Seth drove down the streets without saying a word. I could feel his anger filling the space and suffocating us under its weight. His knuckles were white around the steering wheel and the muscle in his jaw flexed. I had no idea where he was headed, but I didn't want to disrupt him because I was worried about ending up in an accident.

Fifteen minutes of steely silence, and he pulled up outside a house and cut the engine.

"Sorry," he said, staring ahead. "I just needed somewhere safe."

"This is your home?" I asked, and Seth nodded. "Let's get you inside," I told him.

I exited the car and Seth followed suit, letting us into the house. The space was massive for someone who lived alone, and everything was in pristine condition. White walls and pine furnishings. The place looked like a show home rather than one someone lived in.

"I took your advice. Asked her to meet me so we could talk," Seth said, walking through the house, and I followed him. "What a fucking waste of time."

A button fell to the floor, rolling to a stop by my feet. I picked it up and when I straightened, I blushed. Seth had shrugged off his shirt, and I got a view of his sculpted bare back. The muscles moved under his smooth skin as he raked his hands through his thick, dark hair.

"Drink?" he asked gruffly.

"I don't drink," I squeaked in response.

We walked into an opulent kitchen, and Seth gestured to the island, where I took a seat. He grabbed two glasses and poured whiskey into one and water into another before handing it to me.

It was impossible to avoid looking at his body. Seth was a carefully crafted specimen that was a combination of lean muscles and sharp lines. The brush of our fingers intensified my blush, and I was grateful when he pulled a t-shirt from the laundry basket and pulled it over his head. Breathing suddenly became much easier with his body hidden from view.

"Seth," I said, unscrambling my thoughts as he sat beside me. "Are you okay?"

He shook his head. "I never should have met with her."

"I'm sorry," I said, putting a hand on his arm. His bicep twitched beneath my fingers. "But you're safe now. I'm sorry if coming over to you made it worse. I didn't want you all over the headlines tomorrow morning."

"I appreciate it, Kiran. I don't get saved very often."

"Everyone needs saving sometimes."

"I wish you were here when it happened," he said, looking into his glass. "You must think I'm so stupid for not seeing it."

"Not at all."

Seth swilled the liquid around his glass before taking a drink. "You said you were always willing to listen."

"I did," I said, placing my glass on the island and looking at him.

"I'm all those things you called me and more, Kiran. I am pompous and I think everything revolves around me. I used to think I was invincible." He stared ahead at the wall.

"We all think we're untouchable until something happens," I replied, trying not to get caught up in the torrent of memories that rushed to the forefront.

"I met Anna at university. We kind of fell together. Moved up through the circles together and I thought I could trust her."

"What happened?" I whispered.

Seth turned his head slowly to look at me. "I asked her to marry me after I finished my MBA. We'd been together for years and everyone was expecting it."

"Did you ask her because you wanted to or because everyone expected you to?"

"A little of both, I guess. I know that makes me even more of a prick. And then Anna wanted a baby."

"She wanted to start a family with you?"

Seth laughed, and the sound chilled me. It was such a hollow noise, and I wished there weren't moments in his life that drew it out from him.

"No," he said. "She wanted a baby. Her friends were falling pregnant. There were deals on the table for them, and Anna wanted to be part of that club. I wasn't sold on the idea at first but I agreed, eventually."

"Seth." I sighed, running a hand down my face.

"I warmed to the idea, Kiran. I *really* warmed to it. I have six little brothers. I spent my entire life teaching them and leading them. Being a father was something I didn't think about, but when I did…" he trailed off. "I was so excited. I love my family and I wanted to start one of my own. My parents would be grandparents and my brothers would be uncles. The family would be welcoming the next generation."

It warmed my heart to hear him talk about his family. I knew how much I loved my sons, and Seth would make a good parent if his protective nature over his parents and brothers was anything to go by.

"But it didn't happen," he continued. "And it was my fault."

"What do you mean? You changed your mind?"

"No." He shook his head and blew out a breath. "We tried and nothing was happening. I got tested. Unexplained infertility. No kids in my future."

I felt the air get knocked out of my lungs. "Seth, I'm so sorry."

Not just for his diagnosis, but because of my big mouth talking about my boys. I'd told him he would never feel love like love for

101

his children, and he knew the entire time that wasn't a possibility. The guilt violently clawed at my chest.

He shook his head again, and I clamped my mouth shut. It felt like he'd been waiting so long to let it all out.

"She blamed me," he continued. "The reason she cheated was because of the diagnosis, but it started before that. Before she left, she told me she didn't want a man who couldn't do his basic biological job. That one stung."

"She's vile," I breathed, feeling my heart break for him.

"We both are." Seth ran a hand over his face and knocked back the rest of his drink. "Sometimes I think I've ended up with everything I deserve."

"That's not it," I said, reaching out and covering his hand with mine. "Life doesn't work like that."

"Are you sure?" he asked, rubbing his thumb over my skin and setting it alight. "Bad things happen to bad people."

"You're not a bad person."

"I'm not exactly a good one either."

"You are. He's just buried underneath a lot of armour, Tin Man."

He held my gaze for a moment and said, "I'm sorry. It's your birthday and I've taken over your evening."

"Please don't apologise. I'm glad you felt like you could trust me."

"You've never given me a reason not to."

The guilt amplified in my chest and crawled up my throat as I removed my hand from his. "If you're alright, I'll call a cab and get home."

"I'll take you."

"No. I don't want you driving around tonight," I said. "You need to unwind and maybe look into a restraining order." It was only partially a joke.

The cab arrived ten minutes later, and Seth walked me to the front door.

With my hand on the doorknob, I said, "If you need anything at all, you have my number, Seth. Call me."

His hand went to my face, cupping my cheek, and I froze. The blood pounded in my ears and my heart thumped against my chest at the tenderness the gesture held.

"You're a good person, Kiran. Your husband is a lucky man."

"I need to go."

Seth dropped his hand from my face and a coolness spread over me before I opened the door. As I slid into the car, I clutched the necklace and swallowed the lump in my throat.

He didn't know how wrong he was.

Chapter Fifteen

- Seth

This was my first Christmas at home for three years.

I had visited my parents on Christmas day when I was with Anna, but old traditions had slowly been thrown out of the window to make space for what she wanted.

This year, I slept at my parents' house on Christmas Eve with the rest of my brothers in the way we had when we were all little children. The entire day was spent in pyjamas instead of dressed up, and the weight I usually carried with me felt lighter. Gifts unwrapped and dinner demolished, we lounged in the living room, sprawled across the sofas and floor. Completely undignified, and wholly content.

"Are you expecting someone to call?" Aiden asked. "You keep looking at your phone like it's a lifeline."

"No," I said, placing it face down on the arm of the sofa.

His lips formed a thin line. "You're not waiting to hear from Anna, are you? Because I didn't say anything the first time, but if you're about to —"

"No," I cut him off. "It's nothing."

"Well, it's not business on Christmas Day so it has to be a woman," he said quietly, smirk settling back into place.

"I don't want to discuss this with you."

Aiden's eyes widened, and the mischievous glint kindled in his irises. "So, there is a woman."

"Keep your voice down," I hissed.

The grin on his face was wide, showing off all his teeth. He leant in conspiratorially, and I regretted looking at my damn phone when he was in the vicinity.

"Tell me everything," he said.

"There's nothing to tell," I told him honestly.

"I don't want details, but who is she? How long?"

"You're getting to be as bad as Mum."

"Does she know?"

"No! No one knows because there is nothing to know."

My phone vibrated and my hand shot to it, but Aiden dived over my lap, knocking it to the floor. A fight ensued as we both scrabbled for the device.

"What is wrong with the both of you?" Noah asked.

"Nothing," we both replied, and Aiden grabbed a hold of my phone, dropping back on the sofa.

He didn't have the passcode, but he didn't need it. The notification banner stretched across the screen and he looked up at me, arching an eyebrow. Despondently, I sat beside him and snatched my phone away.

"Kiran?" he whispered, finally trying to have a private conversation. "I thought you said she was married."

"She is," I said, gritting my teeth.

"Shit," Aiden hissed. "You're —"

"Do I look as stupid as you?"

He balled his hand and punched me in the arm, leaving a dull ache.

"There's no affair," I clarified. "I enjoy her company."

Aiden narrowed his eyes. "Seth."

"I don't want to hear it, Aiden."

"This doesn't feel like a smart move."

"I'm not doing anything wrong."

"I know. That's not my concern."

Aiden was the most light-hearted brother. His job forced him to be a serious professional, but the moment he stepped out of the hospital, he became a child. So watching the way his face fell made a heavy weight settle in my stomach.

"What?" I snapped, avoiding his eyes.

After a few moments of silence, he said quietly, "I hope you know what you're doing, bro. I don't want you to get hurt."

Aiden's words stuck with me through the holidays, but I clung to the small ray of sunshine that broke into my life. One message to wish her a Merry Christmas soon led to a thread of exchanges about our days, and with each notification, I felt my heart tumble further past the point of no return.

I took it a step too far on her birthday. Pouring out my soul in the kitchen, Kiran had watched me intently and listened to every word. There was no judgement. She didn't recoil.

I would have kissed her. If she showed any indication of wanting it as badly as I did, I would have pulled her in and kept her with me all night. Every day, the urge to ask her for a single tryst grew stronger. One dip into the pool of sunshine and kindness so I could feel worthy of it.

But Kiran wouldn't cheat.

A flirty comment and a shoulder to cry on didn't mean she would come to bed with me. And deep down, I didn't want her to. Not when she wasn't mine. Not when I couldn't keep her.

"Where's your head at?" Dad asked as we arrived at the activity centre on a brisk January afternoon.

"Nowhere," I lied.

"You've been awfully quiet. Are you sure there's nothing you want to talk about?"

I think I've accidentally developed feelings for the ray of sunshine you hired, and now I want to flee the country again before I make a giant fucking mistake.

"You worry too much, old man," I said.

The lobby of the lodge was filled with Sinclair Technologies' employees for the start of year team building day. Dad always encouraged employees and their families to come out and spend the day doing a range of activities to keep us grounded and allow networking between different companies.

I hadn't attended one of these days in the past five years but pulled on my boots and joined my family today. I told Kiran I was trying kindness and although she might not hold me to it, I felt better if I actually made an effort.

"You didn't tell me she was a yummy mummy," Aiden said, slinging an arm around my shoulders and jerking his chin towards the corner of the room.

Kiran stood with her sons, talking to Maaz in the mixture of words and sign. Her hair was scraped back into a ponytail and she wore the fucking yoga pants that instantly made the day, and my dick, harder.

"I'm going to say hello and introduce myself to the kids," Aiden said, starting to move.

I caught his arm roughly. "Leave her alone. She's off limits."

"Just going to ask how her holidays went."

"You're nothing special," I reminded him with a shove.

The rabble was unleashed out on the grounds where instructors stood all around at different stations. Water sports, rock climbing, archery, biking. There was something for everyone to try their hand at.

As I walked with my brothers towards the bikes, I saw Kiran kneeling on the ground beside Maaz.

"Maaz," Kiran said, looking up at the rock wall nervously. "I'm not sure, baby. It's high, and I don't want you to fall."

"I won't fall," he argued confidently. "Please, Ma."

"I don't know," she replied, looking torn.

"He'll be harnessed in," I said, stopping by her.

Kiran rose from the ground. "Is it safe?"

"They wouldn't run the activity if it wasn't. I'll stay with you if you want."

"Seth!" Aiden hollered. "Are you coming?"

I waved him off, and he narrowed his eyes before flipping me off and continuing with the rest of the Sinclair brood.

Crouching down to Maaz's level, I spoke to the little boy, "You have to promise to listen to everything the instructor says, okay?"

He nodded enthusiastically, black curls bouncing.

"Cross your heart?" I asked.

"Cross my heart!" He drew a cross over his stomach.

"Trust me," Kiran mumbled. "That's where his heart is."

Maaz joined the queue and practically bounced into the harness. He looked at me and I tugged my ear as a gesture for him to listen. He nodded and turned back to the instructor.

I jumped when Kiran grabbed a hold of my arm in a death grip. Maaz had only put his foot on the first hold.

"He'll be fine," I said to her. "He's got a lot of confidence."

"Too much," she muttered in response.

Maaz scaled the wall and Kiran stayed glued to my side. The higher he got, the closer she buried herself into my body, and I tried my hardest not to react. This was not helping the tangled mixture of emotions I'd tripped into. And it certainly wasn't helping to keep my mind out of the gutter with her body pressed against mine.

The ringing of the bell made us both look up to see Maaz had reached the top of the wall.

"Oh, God," Kiran breathed as he laughed and started his descent. "I think I'm going to be sick."

I laughed and hugged her to my side. "He'll be back on the ground in a few seconds."

Once Maaz was out of the harness, he ran back over to us, smile wide enough that it could split his face. Kiran dropped to his height, hugging him tight.

"Did you see?" he asked, words muffled against her shoulder.

"Yes. I'm very proud of you." Kiran kissed his cheek, and he immediately wiped it off.

"Did you see?" Maaz asked, looking up at me.

"I saw, and I think you're braver than I am because I've never reached the top of the wall," I replied.

If possible, his smile grew wider.

With my brothers long gone down the bike trail, and Shah off with some other teens he'd met, Kiran and I fell into step together. No matter how much I told myself to stay away from her, the universe continued to place us in each other's paths. It was a cruel and twisted cosmic punishment.

The last activity of the day was a tug of war over a mud pit.

"Go on, Ma," Shah said, giving Kiran a push. "Go show off some muscle."

She pulled a face but went over and held one side of the rope. Her short frame took the lead, with Mike behind her and most of her team following her lead.

I sat on the grass, watching as the other side of the rope filled up, and the war began. Kiran's side leant back and tugged with all their might, but they were the weaker side. Her feet slid across the ground and Kiran let out a scream as she fell face first into the mud alone.

"Shit!" I pushed myself up and ran towards her.

"Ma!" Shah said, following after me.

Kiran pushed herself out of the mud and I stepped into the pit, pulling her up to her feet. She laughed so hard she could barely hold herself upright.

"You're such a fucking mess," I muttered through laughter.

She looked at me for a few seconds and then reached out, wiping a hand down my face and covering me in mud. Kiran cackled as she ran to her eldest son for safety.

This woman would be the end of me in one way or another.

By the end of the day, everyone piled into the canteen for dinner. I heard Maaz as he chattered away and saw Shah nearby. A quick scan of the room alerted me to the fact that Kiran wasn't here. I couldn't hear her laughter or see the swinging ponytail.

"She went outside," Aiden said, coming up behind me.

"Fuck off," I snapped.

"You're looking for Kiran, right?"

I thumped his arm, trying to avoid having this conversation with him. Aiden laughed and shoved me.

"You're completely fucked," he told me. "Planning on becoming a homewrecker?"

"No."

"Because I wouldn't blame you."

"Stop."

"Tiffy would probably kill you."

"I'm not going to do anything," I told him sharply. "I just want to check if she's alright."

"Whatever." Aiden shrugged. "And I want my Gyarados."

My cheeks heated, and it spread down my neck.

"I know, bro," Aiden continued. "She asked if you'd given it to me. Face it, Seth. I'm the favourite Sinclair." He shot me a shit-eating grin, and I turned on my heels and left before I could punch him in the mouth.

Outside, the air was bitterly cold and illuminated only by the lights of the building I'd walked out of. I spotted a tiny figure sitting out on the grass. She had her head tipped back, staring up at the sky.

"Mind if I join you?" I asked, dropping next to her.

Kiran bumped her shoulder against mine. "I thought you'd be stuffing your face with the rest of them."

"That was the plan, but I noticed you weren't there. Is everything okay?"

"It's not very often I get a peaceful moment," she explained, turning her head to me. "Between work and the boys, there's always something else going on. Thank you for helping Maaz today."

"It's my pleasure. He's a good kid."

"One of the best," she said, smiling.

"Why didn't Jamal come with you?"

I felt her body stiffen beside me, and the uncomfortable feeling knotted in the pit of my stomach. Something wasn't right with her marriage.

"Is this not his thing?" I asked. "It would have been good to meet him."

"Seth, I need to tell you something."

The acidic tang filled my mouth as I prepared to hear what she had to say. "You can trust me," I encouraged her.

Kiran looked back up at the sky, and a silence stretched out between us. I wanted to reach out and touch her. To pull her in and tell her that this was a safe space. If she needed help, then I would figure it out, but I couldn't do anything until she opened up to me.

"Has he hurt you, Kiran?" I whispered, gaze dropping to the scar on her face.

She shook her head and let out a shuddering breath. When she spoke, it was a broken whisper. "My husband died five years ago."

It was so quiet you could have heard a pin drop. My mind looped over every time I brought up her husband in conversation, and she took it all when she knew the truth of her situation.

"Kiran. I am so sorry," I choked out.

"You shouldn't be. It's not your fault he took his life. It's mine."

She delivered the second blow, still staring up at the stars, and I saw her breath materialise in the air as she let out a shaky sigh.

Her husband, Jamal, took his life.

I didn't know what to say to her. I was trying to understand how that information slotted into her life. Kiran, who was always so positive, carried a weight like this with her wherever she went.

"Kiran," I said, reaching for her hand.

"Ma?"

She sniffed and looked over her shoulder. Shah waded across the grass towards us.

"What are you doing out here?" he asked, holding a hand out to her. "You're going to get sick. Come inside and eat something."

Kiran took his hand and got to her feet, but I didn't miss the look Shah gave me. His hesitancy towards me made more sense now. Shah had filled his father's shoes and become the man of the house. He was looking out for his mother and brother the best he could, and I was a threat to their unit.

As she walked away with her eldest son, I saw Kiran Jafri in a whole new light.

Chapter Sixteen
- Kiran

The office felt too daunting after my admission to Seth. I had never been so grateful to have Shah as I did in that moment when he came out to find me. My son had stopped me from falling apart without even realising it.

As I walked back into the living room with a cup of coffee in hand, more syrup than coffee by the time I'd finished, there was a knock on the door. I contemplated ignoring it, wanting to wallow on my own, but my feet led me to it before I could decide otherwise.

Mike stood on my doorstep holding up a bag, and my stomach growled at the smell that came from it.

"I brought chicken soup for the patient," he said as I let him in. "Do you need to see a doctor?"

"I'm okay," I said quietly.

He followed me into the living room and set the bag on the table. "You rarely take a sick day," Mike commented. "Did you pick it up from the boys? Are they in sch —"

He stopped mid-sentence as he took in the cream photo album that sat on the coffee table. I set down my mug and pulled the soup out of the bag, rummaging around for a spoon. When I found it, I sat on the sofa, tucking my legs underneath me, and avoiding Mike's stare.

"You don't bring this out much anymore," he said, picking the album off the table and sitting next to me.

I spooned hot soup into my mouth, trying to ignore the burning prick of tears in my eyes.

"This soup is good," I muttered after I swallowed. "I love chicken noodle."

"I know," he said.

Mike's fingers twitched against the cover of the album, and I sighed.

"You can open it," I whispered.

He didn't hesitate, flipping open the cover and turning over the pages gently. Photographs were neatly stuck inside. Some of the colour had started to fade, making them less vivid, but in my mind, I could see them all perfectly.

"It was a beautiful day," Mike said.

I dropped the spoon into the carton and ran my fingers over the page. "We didn't need anything apart from each other."

A large photo of me and Jamal took up the page. He had lost his suit jacket and his tie sat awkwardly around his neck. I sat next to him in the registry office, draped in a red saree, smile wide on my face. Between us, Shah blew a raspberry at the camera. We never had much, but we had all we needed in our little family.

"He adored you," Mike said, turning the page slowly.

Photographs of our reception at a small restaurant. Mike wrestled with Shah as Jamal fed me cake from his fork. Our guest list had consisted of a total of ten people, including ourselves. People would probably laugh at what we called our wedding. Barely any planning and on a shoestring budget, but it was perfect.

"I loved him with everything," I said, voice breaking.

Leaning forward, I put the soup on the table and jammed the heels of my palms into my eyes. I heard the album shut before Mike pulled me to his side. When I tried to push away, he pulled me closer, and I sobbed.

"It's okay, Kiran," he whispered into my hair. "It's okay."

In the months after Jamal's death, Mike had helped me through the haze of grief. He helped with Shah and walked through the arrangements. Mike cemented himself as family when everyone else was against me.

When I finally unburied my face from his chest, he pressed a kiss against my forehead. "You're missing him?" Mike asked. "That's why you brought out the albums?"

The guilt was so strong it made my chest tighten and I pushed away from Mike, needing the space to breathe.

"Kiran." Mike looked worried. "In through your nose and out through your mouth," he coached.

I followed his instructions as my vision started to get blurry. His words sounded muffled in my ears, but I clung to his arms, and slowly, my breathing settled back into a regular pattern.

"It's okay to miss him," Mike assured me.

"It's not that," I admitted. "I miss him. I miss him every day. But I think I've messed up."

"How?"

"I think…"

"There's nothing we can't fix."

I shook my head and dropped it into my hands. "I feel like I'm betraying him."

Mike gently pried my hands away from my face and fresh tears spilled onto my cheeks. "Do you want to tell me what happened between you and Seth?"

"How did you know it's Seth?"

"That man ran to you quicker than any of us when you fell in the mud," Mike said. "And your dirty laugh came out when you wiped mud down his face. I haven't heard it in years."

"Nothing's happened between us. Not really."

"Not really?"

I let out a shuddering breath. "We spend time together. I don't know. He's said things like how my husband is lucky to have me." I swallowed the lump that was making it difficult to talk. "Every time I touch him, it's like I've stuck my fingers in an electrical socket."

"But nothing's happened?"

"No. But I want it to. Sometimes, I want to kiss him, Mike. I want to give him the small pockets of spare time that I have and learn more about him." A small pulse began behind my eyes. "I want it so bad that I finally told him about Jamal. That he died. I feel like I sold out my husband because I saw a pretty face. What is wrong with me?"

"Nothing is wrong with you," Mike told me firmly. "Kiran, you have to stop punishing yourself. It's been years. You're allowed to fancy someone else."

"I feel like I'm doing wrong by him."

Mike squeezed my hands tight. "Neither of us knows what Jamal was thinking, but he loved you. He wanted you to be happy. He wouldn't want you sitting here, forcing yourself to hide away because you think you're hurting him."

"What if I forget him?" I whispered.

"I don't think that's possible," Mike said, laughing under his breath. "What you both had was special."

My bottom lip trembled at his words.

"But," Mike pressed on, "that doesn't mean you stop living when it's lost."

"I don't know what to do with myself."

"Will you answer me something?" Mike asked gently. "How does he make you feel? Seth. When you're with him, how do you feel?"

Taking a deep breath, I thought about Seth and the time we spent together, the messages we exchanged.

"He's a prick," I said without thinking, and Mike laughed. "No, I mean it. He can be such an asshole when he wants to be. I can see exactly why there are stories in the building about him."

"But?"

"There's something underneath all that and I get to see it when it's just me and him. And in those moments, I feel lighter than I have in years. I feel lucky to get a glimpse of him like that."

"Sounds like he's selective about who sees that side of him."

"He protects himself," I said, defending him.

"Kiran, if he makes you feel that way, what would be so bad about seeing what could happen between you both?"

"Because he probably thinks I'm this awful liar, making him believe I was married."

There was another reason, but I didn't want to admit it.

For so many years, Jamal's family blamed me for his death, and I couldn't shake the feeling that I was a contributing factor. Something had been wrong, and I didn't notice. How was I meant to feel comfortable in another relationship when I'd failed so spectacularly at the one that I had vowed to remain in until the end of time?

"I'm not going to push you, Kiran," Mike said, pulling me in and hugging me. "But don't close yourself off to the idea of meeting someone. It doesn't have to be Seth. But you deserve to be happy. You deserve someone who will look after you."

Mike might have felt like I deserved those things, but I wasn't sure I was built for happiness in the form of love after destroying it for the first time.

Chapter Seventeen

- Seth

The door to Kiran's home was a deep green colour and to the left of it, against the wall, was a trellis with twisting plants climbing high. I stared at the image for twenty minutes.

She hadn't turned up to work for the past three days. Astra said she was sick and when she didn't reply to any of my messages, I took the afternoon off work to find her. But now that I was outside, my courage wavered. This would definitely be classified as overstepping the mark.

All I needed to do was knock on the door, check she was alive, and then I would leave. There was nothing weird about this.

Stepping out of the car, I walked up to the door and knocked. A few moments later, Kiran opened it, dressed in a black t-shirt, and pyjama trousers that had illustrated avocados all over them.

"Seth? Shit," she said and tried to close the door.

My hand shot out to stop her. "Don't shut me out."

She held my gaze before opening it wider with a heavy sigh. "Come in."

"Is Shah home?" I asked, stepping over the threshold.

"No, he's at school. Why?"

"He looks ready to fight me."

Kiran laughed softly and shook her head. "He's a little untrusting and very protective. You should be more worried about Maaz. That boy will bite without warning. Sometimes I have children and sometimes I have feral heathens, but for now, you're safe."

Her home was exactly what I expected it to be. The living room was painted in lavender and her furniture was bright paisley prints. Sticky notes were dotted randomly across the walls and stacks of books took up the surfaces. A half-finished Lego structure sat on the coffee table.

It was a stark contrast to my house that was white and marble and in pristine condition. My house that looked empty.

"I'm sorry about the mess," she said, glancing over her shoulder. "Tea? Coffee?"

"I would appreciate coffee," I replied, and followed her into the kitchen.

Another burst of colour. This time, the walls were tangerine and reminded me of her office.

Kiran went over to a pot on the counter. "Just brewed, but I can make a fresh pot if you prefer."

"No, that'll be fine."

"Could you grab me the milk from the fridge, please?"

I crossed over to the fridge and pulled open the door before my brows drew together. "Um, Kiran," I started.

In the fridge's door sat four cartons of milk.

"The one closest to the outside," she said over the sound of the spoon clinking against the mug. I grabbed it as she continued, "I always forget if we have milk or not, so I have a note. Then I end up buying it when we have enough. It's a vicious cycle."

I bit the insides of my cheeks to stop myself from laughing. Kiran was highly intelligent, but behind closed doors, she was a little scatter brained.

Coffee in hand, we traipsed back into the living room and she took a seat on the sofa, curling her legs beneath her. I sat down beside her instead of choosing one of the chairs.

"You haven't been at work the past few days," I commented. "You didn't reply to my messages."

She looked down at her avocado-covered pyjamas. "Sorry," she mumbled. "I wanted to, but I deleted them. I feel like there's a conversation brewing, and I don't know if I want to have it with you."

"You don't have to tell me anything, Kiran. You don't owe me an explanation. But I would rather you didn't avoid me."

"I know, but I also feel you probably have a dozen questions, and I'd rather you talk to me than go searching or come up with your own conclusions."

"I'm not going to hunt," I told her.

The urge had been there. It would have been easy to search for Jamal Jafri and see if anything turned up. To learn the story without Kiran having to relive it. But it was fleeting and my search history remained clean.

"I hate it when people do it to me," I continued. "If you want to talk, I'll listen. And if you'd rather not, that's fine. I just wanted to make sure you were okay."

There wasn't a speck of makeup on her face. The scar on her cheek stood out and the area under her eyes looked dark. My fingers twitched on the seat between us, begging to reach out and touch her. Wanting to offer her the same comfort she gave me when I bared my soul.

Kiran didn't look at me when she spoke. Her focus remained on her legs. "I don't live in a fairy-tale."

It had been flippant of me to say that to her when I didn't know anything about her personal life.

"I was pregnant with Maaz when it happened," she said and sank back against the cushions, clutching the mug in her hands. "He didn't leave a note or anything like that. It's not like books and films." She lifted a hand and brushed the scar under her eye. "His mum threw a photo frame at me after the funeral. They blame me for it," she explained.

"It's not your fault," I argued firmly.

When Kiran looked at me, her eyes were glassy, and my chest tightened.

"But it is," she whispered. "I was his wife. We were together since we were fourteen. A decade. And I never saw any signs. I was too wrapped up in setting up the company, and he didn't feel like he could come and talk to me. What kind of person am I that he couldn't tell me how he was feeling or what was going on inside?"

A tear spilled over and she brushed it away quickly. At that moment, I knew there was a heart in my chest because it shattered for her.

"It's not your fault," I repeated. "You're filling in all these blanks with no proper answers."

"It is," Kiran told me. "He wasn't happy about setting up the company. He was worried about money and the boys. I told him we'd figure it out, but I can't help thinking if that was what plagued him. I wish he could be here now and see the boys and how everything turned out."

"You don't know if that was the reason."

"I've tried to be a better person every day since," she whispered, lost under a current of memories. "I'll listen to anyone if they need it. I keep my office door open so people know they have a space to go."

Kiran had become a product of her tragedy. She moulded herself around it instead of falling apart and becoming bitter.

"I make sure the boys talk to me. It's getting more difficult with Shah. He's sixteen, and I guess it's embarrassing to talk to your mum. But I need to look after the people I have in my life."

"Kiran," I said, reaching out and brushing away another tear from her face. "Who's looking after you?"

She shot me a confused look, nose wrinkling and eyebrows pulling together. "No one," she said, composing herself. "I don't need looking after."

It wasn't flippant or curt. It was delivered with the same gentle confidence that she usually approached life with. Kiran had slid herself to the bottom of her priority list because she worried about everyone else.

"That's not how life works," I reminded her.

How was I meant to tell her she deserved what she gave to others? That she needed to stop punishing herself for what happened.

"Do you know why I still wear my ring?" she asked, twisting it on her finger. "Why I let people assume I'm married?"

"Why?"

"I took it off last year. I felt ready to put it away and focus on my future. But I work and network with so many men. They respect the rings more than they do me saying no." Kiran blew out a breath. "I know that makes me a terrible person. That I wear my rings just to keep people away."

"We're assholes," I told her. "And now I really am sorry about Aiden."

"Your brother is harmless."

"He should know better. We all should if you aren't looking to date."

"I don't think I'll date," she admitted. "I wouldn't trust myself with someone again. Wouldn't know if I was fucking it up or not."

I always knew there could be nothing between us. Not really. But hearing her admit she would never date popped a small bubble of hope in my chest.

When the door slammed open, Kiran yelled, "Maaz Jafri! Do *not* bring the boots —"

But it was too late as the sound of studs against wooden flooring sounded in the room. Maaz appeared in front of us, caked in mud and grinning.

"Seth!" he said, seeing me. "Why are you here?"

"Yeah. Why are you here?" Shah asked, following his little brother into the room.

"I came by to check on your mum," I explained, putting the mug on the table.

"She's fine," Shah replied.

"Shah," Kiran warned quietly.

"Have you been crying?" he asked, looking at her closely. His attention snapped back to me. "What did you say to her?"

Kiran shot up from her seat. "Stop," she said. "He didn't make me cry. I'm a little stressed at work and Seth let me talk to him."

Maaz seemed unbothered by the tension as he stripped off his coat to show even more mud over his kit.

"Why couldn't you choose something like badminton?" Kiran asked, looking at him. She put her mug down. "Why did it have to be rugby? Get upstairs and run a bath. I'll be there now."

Maaz pulled a face but ran off with no verbal complaint.

Kiran turned back to me. "I'll be back in the office tomorrow. Thank you for stopping by and thank you for listening."

"You have my number. Call me if you need anything," I said, repeating the offer she gave me.

She smiled weakly. "Shah, please see Seth out."

Kiran disappeared up the stairs, and I got up from the sofa while her eldest son stared me down.

"I know who you are," he said, just as I stepped out of the house. "I know you spent months sleeping around after your girlfriend left you."

I clenched my teeth together, but it was to be expected. Shah was a teenager, and the internet was probably his second home.

"I'm not sure what that has to do —" I started.

"Stay away from my mum. If you need to talk to her about work, do it in the office or email. You don't need to come to the house."

"I was concerned."

"I don't care," he said sharply. "She doesn't need you to be concerned about her. She's got us."

He slammed the door shut on my face and I blinked a few times. The wrath in me wanted to bang on the wood and ask him who the fuck he was, but the rational side won. Shah was protecting his mother, and I didn't blame him.

Kiran needed people in her corner, and I needed to prove I was worthy of being one of them.

Chapter Eighteen

- Kiran

I stepped into the lift to find Seth already there. He leant casually against the back wall, staring down at his phone. His suit was a charcoal-coloured three-piece, and the shirt was black. He looked positively sinful, and I felt my face heat as I jabbed the button for our floor a few times.

"Have you been on the third floor all day?" he asked, looking up from his phone. A few strands of hair danced along his forehead.

"Yes."

"You need to delegate better."

When he made comments like that, I wanted to snap at him, but I let it go. After his visit, I worried things would change between us. That Seth would look at me as a murderer and freeze me out. Instead, he popped his head around the door to greet me every morning and topped up the herbal tea in the kitchen. He was still Seth, still efficient and traditional, but he hadn't banished me from his life after my admission.

"It's easier to troubleshoot when you're in the thick of it," I told him.

"You're having issues?" He placed the phone in his pocket.

"When do we not?" I mumbled. "AI has a mind of its own." I caught his worried look. "Oh God, not literally. I mean, we want it to do something and it won't listen."

"You're not making it any better. I'm imagining you're fighting robots down there."

The corner of my mouth twitched. It was the first smile I'd cracked all day.

"We'll draft you in if that ever happens," I told him.

The doors barely opened before I shot out the lift and down the hall.

"Astra," I said, not slowing my pace.

"You're out of the office for the rest of the afternoon," she said without looking up from her screen.

"Thank you!"

"Kiran!" Kirsty called, but it was too late.

I walked straight into the glass door with force and rebounded, staggering back into Seth's arms.

"Fuck," I uttered, wincing. He let out a chuckle, and I turned around. "It's not funny."

Seth reached around me and opened the door as I rubbed at the sore spot on my face. The heat of his body made me freeze and the familiar woody scent wrapped around my senses.

"Why are you in such a rush?" he asked, looking down at me.

"Because I messed up," I admitted, walking through the door.

Seth followed me as I entered my office, shoving things into my bag. He leant against the doorframe and watched me, making it difficult to breathe.

"Kiran, slow down," he directed me. "What's happened?"

"Maaz's school has a fundraiser, and I told the PTA I'd help set up and bake some cakes, but I got so obsessed with the grant that I forgot until Maaz mentioned it this morning. So now I need to stop at the supermarket and pick up a million cakes and then break every speed limit to get to the school." My head snapped up. "I'm not actually going to break the speed limit."

"I know," he said. "I might be able to help you."

"Really? You're a master baker?"

"Careful how you say that," Seth said with a smirk, and I flushed. "I can call Noah and see what he has."

The relief flooded through my chest. "Could you? You'd be my hero. I'll pay him whatever he wants."

"Why don't you go to the school and help set up? I'll call Noah and bring the cake to you."

"Aren't you busy?" I asked him, slinging my bag over my shoulder. "Astra can do it."

"I have some spreadsheets that can wait until tomorrow and a meeting that can be rearranged. You'd be doing me a favour."

"Seth, if you can do that for me, I will be forever grateful." I walked towards him, and he moved out of the door.

"Send me the address," he called after me. "I'll get there as soon as I can."

Maaz's school hall was decorated in streamers and stalls as members of the PTA buzzed around.

I shed my bag and coat, and set up the table at the far end of the hall that remained empty. There were a few curious glances, but no one approached me and my stomach flooded with anxiety.

In for four. Hold for seven. Out for eight.

"Hi, Kiran." Angela Watson, head of the PTA, sidled up to the table and ran her finger across it. "Were you too busy to bake?"

It was a veiled insult, and I squirmed in my skin. Truthfully, yes. But I hated it was being used against me.

"I'm just waiting on a friend to bring everything," I said politely.

"We're about to start," Angela replied, looking unimpressed. "Next time, maybe you should leave it to someone who has the time. I don't like letting down the kids."

"I'm not letting them down. He'll be here."

She drummed her fingers across the table, and I felt like I was standing in front of a headteacher being told off for forgetting my homework one too many times. I wanted to be involved, but juggling everything was difficult. Maybe she was right. Maybe I should have left it to someone who wouldn't mess up the schedule.

"Kiran?"

I looked past Angela to see a young woman with curly brown hair walking towards me. In her hands, she held two large boxes. Angela tipped her chin up and left without another word.

"That's me," I said.

"I'm Cleo. Let me make it clear to you I made these. Not Noah Sinclair."

"Um, okay."

"And you let everyone know it was Cleo Saleh at Sugarworks."

A large stack of boxes was placed on the table and Seth stepped out from behind them.

"Give it a rest, Cleo," he said.

"No," she bit back. "Your brother is a pain in the ass and the business wouldn't float without me. I'm not having him steal my thunder."

"Cleo Saleh," I repeated. "Thank you for doing this, and I will let everyone know."

She gave me a curt nod before punching Seth in the arm and walking out of the hall.

"Thank you, Seth," I said, opening the boxes to find beautifully iced cakes.

Each piece looked like a work of art with pastel icing and decorative elements. I couldn't even lie and say I'd made these, but they were a damn sight better than anything I could have picked up from the supermarket.

"How much do I owe?" I asked.

"Noah said not to worry about it."

I looked up at him. "No, no. I'll see him after. I'm not a charity case, just a little forgetful."

"It's for a good cause, Kiran. You'll offend him if you try to pay him."

Seth shrugged off his suit jacket and came behind the table.

"What are you doing?" I asked.

"Helping."

"You've already helped enough. I don't want to disturb your afternoon."

"You're not."

He unbuttoned the cuffs of his shirt and rolled the sleeves up to the elbows. I pulled my gaze from him. I'd seen Seth shirtless, and that image flashed across my mind more than it should have in my spare time. I felt like a teenager with the way I blushed at a glimpse of his skin.

"You didn't send the boys to a private school," he said as we unpacked the cakes.

The doors to the hall opened, and children and parents walked into the hall.

"I thought about it," I admitted. "But decided against it in the end. I wanted them to grow up with their feet on the ground. If I put them in private school, they would be around other privileged kids in a bubble."

"It is a bubble."

"You went to private school? I didn't mean anything bad —"

"I know you didn't," Seth said.

"I don't know if I've done the right thing, but they both seem happy."

"With a mum like you, it would be difficult not to be happy."

"A mum who forgets school events and can't bake to save her life."

"It would be unfair to everyone else if you were made completely perfect."

133

When I looked at him, Seth was still taking the cakes out of the boxes. He'd made the comment without thinking and probably meant nothing by it, but my heart still picked up its pace.

The afternoon wore on and our table garnered a lot of attention. It didn't take me long to realise why. Seth had loosened his tie and was taking orders. He might not have smiled, but it didn't stop the mums from flocking over to get a few words in with the one and only Seth Sinclair.

I stepped back and let him work his magic, tallying up what we had made so far. In one of the lulls, Seth came up to me, and I glanced at him.

"Problem?" I asked.

"Are you planning to help serve?"

"Why would I do that when you have it covered?"

"I have it covered because you've become a banker."

"You have it covered because you are selling. Tell me you're not noticing how many women have come to this table and fluttered their eyelashes before opening their purse."

Seth raised an eyebrow. "You're using me?"

"Incorrect. I'm using your sex appeal." I prodded him in the chest. "I'm a businesswoman, Seth. I look at what works and then use it to my advantage."

"You're lucky that I don't mind you taking advantage of me," he said. Something laid under those words and made my heart stutter slightly.

I told him I wouldn't date, and I meant it, but sometimes, with Seth, there was an undeniable pull. I wondered what a single kiss from him would feel like. All that intensity and anger he harboured poured into something more passionate—

"Ma, can I have one?"

My train of thoughts halted, and I stepped away from Seth to see Maaz standing at the table with some friends. He held up a red velvet cake, and I smiled.

"Sure thing, baby," I said, sighing. "I'll pay for it."

"Hi, Seth," Maaz greeted brightly. "Did you make these? Ma can't bake."

"Thanks, babe," I muttered.

"No. My brother made them," Seth explained.

"You have a big brother like me?" Maaz asked.

"I have lots of little brothers."

"You're bossy like Shah," he concluded.

"He is," I agreed with Maaz. "Come and find me when you're done, and we'll go home together."

"Can I go to Ben's house?"

"Is your mum okay with that?" I asked the little boy beside Maaz.

He nodded. "Mum said to ask you. Please, Mrs Jafri!"

"Please, Ma," Maaz added.

"Okay," I gave in. "Yes."

Both boys looked pleased with themselves as they ran off, cakes in hand.

"Just you and Shah tonight," Seth commented.

"Just me," I corrected him. "Shah's staying at a friend's as well."

"Would you like to grab dinner together after this?" he asked, taking money from a woman and handing it to me.

"You don't have to do that."

"I'd like to."

I bit my lip. "Seth, I..."

How was I meant to phrase this?

"People are very interested in your life and I like to keep mine private," I explained. "Going to dinner with you might cause some questions that I don't want to have asked."

He nodded slowly.

"Come here," I said, seeing that there was no one waiting to be served.

My fingers went to his tie, undoing the knot.

"What are you up to, Jafri?" he said, narrowing his eyes.

"Helping our cause. Shh."

135

I slipped the tie from his neck and opened the first button of his shirt before messing up his hair a little. Dishevelled Seth was a mouth-watering sight in grey and black.

"Much better," I muttered, turning away.

He caught the other end of his tie to stop me, and I faced him again.

"What if I cooked?" Seth offered.

"I don't understand."

"You can come over and I'll cook. No nosey cameras. No questions. Just friends having dinner together."

I should have said no. I should have realised that I was only making things worse for myself, but I couldn't help it.

"Okay," I said. "Dinner at yours."

Chapter Nineteen

- Seth

"I am impressed," Kiran said as she set down her knife and fork. "When did you learn to cook?"

"University. I couldn't live on ready meals and fast food."

"Smart move."

"There's more to me than looks."

"Not according to Astra," Kiran said, giggling. The sound made my heart beat erratically.

"Your personal assistant is a pain in the ass, Kiran," I grumbled, rubbing my chest. "If you don't give her a disciplinary, I will."

"I think she'd enjoy that way too much."

I choked on my sip of wine as Kiran tipped her head back and laughed. This woman had a filthy edge under all the sunshine. I tried to banish the images of disciplining Kiran in a less than professional manner, but they ran unashamed through my mind. My bedroom was on the floor above us, but I'd settle for taking her bent over the dining room table.

Fuck dinner. I'd happily feast on this woman, given half a chance.

"Seriously, if she makes you uncomfortable, I can ask her to stop," Kiran said.

"I'll allow it for now. She's good for my ego."

"Because that needs inflating."

"It took a heavy hit after Anna."

"Not according to Shah."

I stiffened in my seat. Kiran and Maaz had no problem with me being around, but Shah had his reservations about me. He must have spoken to her about what he found.

"What did he say?" I asked curiously.

"Worried?"

Yes.

"No," I replied, shrugging.

Kiran leant back in her chair and regarded me over her glass. "A few models. A professional tennis player. And a diplomat's daughter."

"That one is a lie. The media can be brutal when they want to be, and you shouldn't believe everything they say."

"Doesn't it bother you? The way everything came out about Anna."

"It's part of the lifestyle," I muttered. "They've always taken an interest in my family. It got more intense after Anna and I became a couple. Her job pushed her into the spotlight and I was at her side."

"And you're still there after you've broken up. Don't you want privacy?"

"I would love some privacy, but it's a necessary evil. Me and my brothers always sell ourselves as well as our work."

"I'm not sure I could do that. I get nervous doing scheduled interviews," she said, running a finger around the rim of her glass. "I started as a nobody and I'd like to keep it that way."

"People will take an interest in you, Kiran. The better the company does, the more people will want to know who's behind it."

"That's fine. I'll give them a sound bite or whatever, but I'm not having my pictures splashed across the internet."

"Because of the boys," I said, looking at her from across the table.

"You must think I'm obsessed with them."

"I'd be worried if you weren't."

"I want them to have a normal childhood," she said. "Whatever that is. But it's not being followed around and ending up in magazines where they can't control the narrative."

"What are you planning to do when Shah turns eighteen?"

Kiran's face fell. "I don't want to think about it. He's got a good head on his shoulders, but he'll be an adult. I won't be able to tell him what to do, but I'm hoping he'll know what would be good for him."

"Is he planning on going to university?"

"He says he wants to."

Kiran rose from her seat, picking up her plate and mine.

"What are you doing?" I asked.

"You cooked. I'll clean," she called over her shoulder as she made her way into the kitchen.

"Leave it," I said, following her. "Housekeeping will deal with it tomorrow."

They usually cooked as well but I requested they left early so I could spend the time alone with Kiran. Plus, I had some skills up my sleeve that I hoped she would find impressive.

"I'd be a terrible guest and you'll never invite me over again," Kiran said, brushing me off.

Lies. I would invite her over every night if it was appropriate to do so. I joined her by the sink as she ran the tap.

"What does Shah want to study?" I asked, going back to our conversation.

"Law," Kiran replied, a smile tugging at her lips. "I can see him arguing in a courtroom."

"You must be proud of him."

141

"I am. After Jamal, he was so angry. I worried he wouldn't be able to work past it. That my little boy was going to be swallowed by all this hate and hurt. It hasn't left him. I don't think it ever will completely. I can see it some days, but he is doing better."

"Has he ever talked to someone about what happened?"

"We both did. I spent every spare penny I had on therapy. It never leaves you, but you learn to live with it."

She shut off the tap and grabbed a cloth to dry her hands. Kiran turned around and leant against the counter.

"I forgot what it's like to have adult company." She laughed and dropped her gaze to the floor. "To sit and eat and enjoy conversation."

I took a step towards her, wanting to be closer. Today's dress was powder blue and sported buttons from her neck to her knees.

"You're always welcome here when the boys aren't home," I told her.

"Don't," she said, laughing quietly. She balled her fists and gently pressed them into my stomach. "You'll never get rid of me. I'll claim sanctuary here."

"If that's what you need." I brushed some hair out of her face, fingers lingering over her scar. "I can be your sanctuary."

"That's not a good idea," she whispered, unable to meet my eyes.

"Why not?"

"You're probably sick of seeing me at work. I can't turn up at your door."

Sick of her? I'd started leaving my damn door open in the office so I could catch sight of her. Kiran wheeled around in her chair, sticking notes to her wall. Kiran pacing her office and running her hands through her hair. The few times she'd seen me, she poked her tongue out before disappearing from view.

"You can if you need it," I confirmed.

She took her hands off my body and shook her head. "No. I am not being called a cockblock."

142

Kiran slipped away from me, and I followed her around the island.

"Who called you a cockblock?" I asked, feeling the rage bubbling.

"No one yet, but you will. I can't turn up when you're trying to seduce some underwear model."

My brow furrowed. "I'm not trying to seduce anyone."

Such a fucking lie. There was one woman I would love to draw in, but she fluttered out of my grasp each time I thought I made some progress.

"But you will," she said softly.

"I don't think I'm going to risk loving someone again."

Kiran cocked her head to the side. "You had an awful experience. Anna hurt you, but don't give up on love."

"Tin Man doesn't have a heart. Remember?"

"The Tin Man was looking for a heart. Don't give up because one woman hurt you. Has she been in touch since?"

"No." I shook my head. "The last I saw, she was dating some football player. I'm off her radar again."

"Hmm," she hummed thoughtfully. "That means you need a Victoria's Secret angel."

"How have you come to that conclusion?"

"Law of the universe. You're going to need someone just as beautiful as you are to stand beside you in all those red-carpet photos."

"You think I'm beautiful?" I asked, raising an eyebrow.

"I am not feeding your ego, Seth."

"Would you let me feed yours?" I asked her seriously.

Kiran rolled her eyes. "Let me guess. You liked my avocado pyjamas?"

"They were very cute."

"Please try and control yourself around me," she said jokingly.

Self-deprecation was yet another language she was fluent in. But I didn't find it amusing.

"That's the bit I find most difficult," I said, gazing at her. "Controlling myself around you."

It grew more difficult by the day. And since discovering that she wasn't married, the guilt had completely washed away and there was nothing to rein in the thoughts of how she would feel beneath my body.

Nothing except the fact that she admitted she wouldn't date.

"Seth," Kiran breathed, cheeks pink. "I —"

The sentence was cut off by her phone ringing.

"Ignore it," I told her.

"I can't." She sidestepped around me and picked it up from the table. "It's Maaz." She answered it. "Hey, baby. Of course. I'll come pick you up now. Love you." Kiran hung up and stuffed the phone into her pocket. "I need to go."

"Kiran," I said.

She walked into the dining room and grabbed her bag and coat. "Thank you for having me over. I really appreciate it. I'll see myself out."

"Kiran, wait."

But she wiggled her fingers at me and scarpered from the room as quick as she could.

I should have kept my damn mouth shut.

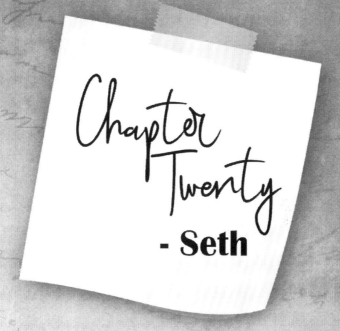

Chapter Twenty
- Seth

"**A**re you even listening to me?" Tiffy asked.

"Yes," I said, keeping a poker face. "Speech. You need me to put something together."

"And you're okay with the content?" she asked, putting her elbows on her desk and steepling her fingers together.

Aiden and Noah snickered from their chairs beside me, and I pushed myself up to sit straight.

Tiffy had scheduled a meeting with the three of us at the Harrington PR offices. Mum and Dad's wedding anniversary was on the horizon, and Tiffy and her father, Henry, had helped us to set up a celebration. With a few days left to go, we were finalising plans, but my mind was elsewhere.

Kiran had moved to the third floor since our dinner. My luck had been terrible in trying to catch her alone. Mike shadowed her everywhere through the building and my temper got progressively worse. I wanted a few moments alone with her. We needed to talk. I needed to explain.

"Mhm," Tiffy said, nodding. "I'm glad that you're willing to discuss the many benefits of adding new kinks into the bedroom to keep a relationship thriving."

I choked on air. "What?" I spluttered.

Aiden howled with laughter, leaning back in his seat and Noah shook his head.

"Pay attention!" Tiffy snapped. "I have plans tonight, and I want you all out of my office as soon as possible."

"What plans, baby girl?" Aiden asked her. "You didn't put anything in the calendar."

"Not with you," she told him. "I'm meeting with Addie."

"Almost had me jealous there, Tiff. Thought someone might be replacing me as number one man in your life."

She flipped him the middle finger, and Noah gagged.

"If you two could stop flirting," Noah said, "some of us have a wedding cake to get back to. I've left Cleo alone with it, which was a bad judgement call on my part."

"I don't think so," Aiden said, shrugging. "Everyone likes her cakes more than yours."

With everyone suitably embarrassed, Tiffy stopped any further arguments and continued with her meeting without interruption.

"What are you doing?" I asked when Aiden trailed me to my car when we finished.

"Checking on you," he answered breezily. "Are you still losing your shit over a married woman?"

Taking a deep breath, I unlocked the car with every intention of driving off and leaving him in the carpark. Unfortunately, Aiden moved at lightning speed and slipped into my passenger seat.

"You can take me home," he said, pushing the seat back and stretching his legs out.

"Are you too old to be adopted?" I muttered, starting the engine.

"Unlucky for you, the answer is yes. Now, tell me you've stopped this obsession with Kiran. You're going to end up fighting her husband and we're going to have to disown you."

"I'm not going to fight her husband," I said, gripping the steering wheel a little tighter. "She's not married."

"Wait, what?" He turned in his seat to look at me properly. "She's single."

"Yes."

"Then why did you say she was married?"

"Because I thought she was. It's a long story, and it's not mine to tell."

"But the short of it is that she's single?"

"Yes."

"Can I get her number?"

"No!"

"Why not?"

We hadn't made it out of the carpark yet when I swerved into another space and slammed on the brakes. Aiden ricocheted between the seat and the seatbelt, hissing as he did so.

"Listen here," I said, pulling the key out of the ignition, and turning on him. "You stay the fuck away from her. Don't even look at her, Aiden."

"Or what?" he asked, looking me in the eye.

I grabbed a fistful of his shirt and pulled him towards me. "Or, what you did to my finger, I'll do to your dick. Test me on this, Aid. I dare you."

The silence lasted in the car for a few seconds before Aiden started to laugh. He pried my fingers away from his shirt and straightened out the creases.

"She's got you good," he remarked. "The sex must be phenomenal."

Another blanket of silence.

"You haven't got that far with her yet?"

"I haven't got anywhere with her yet."

"You're this crazy over a kiss?" he asked, eyes widening.

"Aiden," I said through my teeth. "I haven't kissed her."

"What the fuck?"

I dropped my head against the steering wheel and sighed.

"Shit," Aiden whispered. "You're not messing around here, are you? You seriously like her. Why don't you just date her and see what happens?"

"It's complicated. She has a lot to juggle."

Aiden snorted. "That's never stopped anyone from trying to date one of us before."

"She has children to think about," I muttered into my hands.

Grabbing the back of my collar, Aiden pulled me up again, and I looked at him.

"She told you no?" he asked.

"I haven't even asked her. Every time I get close to telling her how I feel, she backs off or runs away. She's been avoiding me after we had dinner together."

"And you're not reading that as she doesn't want to date you?"

Kiran said that she wouldn't date, but she didn't say she wouldn't date me. Every contract had a loophole and I would exploit it.

I shook my head. "Until she says those words, I'm going to keep trying. There's something there, Aiden. It's been there for months, but it's like she's scared of it. Scared to admit it."

"What are you planning to do?"

"I need to get her to speak to me," I said. "It's difficult to get her on her own."

"Is she coming to the party?"

"I think so. If not, how bad would it be to turn up on her doorstep?"

Aiden pulled a face. "I'll bail you out of prison but a restraining order is going to make it difficult for the both of you to work together."

"This isn't funny!"

"Honestly? It's hilarious. Want me to put in a word for you?"

"I told you to stay away from her."

"What if she doesn't want to stay away from me? Fair game."

I aimed a punch, but Aiden dodged it by leaning back against the door to get away from me.

"Calm down!" he yelled. "I get it. Kiran is off-limits. You staked a claim."

Slamming a hand against the wheel, I let out some of the anger that Aiden had sparked inside of me.

"You know," he said, cautiously sitting properly in the seat. "You never tried to fight me when I flirted with Anna."

I put the key back in the ignition and left the carpark, not trusting that I wouldn't get into a fight with Aiden if we sat alone together.

"Anna didn't like you," I told him.

"Anna didn't like any of us," he said quietly.

"At the risk of sounding like a proper asshole, I don't know if I ever liked her. Loved her, sure. But liked her, I don't think so."

"You wasted a lot of time on that woman."

"We both wasted time in that relationship. Misery loves company," I admitted.

When we were younger, Anna and I enjoyed the social climbing. The photographs and column inches were addictive, and then it changed. Twisted into a game where we were untouchable on the pedestals we were placed on. We drifted apart and rather than either of us facing the facts, we continued on, hoping we would find the smallest spark again. Instead, we ended in ruin, and I was left to pick up the shattered pieces of pride.

"For what it's worth, Seth," Aiden said, "I hope Kiran gives you a chance."

Chapter Twenty One

- Kiran

I nearly tripped over the hem of my saree as I came off the bottom step.

"Ma," Shah said, coming towards me. "You need to be more careful."

"I'm trying. I haven't worn a saree in God knows how long," I mumbled, walking towards the mirror with my earrings clutched tightly in my palm.

"You look beautiful, Ma," Maaz said, coming into the living room from the kitchen. He slurped noisily from the juice carton in his sticky hands.

"You don't think it's too much? Too bright?" I asked, looking down at myself.

Orange was my favourite colour, and I'd wrapped myself in a saree of that colour with delicate flowers printed across the material.

"You look like the sun," Maaz answered, sitting on the couch and watching me. "And who doesn't like the sun?"

"Who doesn't like the sun?" I muttered, securing my earrings into place. "Are you two sure you're going to be okay on your own? I can stay home."

"We're not little kids," Shah said. "Enjoy yourself."

I picked up my clutch and kissed them both on the cheek.

"Wait," Shah said, pulling something from his pocket and holding it towards me.

I took the small black device and turned it over in my hand. "Shah, where did you get this?"

"Online."

"This is ridiculous."

He walked out of the room and I followed, not wanting to discuss this in front of Maaz.

"A rape alarm?" I asked. "Seriously?"

"Ma, I love you and I'm glad you're going out and enjoying yourself a little more, but I don't trust people."

"I don't need this." I held it back out to him.

"Please. It'd make me feel better."

Moments like these, Shah didn't just look like his father. It was almost like Jamal was standing in front of me, asking me to take the damn alarm. Sucking in a deep breath, I opened my clutch and dropped it inside.

"You worry way too much," I said, pulling him into a hug. "I'll keep it on me if it makes you happy."

He kissed my forehead, and I walked out of the door and into my car. Nervously, I played with the pleats on my saree before driving through London.

I almost decided against attending tonight. Arthur and Celeste Sinclair were celebrating forty years of marriage and had kindly extended the invite to everyone they worked with. I'd been excited to attend until my impromptu dinner with Seth.

With great precision and help from Astra and Kirsty, I had managed to avoid bumping into him for the past week. I hoped there were enough people there tonight that I wouldn't get the chance to see him.

Seth had put ripples into my pool of calm. It was safe for me to admire him from a distance. The odd teasing comment seemed harmless, and I never entertained the fact that he might reciprocate the attraction. But Seth had been clear about his feelings and what did I do? I ran and hid.

Parking the car, I stepped out and made my way into the hotel, following the signs for the celebration. The room was packed with guests, photographers, and servers, and I stuck to the wall with my head ducked until I saw Arthur and his wife. Steeling some courage, I made my way towards them.

"Congratulations to you both," I said.

"Thank you! I'm so glad you made it," Arthur said, pulling me into a hug. "This is my wife, Celeste. Love, this is Kiran Jafri."

"Kiran," Celeste said, kissing both my cheeks. "My, you are beautiful. The print on your dress is stunning."

I paled in comparison to Celeste. She had a willowy figure and platinum blonde hair that was cut into a bob that swayed around her chin. If Seth looked like his father, Aiden was the carbon copy of his mum.

"Thank you," I muttered, blushing. "I feel a little too bright."

"The world needs colour," a familiar voice said from behind me.

Turning around, I came face to face with Seth and my breath hitched as the world felt unsteady beneath my feet. He was dressed impeccably in a black suit. His bow tie was perfectly placed at his neck and his hair was slicked back. A model who stepped off the catwalk and straight into the event.

"Hi," I mumbled.

"Hello, Kiran," he greeted me with his deep timbre.

"Doesn't she look beautiful?" Celeste asked him.

"She always does," he replied without taking his eyes off me. "Can we talk?"

If the world could swallow me whole, I would have appreciated it. The world didn't cooperate, but Aiden saved the day. He joined his brother, slinging an arm around him.

"Kiran!" Aiden greeted me. "You're wrapped up like a present. If you need any help to unwrap, I'll graciously offer you a hand."

"Aiden Sinclair!" Celeste scolded.

"Sorry, Mum." He laughed. "Julian Giles is looking for you, bro."

"I'm a little busy," Seth gritted out.

"We can talk later," I lied.

Aiden dragged Seth away, and I turned back to Arthur and Celeste.

"I cannot apologise enough for Aiden. He lacks a filter between his brain and his mouth sometimes," she said.

"You don't need to apologise. Enjoy your evening and congratulations again," I said before leaving them.

I kept myself towards the walls again, away from the bustle of the room and the flash of cameras. I found myself watching people quietly, piecing together their lives from the way they interacted. More than once, my gaze landed on Seth as he moved from guest to guest. No smile and all business. He raked his hands through his hair, the way he always did when he was irritated by something.

Was it any wonder that I struggled to believe he was remotely interested in me? I was a single mum who barely had her shit together, and he was sex-on-legs that turned heads the moment he walked into a room.

Seth cut a course through the room and stepped up onto a small elevated stage, grabbing the microphone.

"If I can have a moment of your time," he said, gaining the room's attention. "I wanted to thank everyone for joining us tonight to celebrate my parents' wedding anniversary. Forty years together is an amazing achievement."

There was a light applause that rippled through the room.

"It's not been without hardship, but you've both worked through everything life threw at you. You've always been a wonderful testament to what love can conquer to me and my brothers. From all of us, we wanted to say thank you for being such brilliant parents and for teaching us that sometimes you need to fight for what you love. Here's to another forty years and more, Mum and Dad. Happy anniversary."

He raised his glass, and we all mimicked the gesture, toasting the couple. I quietly put my champagne flute on the bar and walked out of the room, needing some air.

Forty years. How undeniably lucky they were to have so much time together?

As I stepped outside, the cold air hit me and the rain fell in heavy sheets. Caught up in the way it hit the pavement and cleared the streets, I didn't hear someone join me. An arm slipped around my waist and pulled me into an alcove at the entrance, away from view.

"Get off!" I yelled.

"It's just me, Kiran," Seth said, letting me go.

"You weirdo," I said, hitting his arm with my clutch. "Why didn't you say something?"

"I thought you were leaving."

"I was thinking about it."

"You told me we could talk."

"Seth, there's nothing to talk about."

"I'm sorry if I overstepped the mark," he said, moving a step closer. "You told me you wore your ring to avoid attention and then I say those things to you. You must think I'm an idiot who doesn't listen."

"That's not what I think."

My feet moved backwards, heels clicking against the stone as I tried to put some space between us. But Seth was relentless, matching each of my moves.

"Why else would you avoid me?" Seth asked.

My back bumped the stone column behind me and Seth put his hands against it, caging me in as he stared down at me. My heart thumped erratically in my chest.

"Tell me what you're thinking," he said.

"I don't know why you're doing this," I replied. "I'm not like the women you've been with before. You've seen what a mess my life is."

"Your life might be a mess, but you make the most of it every day."

"I have to."

"Did I overstep?" he asked, bringing his face closer to mine. "Because I'll back off, Kiran. I won't make you uncomfortable."

"I don't know," I admitted.

Seth was not part of my plan when I moved to London. I was going to work on my business and make sure Shah finished his exams. Maaz would get settled in school, and I'd find some hobbies again. A man wasn't in the picture. Should never be in the picture. But Seth made me question that decision.

He nodded slowly. "Kiran." My name sounded so sweet on his lips. "Will you let me kiss you once, please? I need to stop thinking about it. Need to stop obsessing over you."

The way he spoke unleashed butterflies in my stomach.

"One kiss," I agreed shakily.

I knew the feeling. One kiss should eliminate all the curiosity. We would understand whatever tension was between us and be able to carry on like normal.

Seth took his hands off the stone. One went to my bare waist and the other to my neck. His thumb trailed along the curve of my jaw as he brought his face down to mine.

"What have you done to your lashes?" he whispered. "They're curlier than usual."

"You noticed?"

"I notice a lot about you."

I let out a nervous giggle. "I had a lift."

He nodded slowly, lips painfully close to mine, and my blood pulsed in my ears.

"Close your eyes," Seth instructed me.

They fluttered shut, and I felt his breath on my lips. The anticipation made me shake. Seth pressed his lips against mine — softly at first and then with an urgency. My hands gripped the lapels of his jacket to keep me steady.

Five years. It had been five long years since my last kiss. Five years since I wanted to kiss someone this badly. I forgot my heart could do such extraordinary acrobatics.

Seth's kiss lit a fire deep in my stomach and I opened my mouth, needing to taste him. His tongue brushed against mine and his solid, muscular body pinned me to the column.

When we broke apart for air, Seth rested his forehead against mine, and I felt dizzy from the kiss. It was meant to douse my curiosity, but all it had done was make me crave even more of him.

"One more," I whispered, lying to myself.

"If that's what you want," he whispered in return.

Chapter Twenty Two

- Seth

One kiss turned into a flurry of more, hidden in the alcove at the front of the hotel. It pained me to watch Kiran leave so she could go home. Dressed like a sun goddess, I would have worshipped every inch of her in the rain.

Surprisingly, she didn't avoid me at work. Her fingers brushed along my arm when she slipped past me in the kitchen, and I didn't miss an opportunity to have lunch with her when our schedules permitted. Every evening had been filled with messages from her until the early hours of the morning.

Today, her office door was shut with a purple sticky note threatening anyone who disturbed her. Her grant deadline was today, and Kiran had been in her room before I'd even made it into the building.

The sound of something popping outside the office, followed by a scream, made me jump and wrench open my door. Astra stood in the corridor with an empty party popper in her hand with a beaming

Kiran. The smile was enough to stop the world from spinning on its axis and pull me into her orbit.

"She did it!" Astra yelled, and I recoiled at the volume. "She submitted it!"

"Congratulations," I said, looking at Kiran. "I was waiting for you to finish so I could discuss something with you."

"Oh?" Kiran asked, eyebrows rising.

"In my office," I said, walking back into the room.

I heard Astra squeal and kiss Kiran before the door to my office closed again. The scent of patchouli filled the space, and I pulled paper streamers out of Kiran's hair, letting them flutter to the floor.

"You said you needed to —" she started, but I cut her off.

Pulling her into a tight hug, I picked her off the ground. Kiran's arms wrapped around my neck and squeezed me as she laughed.

"You did it," I said. "I'm so proud of you."

"I've just sent it. We won't hear for a while," she replied.

"But you did it. All that hard work and it's in someone else's hands now," I said, placing her back on the floor but refusing to release her from my arms.

"This is what you needed to talk to me about?"

"I haven't seen you all day," I said. Walking over to my desk, I sat on the edge and pulled her between my legs. "And I have matters to discuss with you now that you've met your deadline."

"That makes me nervous. Is something wrong?"

The panic was written all across her beautiful face. Reaching up, I tucked some hair behind her ear. Kiran had been hit with so many curveballs in her life that she was always looking for the next disaster.

"Nothing's wrong. I wanted to ask if you'd let me take you on a date."

I felt her tense underneath my touch.

"Seth, I'm not sure that's such a good idea," she mumbled, looking at my tie.

"Have I misread something?" I asked, thinking about how she'd been with me since the night at the hotel.

We may not have kissed again, but things hadn't exactly cooled off.

Her hands rested on my shoulders. "I told you I didn't plan to date."

"You also said one kiss and look at how that turned out."

She tried to stop herself from smiling. "It's not a good idea."

"Tell me why not."

I refused to give up that easily. Kiran had jumpstarted my heart, and I wanted to have a chance with her. Slipping my arms around her, I pulled her into my body.

"We work together. There must be rules about that," she said, playing with the knot of my tie.

"I'll change the rules."

"Seth," she laughed, bringing her dark eyes up to mine. "You can't do that."

"I can," I assured her confidently. "What else?"

"You are not changing the rules of the company so you can date me."

"We just need to let HR know."

"I like my privacy," Kiran explained. "If we go on a date, everyone will know."

I wanted to take Kiran on a date. Dinner, theatre, museums. I was ready to put in effort and show her how much I was invested in her. But I couldn't guarantee the privacy she adored. Paparazzi liked to turn up where I least expected them.

"And," Kiran continued, "I don't know how the boys would feel about me seeing someone. It's been the three of us for a long time. I can't be selfish."

"Do you want to date me?" I asked.

"I told you, I'm not going to date anyone."

The words date and dating made her throw her walls up. I needed to phrase this differently if I wanted to win.

"Would you like to see me in a less professional sense?" I asked.

"Even if I did —"

"Answer the question, Kiran," I told her sternly.

"Yes."

"Then we'll figure it out. We'll keep it between you and me until you feel comfortable to tell people."

"You're so sure of yourself," Kiran said, shoving me gently.

"What are you afraid of?"

"So many things," she replied softly. "It's all going to fall apart and then we'll be a mess. I like you, Seth. I enjoy having you in my life, and I don't want anything to ruin that."

"I'm not going to leave your life," I assured her. "You're a businesswoman. A smart one. It's all about risk and reward."

"This is not a business deal."

"It's an investment."

"So romantic."

"I'm trying to get you to understand it logically instead of panicking."

Kiran bit her plump bottom lip and asked, "How are we meant to see each other with no one finding out?"

"We have safe spaces. Here. My home," I told her. "No one needs to know. It'll be the two of us."

She ran a hand through my hair, and I closed my eyes. "We'd have to be so careful. I don't want to upset Shah and Maaz."

Opening my eyes, I took her hand from my hair and kissed it gently. "They come first," I agreed.

"They will always be my priority. If I'm with you and they need me, I'll leave."

"I don't expect you to put me first."

"You're saying all the right things, but I'm worried this isn't going to live up to whatever you've been thinking of up here." Kiran placed her finger in the space between my brows. "I think you might have romanticised this."

"Impossible. You'd need a heart to romanticise anything."

She chuckled and then scrunched her nose. "Can we take things slowly?"

"You can set the pace," I said.

The last person she'd been with — the only person — was her husband. They were childhood sweethearts, and no one had turned her head as they grew into adults. I was the first person she was trusting with her heart again, and I would let her dictate how quickly she wanted to move.

Slowly, Kiran nodded her head. "Okay," she said. "Let's see how this goes."

Chapter Twenty Three

- Kiran

Knocking on the back door of Sugarworks, I waited quietly. Seth had told me to meet him here Saturday afternoon. With both the boys deciding to spend the day at the fair, I had no plans and no willpower to decline.

The door opened, and I was greeted by a beautiful man dressed in chef's whites, dishcloth draped over his shoulder and platinum blonde hair tucked under a hat.

"Aiden?" I asked.

"Oh God, you met him before me? You poor woman," the man muttered. He wiped his hands on his apron and moved aside to let me in. "I'm Noah. Aiden's twin."

"I'm sorry. I didn't mean to assume."

"Don't worry about it."

He led me through to a large industrial kitchen that was kitted out with steel appliances and was empty except for two other people.

Seth was hunched over a table with Cleo beside him, heads together as they whispered.

"Oi!" Noah barked.

Cleo straightened up, looking concerned for a moment, before her eyes narrowed. "What, Sinclair?"

"Are you helping him cheat? Get your ass out of here, Saleh. Now!"

Cleo gave him the middle finger before she flounced out of the room, doors swinging in her wake.

"Cheat?" I asked, feeling my stomach sink.

Seth straightened up. He was dressed casually in a pair of chinos and a polo shirt. His casual attire put mine to shame, and I tugged on my oversized jumper, wanting to disappear.

"We're going to have a friendly competition," Seth announced, walking over to me. "Maaz said you couldn't bake."

"And you decided to use that against me?" I asked, jaw dropping open.

"I take every advantage I have. Noah agreed to let us use the kitchen, and he and Cleo are going to judge."

"And you were getting tips from her," I said, narrowing my eyes.

"She has favourites, and I happen to be one of them."

"She has poor taste," Noah remarked.

"Tell her that," Seth muttered.

"Do not destroy my kitchen because I will kill you and show no remorse. Good luck." Noah patted me on the shoulder and walked out the doors.

The moment he was gone, Seth put his hands on my hips and pulled me towards him. Instantly, my hands went to his chest, feeling the muscles beneath his shirt.

"I hope this is okay," he said.

"I think you're ridiculous, Tin Man. And I'm planning to kick your ass because you tried to cheat."

I sidestepped him and pulled my hair into a ponytail. The counter was set up with mixers, ingredients, and a laminated sheet.

"Red velvet," I said, reading the top of the recipe.

"It's your favourite," Seth replied, coming up behind me.

His body pressed against mine gently as he looked over my shoulder. I tensed before relaxing back against him. Seth was a safe space. He'd gone to all this trouble so we could spend time together. My brain struggled to process that someone would do this for me.

"It's your favourite as well," I commented.

He brushed his lips against my cheek, and I blushed. "And today we get to see who bakes the best one."

Seth pulled away from me, and I had to stop myself from grabbing him and keeping him close. I told him I wanted to take it slow, but there was a feeling of comfort I didn't realise I wanted when he placed his hands on me.

"Noah and Cleo," I said, turning back to the recipe and adding the butter and sugar into the mixer. "How long have they been together?"

Seth looked at me and let out a bark of laughter. "They aren't dating. Noah professes he doesn't have time for that, and Cleo would be the last person on his list."

"Oh. I thought —"

"Cleo started here on an apprenticeship last year, and she's talented. Noah hates it, but he can't deny that she's the best he's got."

"Why does he hate it?"

"He went to Buenos Aires for pastry school."

"He went to Argentina?"

"Loved it out there. Learned a lot. I would have gained a few stones if Anna let me eat anything he made." Seth frowned and then shook his head. "Cleo... she dropped out of school and started working. Sugar runs through her veins."

It clicked. "He doesn't like that she might be better than him."

Seth shrugged, turning on his mixer. I did the same, and then walked the few steps, so I was beside him again.

"Do all the Sinclairs think they're God's gift?" I asked him curiously.

"Yes," Seth answered honestly. "There's no reason to believe otherwise."

I rolled my eyes, and Seth's fingers gripped my chin firmly. "You're going to argue with me on this?"

When Seth looked at me like that with his icy blue eyes, I wasn't sure I was capable of forming a sentence, let alone arguing with him.

"Jury's still out," I managed to utter.

Seth released me from his grip and arched an eyebrow. "You'll learn soon enough that it's not a lie."

He grabbed the flour and went to tip it into the mixer.

"Wait!" I called. "You need to turn off the —"

But God's gift had dumped it into the bowl and a mushroom cloud of flour rose into the air, covering both of us and the surfaces.

"Fuck!" Seth hissed, slicing through the air with his hand as I spluttered. "Are you okay?"

The clouds of flour settled, and I blinked at him. Seth's face broke into a smile before he laughed.

"You look a state, flower." He chuckled.

"Because of you, genius," I said, shoving him and walking back to my mixer.

Seth grabbed me around the waist, picking me up from the floor. "Put me down!" I laughed.

"This was your fault," he whispered in my ear. "You're too distracting for your own good."

"I didn't do anything," I said, clinging to his arms.

Gently, he lowered me back to the ground and turned me around to face him. His hair was dusty white from the explosion. I reached up to brush some of it away, but Seth caught my hand and kissed the inside of my wrist.

"That's the problem, flower. You don't have to do anything to be completely and utterly distracting." He dropped my wrist and his fingers brushed against my cheek. "It's maddening."

"Walk around with your eyes closed."

"And miss all of this?" he asked, dragging his eyes down my body, which was hidden under baggy layers of clothing. "I don't think so."

Leaning down, Seth pressed his lips against mine and I melted against his body. Static electricity coursed through my veins and made me hyperaware of every inch of my being. Every time we kissed, Seth made me feel alive. He woke me up from the mundane routine I'd placed myself in that allowed me to get through every day.

His tongue teased along my bottom lip and I opened my mouth, letting it brush along mine. Seth's hand came up behind my neck, the other arm tight around my waist. I clung to him before breaking the kiss. His pupils were dilated as he stared down at me, banishing the blue.

"Now who's distracting?" I whispered.

"All part of the plan to win," he said, winking.

Seth let go of me, and my eyes widened. The cake! He was already a step ahead. Giving him a shove, I went back to my mixer.

"What does your mum do?" I asked, adding eggs into the bowl.

"She's a theatre director."

"Oh, wow. That's impressive."

"She used to be an actress," Seth explained. "That's how she and Dad met. She played Juliet in a production of *Romeo and Juliet*."

"And your dad was Romeo?"

"He wishes. No. He went on a date, saw Mum, and said he fell in love instantly. He spent three months with her before he proposed."

"That quick?"

"He says when you know, you know. And he knew. Forty years later, I guess he made the right decision."

"They're lucky. Most people can't last two weeks these days. Always looking for the next best thing. Running at the first sign of trouble."

I carefully tipped in the flour and turned my head to see Seth watching me.

"What?" I asked.

"Nothing."

"Are you sure?"

"Yeah."

I dropped it and we both continued with the recipe. Seth told me more about his family, and I told him a little more about the boys. They were my world, and I was always cautious about letting people in, but Seth had met them more than once.

By the time we walked out onto the restaurant floor, plates of cupcakes in hand, my cheeks ached from smiling so much.

"What the fuck are those?" Noah asked from his chair, looking thoroughly disturbed.

Seth had refused to let his cakes cool before he iced them, leaving it to drip down the cases and onto the plate. Mine was only marginally better — solid but lumpy and unappetising to the eye.

"No. Fuck it," Noah said, shaking his head. "I'm not eating that shit."

Even Cleo looked sceptical as I placed the plate down in front of them.

"There are easier ways to kill me," she muttered. "Dying by food poisoning seems ironic so I'm going to pass."

"So, who won?" Seth asked, folding his arms across his chest.

Noah opened his mouth to respond, but Cleo beat him to it.

"Kiran!" she announced. "She didn't melt the icing, and she looks cute as fuck. You" — Cleo pointed at Seth — "are related to Noah and that automatically gives you minus one hundred points."

I stifled my laughter behind a hand. "Looks like someone else doesn't think the Sinclairs are God's gift."

"Zip it, you," Seth said, but the corner of his mouth lifted. "Thanks for the kitchen," he said, nodding to Noah. "But we're going to hand it back over now."

"Good plan," Noah said, getting out of his seat, and Cleo followed.

She stopped beside me and put a hand on my elbow. "Kiran, you have a flour handprint on your ass. Might want to get rid of that before you hit the street."

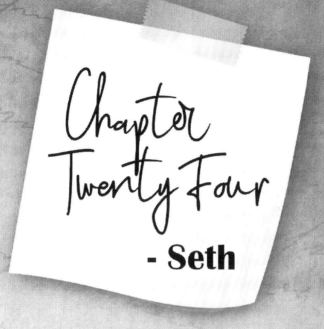

Chapter Twenty Four

- Seth

Business dinners made me itch. It meant extra hours in a suit, being polite as possible when I shouldn't be required to. But Dad insisted I come along instead of hiding in the office. He silently primed me to takeover when he was ready to retire. Something that would have happened sooner if I hadn't lost my shit and fled the country.

Although the dinner was another step towards securing my future, there were other things I'd rather be doing out of office hours. Kiran was never far from my mind. I stole as much time from her as I could, but it never felt enough. My flower was addictive, and I was unashamedly hooked. Every laugh, every blush thawed my heart and made me think about possibilities that I promised myself to never entertain again.

With dinner finally finished and a contract to be drawn up, we settled the bill and prepared to move on for celebratory drinks.

My phone vibrated, and I pulled it out of my pocket to find a missed call from Kiran. She called again, and I picked it up, but couldn't get a word out.

"Seth. It's Shah, Kiran's son. Can you —" He must have pulled the phone away from his ear because he sounded distant. "Maaz, wait. Fuck."

"Shah? What's going on?" I stopped in my tracks, and Dad looked back at me. "Shah?"

"We're at the hospital. Ma got taken into surgery, and Mike's not here. Maaz —"

"Which hospital?" I asked, my stomach coiling into knots. He gave the information, and I said, "I'm coming now. Don't move. I won't be long."

"Son?" Dad asked as I hung up.

"I need to go."

"What's happened?"

"I don't know. Kiran's in hospital and her sons are there. I need to go," I said, racing towards the car.

"I'll drive," Dad said, and I tossed him the keys without argument.

Twenty minutes later, I jumped out of the car, sending Dad back home. Walking into the hospital, it didn't take long to find Shah and Maaz. They were tucked up in the corner of a waiting room, away from anyone else, and Maaz's little body shook.

"Hey," I said, reaching them. "What's happened?"

Maaz looked up at me, and I was alarmed to see the usually bubbly kid crying.

"They took her into surgery," Shah said. He looked pale and drawn out. So much older than sixteen.

"What happened?" I asked, sitting down next to Shah and unbuttoning my jacket. "Come here," I said to Maaz.

He came towards me and I picked him up, setting him on my lap. Leaning against my chest, he sniffed.

"She was having stomach pains the past two days. She said she was fine, but then she couldn't stand properly. Doctor told her to go straight to the hospital. It's her appendix. They wanted to take it out and Mum agreed," Shah explained, looking more panicked by the second.

My heart calmed down, and I hugged Maaz closer. "She's in the best place. I'm sure an appendectomy should go smoothly."

"How would you know?" Shah bit back.

"My brother is a doctor. We can call him if you want."

"Oh."

"She'll be okay?" Maaz asked, wiping his face and nose on the sleeve of his pyjamas. "Can I see Ma?"

"Not yet," I told him gently. "They need to make her better, but as soon as they're done, you can see her."

"Promise?"

The word made me nervous. Both of the boys were looking at me, waiting for an answer. It hit me they were kids who only had their mum. Shah had grown up quicker than his peers, and Maaz had no other figure at home.

"Promise," I said. "You know, time might go quicker if you get some sleep."

"Are you going to leave?" Maaz asked.

"I'll be right here."

I rubbed his back gently, and a silence settled over us. Nurses and doctors walked in and out of the space, and I leant back in the chair, making myself comfortable.

"Sorry for calling you," Shah said eventually. "Mike's in France for work and you were Ma's most recent call."

"It's okay. You can call me anytime you need me."

"I just panicked," he said through gritted teeth. His hands were balled into fists and he stared at the empty seats in front of him.

"You haven't seen her ill before?"

"I have. Food poisoning. Flu. But not like this. I panicked. I thought maybe something was really wrong with her." His body slumped and he dipped his head, shaking it. "We can't lose her like we lost —"

He stopped himself abruptly. I glanced down to see Maaz asleep in my arms and finished Shah's sentence quietly.

"Like you lost your dad."

His head snapped towards me. "You know?"

"Your mum told me what happened."

A range of emotions flickered across his face. "It's not her fault," he said sharply. "Everyone blames her, but it wasn't her fault."

Reaching out, I placed a hand on the back of his neck gently. "Mate, I never thought it was."

Shah nodded slowly. "You spend a lot of time with her. Maaz said you were at the school fundraiser."

"She needed cakes."

"You bake?"

"My brother is a pastry chef."

"You have like four of them, right?"

"Six. All younger."

"Maaz is a handful. I don't know how you cope with six."

I showed him my left hand where I was missing half a middle finger, and Shah sucked in a breath, eyes widening.

"Wasn't so easy when we were younger," I admitted. "And I haven't appreciated them much over the past few years."

I spent all my time on Anna. I defended her at every turn, even when she didn't deserve it, and that put a strain on my relationship with my family. Thinking back, I was ashamed at how I behaved. But it wasn't Anna's fault. That all boiled down to me and my choices, but I was trying to fix it.

"Do you like her?" Shah asked bluntly.

I could lie, but this was the most conversation I'd been able to get from him, and I didn't think it would do me any favours to be dishonest.

"I like her a lot," I replied.

He rubbed his hands down his face. "There's a lot of stuff about you on the internet. You were with loads of different women after

178

you broke up with your fiancée. That was shit, by the way. She shouldn't have done that to you."

"She shouldn't have but she did, and I didn't cope with it well."

Maaz started to snore quietly, and I chuckled at the little boy, who was unaware of the conversation that was happening around him.

"I was hurting," I explained. "And I made a lot of stupid decisions. But then I met your mum, and she reminded me of a lot of things."

Kiran had placed everything into perspective, and I was grateful to have met someone who could pull my head out of my ass.

"Shah," I said.

"You want to date her, don't you?"

He was a smart kid, and I wasn't subtle. Shah had clocked on early that I'd taken an unhealthy interest in his mum.

"I would like to spend more time with her and get to know her better," I said, trying to phrase it in a palatable way. "I know that might be a little worrying since I don't think Kiran's dated since…"

"She hasn't. She's always with us or working." Shah's leg bounced as he looked ahead. "You can't hurt her. You can't hurt Maaz either."

"What do you mean?"

"She's kind of a package deal. If it works out, then you have Maaz in the picture as well."

"And you."

Shah shrugged. "Whatever. But Maaz is a good kid, and he doesn't need people walking in and out of his life."

I thought Maaz was most like Kiran. They both laughed constantly and possessed a personality that drew you in. Shah was a lot colder than the rest of his family. Quiet and withdrawn. But hearing him talk about his mum and brother reminded me of the warning that Kiran gave me. They were protective of their small unit.

"Neither do you," I pointed out.

"I'm not a kid."

Sixteen and forced to be the man of the house when it should never have fallen on his shoulders.

"Even grown men need people they can rely on," I said.

He shrugged again. There was only so much progress I could expect in one night.

"Would it be okay with you if I took some time to get to know Kiran?" I asked.

"I want to say no, but she must like you if she told you about what happened," Shah said. "I want her to be happy. Not the way she puts it on for everyone else. I want her to be happy inside."

"Shah, I don't know what might happen between us because it's all new, but I want her to be happy as well."

"Okay. I guess you can date her."

"Thanks," I said, biting back on a smile as relief flooded my chest. If Shah had refused, things would have an extra layer of complication, but karma decided to deal me a good hand for once.

A doctor walked into the room and I recognised her instantly as one of Aiden's old classmates.

"Seth," she asked, smiling. "What are you doing here? Is everyone okay?"

"Hi, Claire. Family's fine. You have a friend of mine. Kiran Jafri."

She looked at Maaz and Shah and blinked a few times. "Yes."

Shah got up from his seat, and I followed, picking Maaz up as I went. He stirred in my arms and wrapped his around my neck.

"Is she okay?" Shah asked.

"Are you comfortable discussing this with Seth present?" Claire asked.

He looked up at me and then nodded.

"She just got out of surgery. Everything went well, as can be expected. We're going to keep her in for a day or two to monitor her."

"But she's okay?" Shah asked.

"She's doing good. Do you want to come through and see her?" Claire said.

"Please," Shah said and then turned to look at me. "Are you coming?"

"Do you need me?" I asked in return.

"I don't know. I don't think so."

"Then maybe it should be you and Maaz. Some family time. But take my number from your mum's phone and if you need anything, you can call me."

I ran a hand along Maaz's dark curls gently, and he stirred.

"Maaz," I whispered. "Time to wake up."

He rubbed his face against my shoulder, and I laughed.

"Mum's out of surgery and you can see her now," I told him.

"Ma?" He whipped his head up and caught me on the chin. I hissed, and he said, "Ow."

Rubbing the sore spot on his head gently, I crouched down and set him on the ground. "Are you okay?"

"Mhm. Where's Ma?"

Shah held out his hand and Maaz took it.

"She's on the ward," Claire said. "I can take you to the room."

Shah and Maaz followed Claire out of the room and I straightened up, knees cracking as I went. By the time I got home, it was late and as I crawled into bed, I had a text from a number I didn't recognise.

Unknown number: Ma's doing good. Thanks for tonight – Shah.

Chapter Twenty Five

- Seth

hah informed me that Kiran had been discharged from hospital and Kirsty mentioned Kiran was taking a week of sick leave. I didn't tell her I knew why. There would be too many questions that Kiran wouldn't be comfortable with. A few weeks together had coaxed her from her shell, but she was still hesitant to be seen with me in public or let anyone know we were together.

"How's she doing?" I asked, stepping into her home, carrying sunflowers in one hand and two large pizzas in the other.

Shah took the food from me, and I kicked off my shoes.

"She's on the sofa with Maaz."

"Shah, who is it?" Kiran called as we walked into the living room.

She was propped up on the sofa with Maaz tucked into her side. He held a book in his hands and one finger pointed at the page.

"Seth, what are you doing here?" She went to sit up and hissed at the sudden movement.

Shah dropped the pizza on the coffee table and went to her side. "Ma," he scolded. "Be careful."

"What's the pizza?" Maaz asked, sliding off the sofa and sniffing the air.

The book landed with a thunk on the floor, and he lifted the lid of the box.

"Maaz," Kiran said. "You're so rude sometimes. People are going to think I dragged you up."

"Come get plates and a vase," Shah said, holding out his hand to his brother. "Now."

Maaz ran past him and through the house, and Shah muttered something under his breath before following.

"I was going to message you," Kiran said. "I've just been so tired and then Maaz got in from school and he wouldn't leave my side."

I placed the flowers on the table and carefully sat beside her. Glancing at where the boys left and seeing the coast was clear, I leant in and kissed her quickly.

"Seth," she mumbled, turning red.

"They didn't see. Were you planning on telling me you weren't feeling well?"

"It's not a big deal."

"You just had your appendix removed."

"I thought it was a weird stomach ache. I didn't know something had exploded inside me."

"You should have said something."

"I can look after myself."

"But you don't have to," I said, grabbing her hand. Looking down, I raised an eyebrow. "Where are your rings?"

Kiran pulled her hand away and hid it. "I took them off in hospital," she muttered. "It didn't feel right to put them back on when I'm seeing you."

184

I couldn't lie; it felt like a step forward to see Kiran's ring finger bare. In the back of my mind, I accepted she would never fully let go of Jamal, but this felt like a positive sign for our future. Like she was accepting that I was a part of her life and what we had was materialising into something real.

The boys came back into the room with plates, and Maaz dived straight for the pizza box.

"I thought you might appreciate not having to cook," I said as he ripped off a large slice and took a bite.

"Maaz Jafri, chew your food." Kiran laughed and then winced.

"Good luck," Shah muttered, taking a slice and offering me a plate. I declined, and he grabbed himself a slice.

"I wanted to stop by and make sure you're healing up. I should let you rest," I said to Kiran.

"You're leaving?" Maaz asked with his mouth full. "Why do you always leave?"

"Always leave?" Kiran repeated.

"Seth left the hospital when you woke up."

Shah's expression mirrored mine — panicked at the fact Maaz had unleashed our little secret into the world.

"You were at the hospital?" Kiran asked, looking flustered.

"I —" I started.

"I called him," Shah admitted. "I didn't know what to do, so I called him. I'm sorry, Ma. I just —"

"Baby," Kiran said, voice breaking. "You don't need to apologise to me. Come here." She opened up her arms and Shah put down his plate to come and hug her gently. His frame enveloped hers with ease. "I'm sorry. You shouldn't have had to deal with that."

"You couldn't help it. It's fine. Seth was there."

She let go of him, kissing his cheek. "Why don't you take Maaz and the pizza and head upstairs? I need to talk to Seth."

"He didn't do anything wrong," Shah said.

A flicker of warmth sparked in my chest as the sullen teen defended me. Unnecessary but appreciated.

"I know, sweetheart. I need to talk to him."

My stomach knotted as the boys disappeared, and Kiran turned her full attention to me. Dark eyes drank me in curiously.

"Do you want to tell me what happened?" she asked.

"He had your phone, and he panicked," I explained. "Told me you were in hospital and it sounded like he was struggling with Maaz."

Kiran sighed and leant against the back of the sofa. "I'm such an idiot. He shouldn't have to deal with this right now. He should worry about his exams and not me." She pinched the bridge of her nose and closed her eyes.

"Woah," I said. "He's always going to worry about you. He was okay. They both were."

"Did he say anything? Shah."

"He thought he was going to lose you."

She took a deep breath through her nose, and I ran a hand over her hair before she opened her eyes again.

"Thank you for being there for them. It shouldn't have been you. Mike's away, and I don't know why he called you."

"I was your most recent phone call. That's why."

"Oh God." Kiran's eyes grew and her face drained of colour. "Does he know?"

The panic on her features forced me to lie. If Shah hadn't mentioned anything to her, then Kiran remained clueless about our little heart to heart.

"I don't think so," I said quietly. "But if he does, would it be such a bad thing?"

"He's got enough on his plate without adding me dating to it."

"I thought you said it wasn't dating."

Kiran flicked my thigh. "It's sort of dating."

"Sort of?"

"Okay, fine," she whispered, exasperated. "We're dating."

Leaning in, I kissed her again and she reciprocated before pulling away.

"Stop it," she said. "You're a bad influence."

"You have no idea."

She blushed. "If you aren't busy, you don't have to rush off."

"I don't want to intrude."

"I think Maaz enjoys having you around. He'll try and read to you. He's loving it at the moment, although apparently pizza beat it."

I laughed and grabbed her a slice, putting it on the plate and handing it over. "It's good pizza."

"Did Noah make it?"

"Dessert is his thing."

"What about the others?" she asked.

"I've told you Aiden's the doctor and Noah is the pastry chef."

"That leaves four other mysterious Sinclairs."

"What if you prefer them to me?"

Kiran looked thoughtful. "I don't think it's possible."

"I hope not," I teased, but there was a sliver of truth.

One woman had already proven I wasn't enough and the residual fear remained.

"Ethan works in investment banking," I said as she nibbled on the end of her pizza. "Then we have the second set of twins."

"Second set. Your mum is a hero."

"She is, for dealing with all of us. You'll meet Warren when he gets back from the States. He's been working on something out there for the past year."

"What is it?"

"I have no idea, and we're not allowed to know because I think he might actually get killed."

"What field does he work in?"

"He's a coder. Ethical hacking."

She let out a low whistle and fanned herself.

"Kiran," I warned her sternly.

"Is he single?" she teased.

"Don't even think about it," I said, leaning in and cupping her face.

"I'm joking," she said, rubbing her nose against mine. "What about his twin?"

"Mason is a law unto himself," I said, rolling my eyes. "He's been travelling for the past three years. We see him at Christmas and that's it."

"That leaves one more."

"Zane. Baby brother who just started his PhD."

"It must be nice to have such a large family," she commented.

"When they're not breaking your fingers, it can be good." I sniffed and looked at my lap. "I haven't been the best brother over the past few years. My priorities were a little messed up."

"Have you sorted them now?"

"I think so."

"Then appreciate them while you still have time," she said. "Life's short, Seth. Don't sit in regret."

A loud thump sounded from upstairs, followed by a frustrated scream.

"I'm going to kill you!"

The sound of footsteps grew louder before Maaz flew back into the room.

"Ma!" he yelled, making a beeline for her.

"She's still hurting, Maaz," I called, seeing his next moves.

His steps faltered, and he tripped before continuing his trajectory towards me. Maaz slammed into my legs and scrambled onto the sofa, squeezing in between me and the arm. Shah appeared in the door of the room, eyes narrowed at his brother.

"Seth's den!" Maaz yelled. "Seth's den!"

"You really can't leave now," Kiran said, laughing.

Chapter Twenty Six

- Kiran

"**Y**ou need to keep holding my hand," I reminded Maaz as we walked through the stadium. We joined a large crowd of people, all locating their seats.

The move to London had not fazed Maaz the way I thought it would because of one simple promise — we would watch the rugby at Twickenham.

My ruptured appendix had nearly thrown those plans out the window, but I was healing fine and I couldn't let Maaz down. What was meant to be an afternoon with my baby and Mike had suddenly become less relaxing and more stress inducing, and it had nothing to do with the fixture.

When I asked Maaz if he wanted a friend to come to the match with us, he immediately mentioned Seth and was like a dog with a bone. Nothing I said could deter him, and nervously, I stuttered through a request for him to join us, fully expecting him to decline.

But Seth cracked a rare smile and told me to transfer him the ticket so he could meet us there.

Maaz bounced along beside me, chattering away. His England rugby shirt was pristine white, but it wouldn't last. The smile on his face was so wide I worried about the ache setting in on his cheeks. But this was what I lived for. I loved seeing my sons happy. Even if I didn't share their passion for sports.

"Ma, look!" Maaz said, pointing ahead of us and laughing.

Welsh fans dressed in red, donned daffodil heads and wrapped in flags, bobbed ahead of us, and I smiled at the sight.

"Do you think we'll beat them?" I asked him.

He nodded confidently, and we climbed the stairs towards our seats. Seth was already sitting in the middle of the row, long legs spread and staring down at his phone. He was dressed casually in jeans and wore the white jersey that showed off his trim figure. I blushed at the thought of what laid underneath.

Maaz stumbled his way through the row with me, apologising to the spectators in their seats.

"Seth!" Maaz called.

My little boy tripped over his feet and crashed into Seth's legs. Seth jumped before laughing and stuffing his phone away.

"Mate, we're going to need to practise on that footwork if you're planning to play on this pitch in the future," Seth said, moving his hands slowly.

"I'm better in my boots."

"I'll have to watch you play."

Seth pushed down the seat and Maaz clambered onto it, swinging his legs.

"Hello, beautiful," Seth said, standing up and kissing my cheek.

"What are you doing?" I asked, blinking and feeling like the world was spinning too fast.

"I can't call you beautiful?" he asked, looking confused. "Or the kiss?"

We both sat down on either side of Maaz.

"Not that," I said to him.

"Ma, have you got the flag?" Maaz asked, tugging my sleeve.

"Yes, baby," I answered.

Unzipping my bag, I pulled out the folded flag and handed it to Maaz. He took it from me and shook it out.

"I forgot mine," Seth said to Maaz. Once again, his hands moved hesitantly. "Can we share?"

"Are you signing?" I asked, cutting across them.

Seth brought his gaze up to me. "I'm not sure. I think I am. Am I?"

Maaz tugged on my sleeve again, pulling my attention to him. "He's a little slow," Maaz signed without anything verbal.

"We all were when we started learning," I returned.

"I can teach you better," Maaz said, suddenly swinging his body towards Seth.

"I'm not doing a good job?" Seth looked crestfallen.

"You're slow," Maaz told him matter-of-factly.

"How have you been learning?" I asked. "How long have you been learning?"

"After the fundraiser," Seth said, rubbing the back of his neck. "I found someone to teach me through video sessions. Three times a week. There's a lot to learn. It's an entire language."

"Yeah," I replied, but it was swallowed by the stadium announcer booming over the speakers.

As we stood for the national anthems, I felt the tears prick my eyes. Seth had been learning sign language without telling us. Maaz was right. He was slow and hesitant, but that was likely because of his lack of practice outside whoever was teaching him. My heart stumbled in my chest, trying to figure out why he would make such an effort.

The match kicked off, and I stared out at the pitch, but my brain continued to focus on my life. I was selective about who I let in and how close they got. Seth was meant to be a colleague kept at arm's length. A hello in the corridor or a knock on the office door to ask for a pen. But Seth wasn't a man who faded into the background. He demanded to be noticed.

I just hadn't expected him to notice me or my boys. Maaz was growing attached to him. Seth's appearances in our life had impacted my youngest, but it was Shah who took me by surprise. Shahzad was guarded and observant. He rarely asked anyone for anything, but hearing he had reached out to Seth while I was in hospital made me wonder what had gone on between the pair. It was a question that I wasn't brave enough to ask.

Things were converging quickly. I wanted to keep them separate and minimise any oncoming damage, but it was clear that wasn't the case. And although my primary concern was my sons becoming invested in Seth, apparently it was reciprocated.

"Kiran," Seth said my name, his large hand landing on my shoulder and spreading warmth across the joint. "Are you enjoying the match?"

People were shuffling away from their seats, and I nodded. "Mhm. Yes."

"What's the score, flower?"

I blushed at being caught out.

"Maaz," I said, trying to get out of the hole I found myself in. "Are you hungry? Do you want anything?"

He scrunched his face before he said, "Yes, please."

"I can take him," Seth offered.

"That's okay," I said, standing up and waiting for Maaz. "Do you want anything?"

"No, thanks," Seth replied.

I shot him a smile, and Maaz clambered past me to get out of the aisle. I trailed after him, thankful that the rush of people meant he couldn't get too far away. Maaz opted for a bottle of water, ignoring my warning that it wasn't food, and we eventually got back to our seats.

Seth was engaged in conversation with a few men in the row in front of us, but the moment he spotted us, he cut the conversation short.

"Sorry, gents," he said, and they glanced in my direction. "That doesn't look like food," Seth continued, helping Maaz back into his seat.

"I'm not hungry," Maaz told him, trying to open the bottle.

I reached for it at the same time as Seth, and our fingers brushed. Every time his skin touched mine, thousands of volts shot through me, waking up every nerve in my body.

"I've got it," he said, taking the bottle and twisting the cap open.

There was a little spark of jealousy in my chest as Maaz turned his body away from mine to talk to Seth. I played with the curls on the back of his head as he chatted away about the game.

When he was born, I worried more than when I had Shah. I may have only been shy of sixteen when I had my first son, but we had family to help. With Maaz, I was still grieving, and I thought it would affect him. That I would mess up and ruin him somehow. But my baby grew up with more confidence than most and refused to hide away.

"I'm not sure I like you very much," I said to Seth when Maaz stopped to take a drink.

"Oh?" he asked, arching a dark eyebrow.

"I'm meant to be his favourite person, but it feels like you're trying to take that spot."

"I don't think you have to worry. I just appreciate the rugby enough to pay attention."

The second half started, and I capped Maaz's drink so he could wave his flag wildly. I forced myself to pay attention to thirty men running up and down the pitch.

As the closing minutes of the match ticked down on the clock, the score was tied. People rose to their feet as the ball changed hands and England won possession. Maaz dropped the flag and stood on his seat to see over heads.

"Come here," Seth said to him.

He grabbed Maaz, lifting him up in his arms so he could see the pitch properly, and my heart skipped a beat. Seth didn't look uncomfortable. He looked like he'd been dealing with Maaz his entire life, and the sight of both of them together made butterflies swarm in my stomach.

The noise erupted around me and I looked down at the pitch to see we had scored a try. Seth's deep timbre sounded in my ears as he cheered and Maaz's arms shot up in the air.

"We won!" Maaz screamed as the conversion was kicked. He hugged Seth around the neck.

"We won!" Seth echoed, grinning and ruffling his curls.

We trekked out of the stadium with a jubilant home crowd and Seth walked us to the car that was parked streets away.

"Can we do this again?" Maaz asked. "Will you come to the rugby with us next time? It's more fun to watch with you than Ma."

"Thanks, champ," I muttered under my breath. "Seth might be busy, so I'm not sure —"

"You let me know what match you want to go to and I'll be there if I can," Seth said.

"You don't have to do that," I replied.

"I want to. It's been years since I sat in the stands and watched a match."

"We better go," I said, unlocking the car.

"I'll see you on Monday." Seth closed the space and kissed my cheek. He opened the car door for me and I slipped in before he closed it and left us.

Maaz clipped his seatbelt into position and turned to me. "I really like Seth."

I watched as Seth's tall form disappeared down the street and replied, "I really like him too."

Chapter Twenty Seven

- Seth

"**W**hat I don't understand," Aiden said over dinner at our parents' home, "is how she's met me, but decides to spend her time with you."

Our little outing to the match yesterday hadn't gone unnoticed. A few members of the public fancied themselves as amateur reporters and snapped photos of the three of us which had since been plastered over the internet.

I'd spent most of my day messaging a very panicked Kiran and then on the phone to Tiffy. Maaz's face was clear in the pictures and no one had bothered to blur out the identity of the tiny five-year-old who just wanted to enjoy watching England win.

"Are you going to introduce her to the family?" Noah asked, pushing his dessert plate away.

"Why would I do that?" I asked.

"She's your girlfriend, right?" Ethan asked, pointing his spoon at me.

"No," I snapped. "She's a friend. Do you idiots remember what it's like to have friends of the opposite sex?"

Aiden looked at Noah and cocked his head to the side. "Noah, do you remember what it's like to have friends?"

A piece of silverware was thrown across the table, narrowly missing Aiden's head.

"Boys," Mum called from the head of the table. "You're adults. Why does every dinner end this way?"

There was a collective "Sorry, Mum."

"Her son is a beautiful little boy," Mum said, looking at me. "Just the one?"

"Two," I replied. "Maaz is her youngest. Shahzad is sixteen."

"Oh." Mum's eyebrows rose towards her hairline and I tensed, sitting up straight in my chair, ready to defend Kiran. "She was a young, Mum."

"She's done well with two children," Ethan said, sensing my mood.

"She has," I said curtly. "And she likes her privacy, so this conversation is done."

Getting up from the table, I picked up my plate and walked into the kitchen, ignoring the staff.

"She's just a friend?" Dad asked quietly as I placed plates into the dishwasher. When I didn't reply, he continued, "Come to the study."

Gritting my teeth, I left the kitchen and followed Dad into the study. The invite had only been extended to me, which meant that this was a conversation he didn't want to share.

"Is the interrogation necessary?" I asked, closing the door to make sure we were left alone.

"You tell me."

He popped the stopper out of a decanter and poured two glasses. I took the one he offered to me and drank from it.

"Did you know about her husband?" I asked him curiously, turning the questions on him before he could start.

Dad sat in the chair behind his desk. "Yes. We met a few times before everything was signed off. She had concerns and spoke to me about them. I'm glad she did or we wouldn't have her under our wing. She's a remarkable woman, even if she doesn't see it."

He put his glass on the table and gestured to the chair in front of him. Reluctantly, I sat and waited for the inevitable.

"There's something going on between you both?" Dad continued.

"She wants to keep things quiet," I explained why I'd just lied through my teeth at the dinner table.

Dad snorted. "Yes, well, attending a large rugby match and playing happy families isn't exactly subtle."

My cheeks heated, and I stared into my glass. "Maaz asked her to ask me and I couldn't say no."

I could have. I could have made any excuse, but I didn't want to. Something inside of me lit up to hear that Maaz had specifically requested the ticket went to me.

"Seth, I want to make sure you understand what you're doing."

I looked up. "I'm not an idiot."

"I'm not saying you are. But you have a tendency to bulldoze through life with little care about the collateral damage."

It was a stinging assessment, but the truth.

"That's how we work," I said to him.

"And it's not a bad attribute for business. Maybe not so much in your personal life."

"I really don't see how this has anything to do with you."

"Really?" he asked. "I watched you fall apart after Anna. You hit self-destruct and left."

"I came back."

"Are you any less destructive?"

"I'm learning."

"I'm not sure Kiran should be a test run."

"She's not," I said, gripping the glass tightly. "I can't explain it. She… she makes me want to be a better person."

Dad cocked an eyebrow. "You have an issue with who you are?"

"I didn't. Not really. She said a few things that made me think about how I behave sometimes."

He nodded slowly. "What are the boys like?"

A smile tugged on my lips. "Maaz is a ball of energy. He doesn't stop. I keep thinking him and Aiden are going to get on when they meet."

"So, you plan on having us meet her as more than an employee?"

"Maybe."

"And her older son?"

"Shah's a little more difficult to crack. He's not so trusting."

"I'm not sure sneaking around is going to give you any points with them."

"He knows. I sort of asked his permission."

"You must see something with her if you've spoken to her son."

"It's still early days."

"I asked your mother to marry me after three months of knowing her."

"She's hesitant, and I understand. We're coming from two different worlds. She likes her privacy. The photos have made her uneasy, and I'm trying to do damage control."

"I'm not sure how much you're going to be able to avoid pictures when you've lived half your life in the public eye."

"Maybe that's the problem," I mumbled. "Spending so much time letting everyone in instead of focusing on letting one person in."

"You're letting three people in by the sounds of it," Dad mused. "Seth, I'm not telling you to stop seeing her. I just want you to be careful."

"I plan to be."

"Good," he said and got up from his seat. "I look forward to meeting them all properly when you're both ready. Your mother wouldn't stop talking about her after she came to the anniversary party."

"She's going to run a mile when she meets everyone."

"Then I hope you're ready to chase her."

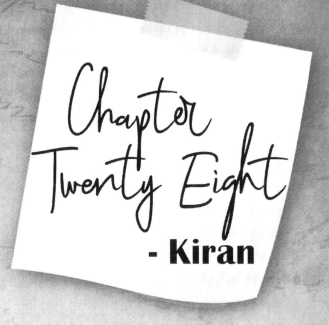

Chapter Twenty Eight

- Kiran

Leaving yoga this morning had been a shock. As I slipped into the car to head to the office, someone knocked on my window. I lowered it to be greeted with a camera in the face and a lot of questions. Quickly bringing up the glass again, my heart pounded violently against my chest and I drove towards the office and rushed inside.

"Morning, Kiran," Astra greeted breezily from her desk.

I raised a hand and hurried into my office, shutting the door behind me. The entire weekend had been tainted by photographs that appeared online of Seth and me. And whereas that had put me into panic mode, the fact that Maaz was front and centre in most of the pictures had me in tears.

It had been stupid to think we could get away with a simple trip out. I didn't expect someone to intrude and sell stories to anyone who wanted it, but that had been wishful thinking.

The articles ranged from dismissive — I was nothing special and a pit stop for Seth before he found someone more glamorous — to brutal — I was a gold digger who was attempting to trap him with my child.

Neither side of the line made me comfortable and I spent most of the weekend in bed, scrolling through articles and figuring out how to get out of the mess I created.

"You look exhausted," Mike said as I walked onto the third floor. He pulled a chair from behind him and I dropped into it.

"It's been a long weekend," I replied.

"I saw."

The tears pricked my eyes, and Mike wrapped an arm around my shoulder. "This can wait. Why don't we grab a coffee?"

It felt safer to be out on the street with Mike by my side. Like if anyone was to jump out at me again, I would have some backup.

"You look like you have a lot on your mind," Mike said when we had coffee cups in hand.

"Just wondering why we ever thought AI would bring us happiness," I joked.

"It's a pain, but look at what it pays," he replied. "I don't think it's work that's bothering you."

"You saw what happened this weekend."

"I saw you, Seth, and Maaz enjoying yourselves. There's nothing wrong with that."

"Isn't there?"

"You went to the match with a friend because I couldn't make it."

I shot him a look, and Mike shrugged.

"Kiran, how long have I known you?" he asked.

"Since we were eighteen and taking those stupid catch-up classes together."

"Then tell me what's going on."

I let out a shuddering breath as a light rain started to fall over London.

Mike was a safe space. He already knew most of the story, but I hadn't caught him up on the recent developments. It felt better to keep Seth in a separate bubble in my life, away from everything I deemed stable until I really understood what was happening between us. That had been blown out of the water in a single afternoon.

"Seth and I sort of started seeing each other," I mumbled.

"I guessed as much," he said with a soft smile. "Are you upset about what the press are saying?"

"Kind of." I bit my bottom lip. "There's a lot going on in my head."

"Talk to me about it."

"I don't want people taking pictures of the boys. I don't want cameras in my face when I leave the gym," I explained. "And I don't know why, but I feel so guilty, Mike."

"Guilty," Mike repeated the word.

"He's the first man I've given any real time to since Jamal," I said quietly. "I took off my rings, thinking it might help. And it did. It felt okay when it was private, but now it feels more…"

"Real?"

"Yes. Real. And I have this overwhelming sense of guilt about how happy he makes me, Mike. Did you know he's been learning sign language for Maaz? Who does that?"

"I didn't know, but that's a good effort."

"I shouldn't be this happy."

"Why not?"

"Mike, I lost my husband, and I don't even know why. I don't know what he was thinking, and I'm here, taking my kids out with this new guy. It's like I'm trying to replace Jamal and that makes me this awful human being —"

"Stop," Mike said, grabbing my arm. "Kiran, when are you going to stop blaming yourself?"

"I don't think I can."

"Listen to me," he said and started to walk again. "I don't know how it feels. I told you that years ago. But I know who you are and you were not the reason Jamal left. He loved you."

"And look at how I'm repaying that."

"By being happy? Yeah, Kiran. You're terrible for wanting to continue living your life."

"The boys should be my priority. I shouldn't have even entertained the idea of dating someone. I don't know what I was thinking."

"You were thinking about yourself for once in your life," Mike said, walking through the revolving door of the building. "That's not a bad thing, Kiran. You're allowed to date. You're allowed to fall in love."

"No one said anything about love."

"One day, it might happen again. That doesn't mean you forgot Jamal." He stepped into the lift and I walked in, leaning against the wall. "Kiran, you tell everyone to do what brings them joy in their life, but you need to take your own advice. Talk to Seth and figure out all these little things."

"What if he runs?" I asked, voicing another worry.

"It doesn't sound like he's planning to bolt if he's been learning how to sign for Maaz."

The lift doors opened, and I jumped, spilling coffee out of the lip when I saw Seth standing there.

"Kiran, I've been looking for you," he said.

"I'll get started on cleaning up the code and send you an email," Mike said to me.

"I'll come down later and check," I said, watching as both men passed each other.

Seth hit the button for our floor and the door closed. The moment they did, he crowded my space, bringing his hands to my face and cupping it.

"How are you doing?" he asked. "Astra said you were rushing around this morning."

"I'm okay," I muttered.

"Don't lie to me."

My free hand went to his tie, red and silken, tugging at it gently. Seth lowered his face to mine.

"Tell me how to fix it," he whispered.

"I don't know," I replied.

"I feel like I'm going to lose you."

"You're not," I said. Even with the guilt, I couldn't bring myself to step away from him. "I just want to figure out how to deal with people invading my privacy."

"I haven't given a comment yet, but I can say you're a friend. I can lie if you need more time."

"Do you think they'll believe that?"

"Kiran, they won't believe a word. They'll think whatever they want, but we don't have to confirm it."

My gaze flicked over his shoulder. "Seth, we're almost at our floor."

He let go of me and stepped back before stopping the lift.

"Seth!"

"I need to know what you want to do. If you still want to explore this."

"No more trips with Maaz," I blurted out. "Not yet. Not when people are trying to take pictures of him."

"They should never have fucking run those," Seth seethed, looking pissed.

"It's done, but no more."

"No more," he agreed.

I thought about what Mike said. I spent a lot of my time trying to make sure people were okay and Seth was one of the people in my life who reciprocated it. The adrenaline and butterflies made me feel like I was living again instead of just existing.

"I'd appreciate keeping it between us for now. Please," I said.

Seth nodded and kissed me softly. "Done. But there is one person I want to introduce you to."

"Who?" I asked.

"Tiffy. She can help if you let her. She'll keep away the questions and minimise the press if you hand it over to her."

"I don't know," I said, chewing my bottom lip.

Seth pulled it from between my teeth with his thumb. "Stop that," he scolded. "I'll give you her details and then it's up to you if you use them or not."

Chapter Twenty Nine

- Seth

Dates were difficult when most of them were confined to the house. All the grand gestures I wanted to present Kiran were reduced to simple pleasures. Not that she complained. Kiran was never ungrateful. Every bunch of flowers, every sticky note I left her was met with gratitude, and the panic that had unsettled her after the match slowly subsided.

She had taken my advice and got in touch with Tiffy. Although Tiff swore she wouldn't take on any more clients because she had her hands full with me, Aiden, and Noah, she added Kiran to her roster, and I was thankful.

Kiran currently laid on top of me on my sofa as we watched a documentary on the tombs and pyramids of Egypt.

"You can't go breaking into a pyramid," Kiran said, her fingers running up and down my bare side.

"Why not?" I asked, barely paying attention to the screen.

"Curses, Seth."

"You don't believe in that."

"Of course, I do. There's plenty of proof out there."

"What proof?" I asked, amused by her revelation.

"All the people who died after opening King Tut's tomb."

"Eight of them," I said, looking down at her.

"Eight more than there should have been."

"Kiran, there was a team of around sixty people," I argued with logic.

"Shhh." And she pressed her lips to mine, smiling.

My entire body flooded with desire at the simple action.

It was strange to think that there was a time when being at home left me feeling aggravated and suffocated. I had to be out of the four walls. Had to grab attention. Being home with Anna felt like walking around with a stranger. Both of us were more interested in our phones or email inbox to enjoy time together.

Kiran only checked her phone to make sure the boys didn't need her, and I swapped mine to silent, cherishing the time I had her alone.

Her phone vibrated on the glass coffee table and she groaned, pushing herself up from my body and getting up to grab it. I watched her like a hawk, drinking her in.

Away from the office, Kiran craved comfort, and the moment she stepped into my home, she shed the heels and work attire and slipped into a pair of my sweatpants. Even rolled at the waist, they were too long and dropped low, revealing red lace high around her hips that made my dick twitch.

"Who is it?" I asked, voice gruff.

"Mike, with a work update," she said, putting her phone down again. "I can handle it later."

Mike was a thorn in my side, spending much more time with Kiran than I liked. But it did my ego well to know she would ignore him for me.

I sat up as she turned around and pulled her onto my lap. Kiran's hand went to the back of my neck, nails gently raking my hair.

"So, I have you for a little longer?" I asked, pressing my face into the crook of her neck.

"Mhm," she hummed quietly.

Nipping at her neck gently, she let out a breathy moan.

"How should I keep you occupied?" I mused, trailing kisses back up to her mouth.

Every time I kissed Kiran, it was like someone set fire to every muscle in my body. I couldn't contain myself, and I wanted more. It took so much to hold myself back. To move slowly like she asked. The more time I spent with her, the more difficult it became. But the more time I spent with her, the braver Kiran grew.

As our tongues met, Kiran shifted so that she straddled my lap, knees on either side of me. The bulge in my trousers grew, and I was certain she was aware of it because she smiled into the kiss. She pressed her hips down, grinding her pussy against me, and I bit hard on her bottom lip. All week, she teased me until I felt I would go insane. I'd had enough.

"You look like butter wouldn't melt," I said, letting go of her lip. "But it's all an act."

Kiran looked up at me from under her lashes. "It's not an act."

I flipped her so that she was sitting on the sofa, and I sank to the floor between her legs.

"Isn't it?" I asked. "You've never had any thoughts about me worshipping your body?"

"No," she answered quickly, but the blush stained her cheeks.

"Don't lie, flower."

I stripped the sweatpants from her and trailed kisses up her left leg, stopping when I reached her thigh. My goal was covered in bright red lace, and I couldn't help but stare. The colour was stark against her brown skin, and my dick strained against my trousers.

"Good underwear makes you feel you can conquer the world," she muttered quietly.

I looked up at her. "But they make it difficult for me to conquer you."

My fingers ran along the lace and she let out a shuddering breath. I could smell the scent of her arousal, and my mouth watered. Keeping my eyes on hers, I dipped my fingers under the lace and into her pussy to discover wetness. Kiran whimpered quietly as I brought my glistening fingers back in front of me. My tongue darted out to taste her from my digits, and I let out a deep, low groan.

"Of course you would taste this fucking sweet," I muttered darkly.

"Sorry," she whispered.

My eyes snapped to her, and I grinned wolfishly. "Don't apologise," I said, tugging the thong from her hips and tossing them to the side. "But I need a proper taste."

Forcing her knees apart wider, I felt her tremble under my hands.

"Relax," I told her, moving my face closer.

Kiran leant back against the sofa, looking down at me with her large eyes. I kissed her inner thighs softly and her muscles twitched in anticipation.

"Seth," she breathed my name.

"Yes, Kiran?"

I agreed to take it at her pace and wanted to hear her ask for this. As much as I wanted to desperately feast on this woman, I would back away if she told me to.

"Please," she whispered.

That was the only encouragement I needed. My thumbs spread her lips to reveal her clit and my tongue came out to lap at her eagerly. Kiran gasped before it melted into a moan. Her hands instantly went to the back of my head, fingers threading in my hair. I moved slowly, wanting to savour the taste of her, and her hips bucked against my face.

Pulling away, I asked, "Are you going to be honest with me now?" I pushed a finger into her. "Have you thought about me like this?"

Kiran nodded her head quickly as I curled my finger inside of her. She tipped her head back and shut her eyes.

"How often have you thought about it?" I asked.

"A lot," she breathed.

"When?"

"Seth, please."

"Tell me when." I pumped my finger slowly to encourage her.

"When I'm alone," she said. "At night."

"In bed?" I asked, licking her once.

Her body jerked, and she whimpered when I pulled away from her.

"In bed," she confirmed with a moan.

"Have you masturbated to the thought of me, flower? Have you made yourself come, thinking of me between your legs?"

"Yes. Yes."

"Dirty girl." I laughed, thumb rubbing against her swollen clit.

"I'm sorry," she said, looking at me. Her pupils had dilated, robbing the brown of her irises.

"You don't need to be sorry," I replied. "But this is only for me, understood?"

"Mhm."

"Do you want me to make you come, Kiran?"

"Please, Seth," she begged. "Please."

I fantasised about how she would sound when I got my hands on her. How she would feel and how she would taste. The reality was sweeter than anything I imagined. Kiran's timid nature dissipated. Her grip grew tighter and her moans were louder. The more I ate, the further she pressed my face into her.

My tongue brushed against her again before I bit lightly on her clit.

"Fuck!" she hissed.

I sucked it into my mouth, and she trembled. My gaze shifted to her face to see her mouth open as the pleasure built. How many times had I pictured her like this? Completely and utterly powerless under my touch.

Kiran's body tensed, and her pussy began to tighten around my fingers. I sucked harder on her bundle of nerves, and she screamed my name as she finally reached her orgasm.

217

Slowly, her body relaxed, and Kiran opened her eyes, heavy with lust. I slid my fingers from her and joined her on the sofa. Closing her legs, she curled her body against mine.

"Are you going to help me clean up?" I asked, showing her my fingers.

Kiran looked at them, sticky and glistening from the mess she made. I placed the tips of them on her bottom lip and she took them into her mouth without complaint, licking and sucking them. The next time I had her alone, it wouldn't be my fingers in her mouth.

"Good girl," I said, kissing her head.

She let my fingers out of her mouth and kissed me deeply, tasting herself on my tongue.

"Better than your imagination?" I asked.

"So much better."

Chapter Thirty

- Kiran

"Jack said his dad is coming from work," Maaz said as I tucked him in.

I wished I could crawl into bed as well. Adding Seth into the mix of my routine had sapped the last of my energy. And as our relationship ventured into intimacy, I was left exhausted at trying to balance my desire to dive into sex with self-restraint.

"And," Maaz continued as I stifled a yawn, "he said he's going to run the three-legged race with him."

"So we need to beat Jack and his dad," I said, putting the glass of water on his bedside table.

Maaz scrunched his nose and turned on his side. "I want Dad there."

I felt like I'd been punched in the stomach. Every ounce of exhaustion was replaced with the feeling of anxiety.

I decided early on to be honest with Maaz about Jamal. Not the whole truth. He was still too young for that. But I explained his dad wasn't with us anymore and that he kept watch on all of us from heaven. There were a lot of questions and poring over photo albums, but Maaz grew up knowing that our trio was his version of family.

"Baby, if he could be, then you know he would," I said before running a hand through his curls. "Do you miss him?"

"I don't know."

"Do you want to talk about it?"

Maaz shook his head against the pillow, and I bit the insides of my cheeks.

"I'll be there," I reminded him.

The school sports day had been marked on the calendar for weeks and I was working from home in the morning, so I would be there on time.

"I know, Ma," he said, signing. "I love you."

"I love you too," I returned, pressing a kiss to his cheek.

We gathered on the school fields where brightly coloured cones outlined the track. Maaz tugged at his baseball cap as we walked with other parents, children, and teachers to our designated spot.

"Baby, are you okay?" I asked, bending down.

He kept glancing around and wasn't as bubbly as he usually was.

"Yeah," he said, shaking me off and walking ahead of me.

There was no doubt in my mind that the conversation from last night still weighed on him. I would do anything for my kids, but some things were beyond my control. I couldn't bring his dad back, and that meant I had to fill the role. But often, that wasn't enough.

Whatever Maaz wanted to do this weekend, we would do it. Bowling. The park. Ice cream. I would make it up to him somehow. I hated the fact the smile dropped from his little face.

We parked ourselves on the grass and listened as the teachers walked through health and safety, lining the kids up for the first race — egg and spoon. Maaz ran over to the start line, grabbing a spoon from the box and taking a boiled egg.

I gave him a thumbs up, but his eyes widened, and he waved wildly, beaming. My brow furrowed until a shadow fell over me. Craning my neck, I was met with a tall figure dressed in a pair of shorts and a t-shirt, showing off lean limbs and dark sunglasses covering his eyes. My stomach knotted.

"Hello, flower," he said, sitting on the grass next to me.

"Seth, what are you doing here?"

My cheeks burnt as a few parents threw glances our way.

"I would have been here sooner but needed to wrap up a meeting with Teresa over a patent," he explained.

"What are you doing here?" I repeated.

"Maaz called me."

"Maaz, what?"

"From Shah's phone."

I rubbed my temples, trying to piece together what was happening.

"He told me about his sports day," Seth continued. "Asked if I could be here."

"And you couldn't tell him no?" I asked sharply.

"Not if you heard the way he was down the phone. Talking about some shitty kid, Jack, and his dad winning a race."

"You had no right. He shouldn't have called you and you shouldn't have turned up."

"Maaz has missed out on enough, don't you think? He wanted someone here to run a race with him, Kiran. We're not planning a heist."

"He has me."

"He wants a dad."

"He has a dad, and that's not you!"

Seth recoiled, and I instantly regretted the words that left my mouth.

223

"Seth," I whispered, reaching out to him.

He jerked his hand away. "No. You're right. I'm not his dad, and I never will be," he replied icily. "But he needed something, so I'm here. I'm here for him. Not for you."

Maaz ran over, red in the face and holding a plastic silver medal.

"Did you see?" he asked excitedly. "Did you see?"

"You did brilliant," Seth said to him with a high-five.

"Great, baby," I told him.

But Maaz had lost interest in me being there now since he had Seth. I sat on the grass for the rest of the afternoon, feeling two feet tall. There was a lump in my throat that refused to move, and I pasted on a smile for Maaz, even if it was the last thing I felt like doing.

When they called for the three-legged race, Seth looked at me, and I flinched.

"Maybe your mum should do it with you," Seth explained to Maaz kindly.

"No," Maaz whined. "Please, Seth." He grabbed Seth's hand and tugged it hard, trying to get him to stand up.

"You should race," I said.

"Am I allowed to now?" Seth shot back, and I nodded.

He unfolded himself from the grass and held Maaz's hand as they went to the start line.

I dreamed of days like this. Five years of being a single mother wore on me. The parents' evenings and sports days I battled on my own. I wondered what it would be like to have their dad there with them to share in those moments and make those memories. Jamal and Shah and Maaz — the way it should have been.

But it wasn't Jamal. Slowly but surely, Seth had crept into the picture. Not vindictively or forcefully, but because my boys felt comfortable with him. Because he wanted to be in their life and support them if they needed it.

The whistle was shrill, and I looked on as Seth and Maaz ambled down the course. Seth was easily double the height and Maaz tried to pull ahead. My heart ached as I watched my baby laugh, clinging onto Seth. They tumbled over the finish line a hair's breadth before the others and celebrated, falling in a heap on the ground.

Maaz wore his gold medal proudly around his neck, hanging onto Seth's hand instead of mine as we left the park.

"I can drop you home," Seth said. "If that's not going to cause an issue."

"Yes, please," Maaz answered for me. "My legs are tired."

"You're a champ, that's why."

Seth helped him into the back of the car, and I slipped into the passenger seat. Seth climbed into the driver's side and drove towards my home. His hand left the gearstick and rested on my thigh and my hand immediately covered it. Seth laced our fingers, and I squeezed his hand tight as a tear spilled onto my cheek.

I was grateful that Seth kept the conversation up with Maaz because I couldn't. The tears fell and I couldn't stop them. Wiping them with the heel of my free hand, I tried to pull myself together as we stopped outside the house.

"Thank you," I whispered.

"I'm coming in," Seth told me, and I nodded.

Maaz flopped himself on the sofa, leaving me and Seth to take up the kitchen. Seth shut the door to give us privacy, and I stood at the other end of the room, away from him.

"I'm sorry," I told him without prompt. "I didn't mean what I said." The tears burnt my eyes again. "I knew I was going to mess this up."

Seth crossed the kitchen in a few steps and pulled me into his arms. "Please don't cry," he said, kissing the top of my head. "Kiran, there's no need for tears."

"I messed up," I sobbed into his chest.

"So did I. I should have called and checked with you."

"I shouldn't have been such a cow."

"Kiran, flower, look at me." Seth stepped back and cupped my face. "It's okay."

"It's not. It's not." I was struggling to breathe. "This is how it starts. We're going to fight and you're not going to talk to me about things and then... and then..."

My lungs burnt, and the room grew smaller. I couldn't take in enough air and felt lightheaded.

"Kiran," Seth said. "Kiran, you need to breathe. Breathe."

But it was easier said than done. The panic set in, and I was struggling to focus on anything else.

"Copy me, flower," Seth instructed.

He exaggerated his breathing — in through the nose and out through the mouth. I followed him, still crying, and eventually felt the world steady around me.

Seth relaxed and kissed my forehead gently. "Couples fight, babe. We're going to fight, but that doesn't mean bad things. You're allowed to be mad at me for showing up today. I'm allowed to be pissed at you for just wanting to spend time with your kids. I won't go anywhere. Maybe I'll get drunk at a bar with Aiden or I'll go see one of the others, but I will *always* come back to you. I promise you I will always come back."

"I'm so sorry," I said, hugging him around the middle.

"So am I," he muttered into my hair. "Kiran, you're going to need to let me spend time with them. We don't have to tell them what we are, but it won't be a complete shock if you let me be around them when they ask."

"I know," I replied.

Everything he said made sense. He wasn't getting in contact with my boys or muscling his way into their lives. They asked for him, and he answered. Never once had he complained about them or made it seem like an effort.

"Ma?" Maaz's voice sounded in the space.

Seth wiped a tear away from my face and nodded, giving me the all clear. I stepped away from him to see Maaz looking confused.

"Why are you hugging Seth?" he asked.

"I was just congratulating him for winning the race," I explained, pasting on a smile.

Maaz didn't look like he believed me.

"Did you need something?" I asked.

"Is Seth staying for dinner?"

"Depends on if your mum can cook better than she bakes," Seth said, laughing.

"She makes the best burritos," Maaz boasted.

"Can I stay for dinner?" Seth asked me. "I have a deep love of burritos."

"I'm sure we can squeeze you in at the table," I muttered in response.

"Yes!" Maaz said, grabbing Seth's wrist.

"Where are you taking him?" I asked.

"I want to see if Seth can break the Lego you couldn't pull apart," Maaz replied.

"Good plan, champ. If he's staying, he's got to earn his place."

Seth looked over his shoulder at me as he left the room. "I'll earn it."

Chapter Thirty One
- Seth

"**W**hy do we have to wear a suit?" Maaz asked as the tailor measured around his chest. "Ma said it was black tie."

"That's what black tie means, dippy," Shah replied.

Burrito night at Kiran's had been a slightly awkward affair when Shah joined us. He might have agreed to let me date his mum, but that didn't mean he wanted to see me at the kitchen table. He kept conversation to a minimum until I was ready to leave and swooped in with a request for a suit fitting for the summer gala.

Kiran had given her blessing, and that was how the three of us ended up in a boutique with Maaz complaining about the dress code.

"Can I wear blue?" Maaz asked. "It's my favourite colour."

"Not for this one," I told him. "We have to be in black."

"Black is for funerals," he argued, pulling a face.

Shah stiffened in the chair beside me and dropped his head. I learned every day how the events in the Jafri family's past still affected them. When people said time healed, it wasn't a lie, but it wasn't the truth, either. The odd word or item pulled emotions to the surface and reopened wounds. Just like it had now.

I clapped a hand on Shah's shoulder and he looked at me.

"Everything okay?" I asked.

He shrugged me off. "I haven't worn a suit since Dad's funeral. It's going to be weird."

"Hopefully, you'll make some good memories from the gala. And don't you have prom coming up?"

Shah groaned, "Did Ma say something?"

"She can't wait. She's still trying to figure out if you have a date."

"I asked Roxy Popova," Shah said, looking at his little brother.

"Did she say yes?"

He nodded.

"Your mother is going to lose her shit," I said, chuckling.

"That's why I haven't told her yet."

"Your secret is safe with me."

"I need to buy her one of those flowery wrist things that girls have."

"A corsage?"

"Yeah, but I don't know where to get one from."

"I'll get Kirsty to send you some places."

It was safer to avoid Astra and her big mouth. Nothing would be kept a secret if we told the office pixie.

Shah turned his head to me. "Thanks, Seth. I don't want to mess this up for her."

That sentence alone stood as a testament to how Kiran had raised her sons. I wasn't surprised that Shah was thinking about someone else before himself.

Another hour of measurements and trying on different suits and we finally stepped back out onto the street. The wild child that was Maaz Jafri revelled in the freedom, running off down the street and forcing me and Shah to chase after him.

I caught up with him and grabbed him around the waist.

"Maaz," I scolded. "Your mum is going to kill me if I let you run the streets like a wild boy."

"Freedom!" he yelled.

Picking him off the ground, I locked a squirming Maaz under my arm and strode towards the car.

"He's a nightmare," Shah told me, falling into step.

"Trust me, I've realised," I muttered back.

I messed with Maaz's hair and he beat his fists on my ribs. "Put me down!" He laughed. "I want to be wild."

"That's all Ma," Shah said. "A little unhinged and wanting to do things his own way."

"Your mother's not unhinged," I said, but couldn't help the smile that grew on my face.

Kiran danced to the beat of her own drum. She left a trail of sticky notes in her wake and talked to herself when she thought no one was around. Syrup and sugar were her not-so-secret addictions in tea and coffee. There was always more milk in her fridge than any human needed. Some days, I wished I could take a peek into her brilliant brain to understand what went on inside.

"Let me run wild!" Maaz demanded, still laughing.

"No can do," I replied. "You can go wild after you go to the gala. I'll tell your mum she can't put you in a suit again for a year. Deal?"

"And I want a dog."

I looked down at the wriggling boy. "What?"

"Tell her I want a dog!"

Jostling him under my arm, I said, "A dog? That's not part of the deal."

"Please!" Maaz yelled, giggling to himself. "Please, Dad!"

The word made me halt in the street, and I heard Shah utter the word "shit." Carefully, I lowered Maaz down on the ground and he looked at me nervously. I got onto my knees to talk to him properly. Man to man. Weird awkward man who was dating Kiran to Kiran's youngest son.

"Maaz," I said gently. "You know I love spending time with you. But I'm not your dad. He's —"

"I know. He's in heaven."

"Yeah, and he's always going to be your dad."

"I wish you were," Maaz said, looking straight at me.

A range of emotions bubbled and twisted in my chest. I had a soft spot for Maaz. He was a cheeky little kid with way too much energy, and I wanted to be there for him. But I couldn't take on that role. Not in the way he wanted me to. We couldn't erase Jamal from the position.

"This is my fault," Shah muttered. "We shouldn't have asked you to take us for a fitting."

"You don't want to be my dad?" Maaz asked me.

"I…" I started.

"Dippy," Shah said. "You can't just ask people that."

"Why not?" Maaz argued.

"Because it's awkward. We have a dad."

"*You* have a dad. You met him. I never did. I want a dad."

This had spiralled out of control and I needed to put a lid on it before they got back home and Kiran had to deal with this meltdown.

"He was still your dad, and he still loved you," I said, getting up from the ground. "And your mum loves you enough for two people."

I held a hand out to Maaz, but he folded his arms across his chest and scowled at me.

"I don't like you," he told me bluntly, and it cut deep.

"Maaz," I said, putting a hand on his shoulder.

"No," he replied, shaking it off and sticking to Shah. "I want to go home."

"I think that's the best plan," Shah mumbled.

The boys slid into the back of the car, and I drove them to the house. Shah spent the trip talking Maaz down. He calmed a little by the time I pulled up, but he refused to say goodbye to me, jumping out the car and heading towards the door.

"He'll be fine," Shah said to me. "Thanks again for tonight."

When he closed the door, I took off for the only place that I could think of that might give me answers to how badly I had fucked up.

"I didn't expect to see you tonight," Dad said, letting me into the house. "Is everything okay? Issues with the patent?"

"It's a more social visit," I said, following him into the living room.

"Trouble with Kiran?" he pinpointed, raising an eyebrow.

I rarely made a social call, so it wasn't hard to decipher that I was here for a reason.

"Trouble with Maaz," I admitted. "Her youngest son."

"Is he okay?" Dad asked, looking alarmed.

I dropped onto the sofa and hugged a pillow around my middle. "He's fine. I think I fucked up."

"What happened?" Dad took a seat on the chair opposite me.

"I took the boys out to get fitted for the gala. Everything was fine and then he called me dad. I tried to explain I'm not his dad. Kiran… We haven't discussed that sort of thing, and I'm not sure she would be happy about it."

Kiran had clarified that my position in their life was not paternal. Although it had been said in the heat of the moment, I understood I could never and would never replace Jamal in their lives.

"That's a smart decision," Dad said.

"I thought so, but Maaz didn't." Nausea rolled in my stomach, and I felt uncomfortable. "We've always had a good relationship, but after I told him that, he said he didn't like me much. Wouldn't hold my hand. Didn't say goodbye. I am public enemy number one as far as that kid is concerned."

Dad blinked a few times before he laughed.

"It's not funny," I snapped, putting the pillow aside and sitting up. "He hates me!"

233

"He doesn't hate you. You've always had a flare for the dramatics. I blame your mother," Dad said, shaking his head. "Welcome to parenthood, Seth. Children have their own views on the world and when they don't match ours, they sulk. Maaz is sulking. He'll be fine."

"Will he?"

Dad leant forward and looked at me, smiling. "I'm proud of you. I thought maybe you just wanted Kiran and not her family."

"She doesn't do anything without the boys," I told him. "I thought it would annoy me, but they're good kids, Dad. I really like them."

"Sounds like they're fond of you too."

"This is a mess."

"Is it? Would you want to be a dad to them?"

"Kiran —"

"No, Seth. I'm asking if you would want that. A teenager and a little kid. Would you want that?"

"It's not the traditional route into parenthood," I admitted. "I've never done it, and I'm worried I'm going to fuck it up. I'm not their dad. They aren't related to me in any way."

"Being a dad isn't about sperm," Dad said, voicing my thoughts.

"Please stop."

"It's about being there for them when you're needed. Celebrating all the important milestones."

"I went to Maaz's sports day," I said quietly. "He asked me to be there, and I raced with him. I don't know how to explain it, but seeing him laugh, seeing how proud he was to win with me made me feel... full." I rubbed the spot above my heart.

"Kids have a way of doing that to you." Dad leant back in his seat. "Let me tell you a secret. You'll always think you're doing a terrible job. You're thirty-two, and I still worry about messing up."

"Really?"

"The worry never stops, son. You'll want to protect them from everything, but sometimes we can't. Sometimes they get hurt and you pick up the pieces. You let them work through it until they're ready to come back."

I rubbed the back of my neck. "Like I came back."

"Exactly," he said. "Give it a few days. Maaz will forget about it and want you to do something else with him. How old is he?"

"Five."

Dad laughed again. "Five? You have plenty on the way with that one."

"You're not helping the situation."

"Call it payback for all the stress you've given me over the years."

Chapter Thirty Two

- Kiran

I let out a shrill scream, followed by a laugh. Grabbing the office phone on the desk, I jabbed in the extension and then the number.

Seth appeared at the door, looking panicked, and Astra squeezed in by his side. I raised a finger to stop them as Professor Hargreaves picked up the call.

"Hello," he yawned.

"Kiran Jafri," I said.

"Kiran!" He sounded alert now. "Have you heard anything?"

I heard the distant chime of his laptop starting up.

"We did it," I said. "They awarded us the grant."

The same scream came down the line, and I laughed hard again. The decision was a lot quicker than we expected.

"Yes! Yes!" he yelled down the line.

We finished up the conversation, and I looked at Seth and Astra in the doorway.

"You got it?" Seth asked. I nodded at him and a grin spread across his face. "Congratulations, flower!"

He walked across the room and I rose to meet him. Seth pulled me into a tight hug, my feet leaving the floor as he buried his face in my neck.

"I'm so proud of you," he said, kissing my skin softly.

"Thank you, Tin Man," I replied, dotting a kiss on his cheek.

Astra cleared her throat, and Seth set me down before we both looked at her. She raised a blue eyebrow, and I blushed, straightening out my dress.

"Congratulations, Kiran," she said brightly. "Can I nip out to grab some things to celebrate? Cake? Champagne?"

"Yes," Seth answered and then looked at me. "This deserves to be celebrated."

"Thanks, peaches," Astra said. "Don't break my boss! Unless she likes that shit!" she called before closing the door and walking off.

I should have panicked that Astra had witnessed a more intimate moment between us than I planned to share, but it was becoming harder to keep it under wraps. Seth slowly infiltrated my life, and I cleared a space for him, allowing my heart to open up to possibilities.

"Peaches?" Seth asked, turning back to me and placing his hands on my waist. His touch was always firm, possessive. Like he was making sure I didn't have a chance to run.

"She loves your peach," I told him, reaching around to pinch his ass.

He grabbed my wrists, pulling my hands above my head and walking me back until I hit the wall. Sticky notes fluttered to the ground around our feet.

"Seth," I muttered, glancing at the door.

"I'm going to have to send Astra on a sexual harassment course," he said, pressing his body up against mine.

Adrenaline flushed through my system, causing every cell to ache for him.

"Book yourself a place while you're at it," I replied, trying to free my hands.

The longer he held me in this position, the weaker my resolve grew. It was already dangerously thin whenever I was alone with him.

"Are you saying I'm harassing you?" he asked, running his nose along my face.

I took in a deep breath, trying to ignore the prickle of his stubble against my skin and the way he stole the air from my lungs. He was commanding in every sense of the word, and I was powerless.

"Yes," I whispered.

"Here I was," he said, pressing a kiss to my jaw, "thinking I was just congratulating my girlfriend."

Seth pushed away from me in a fluid motion, and I let the oxygen flood my brain as an ache throbbed between my legs.

"Wait," I said, catching his tie between my fingers and tugging him back.

He cocked his head and settled his icy blue eyes on me. "If you're about to proposition me, that will put three of us on the course."

I slapped his chest. "I don't harass you," I told him haughtily.

"Darling, you started this by trying to pinch my ass."

I bit my lip, realising he was right. "And I'd do it again."

The corners of his mouth tipped upwards.

"But what did you just call me?" I asked, letting go of his tie.

"Darling?"

"I know you're not stupid, so don't start acting like it now."

"What do you think I said?"

Slipping past him, I went to my desk and sat in the chair. I didn't want to repeat it if he wouldn't. What if he suddenly changed his mind? What if it was a slip of the tongue? An accident?

Seth's fingers came under my chin, tipping my head up to see him perched on the edge of the desk.

"I called you my girlfriend," he confirmed confidently. "I'm not planning on seeing anyone else. And I hope you aren't either."

"That would make you my boyfriend," I stuttered.

His hand moved from my chin, fingers brushing along my jaw, until he tucked a lock of hair behind my ear. There were times I thought Seth was incapable of actions that held such gentleness, but beneath the brash exterior he kept for the world, was a man who knew how to be soft.

"If that's what you want," Seth said. "Nothing has to change, Kiran. I'm not asking you to tell people."

"But I'd be your girlfriend?" I asked. "What's the catch?"

"Why are you so suspicious?" He laughed.

"You're a businessman. There's got to be something in it for you."

"There is," he said, shrugging.

"I knew it."

"If you agree, you belong to me and only me."

An undignified squeak left my lips. That was not the answer I was expecting.

Seth rested his palm against the side of my face and I leant into his touch. "What do you say, Kiran?"

Chapter Thirty Three

- Kiran

The more time Seth spent with the boys, the more I realised I was taking second place in their life. The three of them had formed a weird bond that occasionally squeezed me out, and that included getting ready for the gala dinner. Maaz and Shah had been whisked away to Seth's place rather than stay with me, and I didn't have the heart to say no.

"You look beautiful," Mike said, kissing my cheek as he met me in front of the venue.

I held my clutch in front of my stomach. The dress was beautiful on the hanger — black and slinky, but the moment I slid it on, I was full of doubt. There was no room to hide, and aside from being painted on like a second skin, the slit up the side ran all the way to my thigh, and I kept tugging it closed.

"Thank you," I said, brushing lint from his left shoulder.

"Where are Maaz and Shah?" Mike said, looking around me. "I thought you were bringing them for the dinner."

I pulled a face and walked into the building with him. "I was. I am. But they wanted to get ready with Seth rather than hear me ask them if my ass looked too big in this dress."

"With Seth, huh?" Mike said. "They know about you two?"

"Not yet. But… I think they will soon."

"Really?"

"They like him. I like him." The blush crept to my cheeks. "It makes sense for the boys to meet my boyfriend."

If I thought I could get away with an off-the-cuff comment and continue with the night, I was mistaken. Mike grabbed my wrist and pulled me towards the wall, just outside the room where dinner was being held.

"Boyfriend?" he asked, grinning.

"Do not make a big deal out of this," I said, poking him in the stomach with my clutch.

"You're comfortable with everything?"

Slowly, I nodded my head. "Yes. I think so. I still get these weird moments, but it's hard to ignore what I feel about him, and I don't want to lose him."

Mike leant forward and kissed my forehead. "I'm happy for you."

"Thank you," I whispered, ignoring the sudden swell of emotion. "Let's go in."

I looped my arm through Mike's and walked us into the hall. Round tables covered in starched white tablecloths were dotted throughout the room. Large flowers in intricate vases made up the centrepieces. With my free hand, I waved at a few of my colleagues as Mike led us towards the seating chart.

"Would you look at that?" Mike muttered, snorting.

My eyes found my name alongside Shah and Maaz. Mike's name was also at the table, along with Seth and some of his brothers.

"Was that planned?" Mike asked.

"Not by me," I mumbled.

He led us towards the table in front of the room and a few occupants were already seated. No sign of my sons or my boyfriend.

But Noah rose from his seat when he caught my eye and I unlinked myself from Mike to greet him.

"Hey," Noah greeted me, kissing my cheek. "You look beautiful."

"Thank you. Have you seen Seth?" I asked.

"He's teaching your sons about networking. Let me introduce you to the rest of the family."

Turning around, I was met with a man I didn't recognise, but he shared the same dark hair as Seth and his tan made me feel like he had just walked off a beach.

"This is Warren. Warren, this is Kiran," Noah introduced us.

"Warren," I said, shaking his hand. "Pleasure to meet you."

"The pleasure's all mine," he replied, kissing the back of my hand.

"Seth mentioned that you and I might have some overlapping interests in the business world," I said, trying to shake off the nerves. "Maybe we could schedule a meeting."

Warren sat up straighter and nodded. "I'd be a fool to decline that offer. Would you like my details?"

A familiar voice cut across my response, "I can forward them to her."

When I turned around, Seth was standing behind me, glaring at his brother, but my mouth went dry. Whenever he dressed in black tie, Seth could have auditioned to be the next James Bond. My gaze flicked to his left where Shah stood beside him and my eyes watered, tears threatening to spill over.

"Look at you," I whispered, walking over to him.

"Ma," Shah warned, but it was too late.

I took his face in my hands and looked him up and down. "My handsome boy," I said, kissing his cheek. A few chuckles sounded from the table, and Shah wiped his skin but smiled at me.

"Wait," I said, heart hammering. "Where's Maaz?"

"You don't want to know," Shah muttered.

"Shah, Seth, where is Maaz?" I panicked.

Shah went to join the table, sitting himself between Warren and Mike.

"Aiden has him," Seth answered, eyes trailing along my body. "What are you trying to do to me, flower?" he asked, stepping closer.

"Behave," I warned him softly.

"You make it exceptionally difficult."

"How have I ended up at a table with you and your brothers?" I asked, reaching up to straighten his bow tie. Maaz must have got to him at some point because Seth was never messy.

"Mum handled the arrangements. You'll have to take it up with her," he said, taking my hand and looking at my forearm. "Did you run out of sticky notes?"

The pale skin of my inner arm was marked with pen, ink bleeding and smudging the words into something illegible.

"I was in a rush," I said, pulling my arm away.

Seth pulled out a chair, and I sat down before he took the seat next to me. Beneath the table, his hand found my thigh and my skin prickled with goosebumps. I placed a hand over his, squeezing it tight.

"Ma!"

I turned in my seat to see Maaz in Aiden's arms. They both wore wide grins, and as they came closer, I caught sight of the lipstick stains on both of their cheeks.

"Oh my God," I said, shooting up from my chair. "Aiden Sinclair! What have you done?" I marched over, and Aiden continued to grin at me, dimples on display.

"Maaz is the best little wing man, Kiran. Can I keep him?" Aiden asked.

"Absolutely not!" I said, reaching out to wipe Maaz's cheek that was shades of pink and red.

"Please," they both said, drawing out the *e*.

"You have to promise to behave," I said, not sure which one I was directing the sentence to.

"Good luck, Kiran. We've been trying to train him for thirty years," Warren said from the table.

Aiden breezed past me, depositing Maaz into an empty seat at the table and dropping into the space beside him.

"I think you have more competition than just me for their attention," Seth commented as I sat down.

Shah was in conversation with Mike and Warren, and Maaz was being entertained by Aiden. Neither of them looked uncomfortable, like I thought they might, and my heart fluttered wildly in my chest.

Our family had always been small. There were no extended members or large holiday gatherings. Over the years, the family tree had been pruned down until only the three of us remained. I thought that was all we needed. It wasn't ideal, but we made the best of what we had. But watching them both now, I realised just how much they missed out on without a wider family to turn to.

"What is it about the Sinclairs?" I mumbled in return.

"I told you, darling. We're God's gift."

Chapter Thirty Four

- Seth

"Tired, baby?" Kiran asked Maaz.

He yawned in response and finished his last bite of dessert. Miraculously, his white shirt lacked a single stain.

"Maybe we should go home," she continued.

Her fingers brushed through his curls and I watched her intently the way I had all night. I longed to mimic the action, combing my fingers through her hair. Keeping our relationship secret seemed like an easy decision until my feelings had spiralled. Open affection — possession — was what I craved. Especially when she was dressed like a temptress. I wanted people to know she belonged to me.

"You're planning to leave?" Aiden asked. "What about our night of debauchery?"

"I can't exactly sit Maaz on the bar," Kiran said, looking up at my brother.

"I can take him home," Shah said from across the table.

"No, sweetheart. It's okay," she argued.

"Ma, enjoy yourself. Live a little."

I squeezed her thigh under the table and Kiran chewed on her bottom lip, unknowingly making this evening more difficult.

"Are you sure?" she asked him. Shah nodded, and Kiran let out a deep breath. "Okay, then."

Twenty minutes later, Shah and Maaz slipped into a cab and Kiran waved them off from the venue.

She turned back around to face me and my heart stuttered. Black wasn't a colour she wore and for good reason. Kiran, in black, was a man's kryptonite. The flashes of skin at her cleavage and thigh were enough to drive my mind into the gutter.

"We should get back inside," she said, pressing a hand on my chest. "Aiden mentioned a night of debauchery."

"You must be dreaming if you think I'm letting him take you out where other people can see you like this," I told her.

She cocked her head. "You'll be there."

"Where I'm not allowed to break the hands of any guy who wants to hit on you."

Kiran looked at me curiously. I made it clear to her when I called her my girlfriend that we could keep this quiet, but she would belong to me. I didn't share, and I didn't play nice when it came to what was mine.

"So what are we planning to do for the rest of the evening?" she asked quietly.

"You tell me."

Whatever she wanted, I would make it happen. The heels were probably killing her feet and if she wanted to head to a bar, I would make sure there were private booths where no more eyes could land on her.

"We could always leave," she suggested in a whisper. "For a more private party."

My eyes snapped to her face. "Kiran," I warned.

"If it's not something you want —"

"Do you need to get anything from inside?"

She shook her head, looking highly amused. I beckoned her to follow me to the back of the hotel where cars were parked. She slipped into mine without a word and I pulled out of the venue hastily.

The ride back home was quiet, thick with anticipation and want. I helped Kiran out of the car, keeping her hand in mine as I led us into the house. The moment the door closed, I pulled her body into mine, arms sliding around her waist and kissing her deeply.

There was a thud as her clutch fell to the floor and her arms wrapped around my neck, fingers playing with the hair at the nape. Kiran pulled away, a smile on her lips as she gazed up at me. My knuckles ran down the side of her face and she let out a shaky breath.

"Are you sure you want this?" I asked, the tip of my nose meeting hers.

Kiran nodded slowly. "Yes."

Grabbing her hand and lacing our fingers together, I led her upstairs and into my bedroom. The level of self-restraint I was exercising was superhuman. I wanted to rip the dress from her and mark every inch of skin. To finally feel her wrapped around me. But Kiran had displayed the largest form of trust by leading us here tonight.

Kiran's hand came up to my face, pulling me down for a kiss. Our tongues danced together, and the heat coursed through me. I pressed her body against mine so she could feel my erection against her stomach, and she let out a sweet moan.

My clothes disappeared piece by piece until I was left in my trousers. Kiran's gaze ran down my body, fingers following in feather-light touches that made me clench my teeth together.

"It should be a sin to be this perfect," she said, bringing her eyes back up to my face.

"Speak for yourself," I replied huskily. "This is a little unfair, Kiran." I gestured to my semi-naked body. "Turn around."

I could see the doubt clouding her features. "I'm not perfect."

"Turn around and let me prove you wrong."

251

She held my gaze for a moment before slowly turning so that she faced away from me. I pinched the zip of her dress between my thumb and index finger, dragging it down her spine. Pushing the straps from her shoulders, the material fell away from her body, pooling on my bedroom floor. Kiran stepped out of it and turned back to face me, arms wrapped around her middle.

"Don't hide from me," I said, pulling her arms away and taking her in. "Never hide from me."

She opened her mouth to argue, but I silenced her with a kiss, walking her back towards the bed. Kiran dropped onto the mattress, and I followed, trailing kisses down the column of her throat. My hand reached under her back to unclip the strapless bra, removing it from her and tossing it aside.

"There's never a moment I don't want to see this body," I muttered, dragging my tongue across her collarbone.

Kiran's breath hitched. "You'll be asking me to turn up to the office naked," she teased.

My fingers dug into the flesh of her hips. "Don't even think about it."

"Don't introduce casual Fridays."

She stopped the smart remarks when I swirled a tongue around her left nipple, sucking it into my mouth. Her back arched from the bed and she groaned.

"You don't fight fair," she muttered, running her fingers through my hair and tugging at it.

"Who cares about fair when you can win?" I asked, smirking against her skin.

My impatience steadily grew, and I pulled the black lace away from her hips and down her legs before stepping back to look at her.

"Fuck," I uttered, dick painfully hard at the sight of Kiran completely naked on the bed.

How many nights had I dreamed of her like this, soothing blue balls with my hand and my imagination? The image in my head didn't compare to the reality.

Kiran propped herself up on her elbows. "Are you just going to stare?" she asked.

"You can't blame a man for appreciating art."

Her cheeks flushed red as she shifted on the bed, moving onto her knees. Kiran's fingers undid the button and zipper on my trousers before pushing them off my hips. She brushed the tips of her fingers against the fabric of my boxers that covered my dick, and I hissed. Her gaze flicked up to my face and then she pushed my underwear down, finally freeing me.

Kiran sat on her knees, back straight and face flushed as she focused on my dick.

"Are you just going to stare?" I repeated her words darkly.

They jolted her from her thoughts, and she bit her bottom lip before leaning forward. Taking my cock in her hand, her tongue came out to lick the pre-cum away from the head and my eyes rolled back at the contact. My hands went to the back of her head, tangling in her long hair, and Kiran took the encouragement, dragging her tongue down my length before taking me into her mouth.

A guttural groan left my lips as she worked her magic. Kiran kept her eyes up and on me, and I couldn't help but stare back. She was such a pretty sight on her knees as I fucked her mouth. I kept a glimmer of control, but it was waning and I pulled her away from my dick, desperate for something more.

"Lie back," I told her, pressing a searing kiss on her lips.

Kiran listened, moving up the bed as I pulled a condom from the drawer and covered myself.

"Prepared?" she asked, watching me with a lustful gaze.

I climbed onto the bed, kissing her deeply. "I was always going to get you," I muttered against her lips.

She laughed softly, but I felt the way she trembled under my touch. Resting my forehead against her, I stared down into her dark eyes.

"But we can wait," I told her. "If you're not ready, we can wait."

This wasn't about my blue balls or how much I wanted her. Kiran hadn't trusted anyone in her life since her husband died. She

253

wanted to take things slowly. And although things had naturally progressed here, she had every right to deny me and change her mind.

Beneath me, she shook her head, hand moving down between us until it closed around my cock, stroking me.

"I don't want to wait," she said. "I want this. With you."

This woman was going to make me lose my mind. I pulled her hand away from me and nudged her legs wider. My thumb rubbed along her clit, sticky and wet with want. Kiran's eyes fluttered shut as I pushed a finger into her.

"Seth," she moaned. My name never sounded as sweet as when she called it like this.

"Ready for me?"

She opened her eyes and nodded eagerly.

Lining myself up to Kiran, I thrust myself into her gently, groaning in pleasure as I felt her walls around me. Kisses became heated and messy as we adjusted to each other. Skin was bruised under the pressure of fingers and teeth.

Kiran shifted us expertly until I laid on my back and she straddled my waist, sinking back down on my cock. I watched, mesmerised as she tipped her head back, hair cascading down her back, and rode me. My hands landed on her hips, thumb stretching down to play with her clit, and continued to encourage her.

"That's it, baby. Take what you need from me," I groaned, thrusting my hips up into her.

She whimpered and moaned, body stretching and arching in pleasure. I would forever be confused at how Kiran couldn't see herself as perfect.

"Seth," she moaned. "I can't..."

She tightened around me, and I moved us again, pushing her back against the mattress. Hooking one of her legs over my shoulder, I picked up the pace. The sound of skin against skin filled the room.

"Can you wait for me, darling?" I asked, kissing along her chest.

"I don't... I can't," Kiran panted.

Her walls tightened around me, and I smiled, biting at her nipple and forcing her to scream out. Manicured nails dug into my ribs and ripped up my skin as Kiran's body tensed, hitting her high. I continued to fuck her through her orgasm, finding my own, and pressing my face into the crook of her neck as I came.

Kiran's body relaxed, and I slid out of her, taking the space beside her on the bed and pulling her against my body. She nestled herself against my chest, humming contently. The sound made me laugh under my breath.

"Happy there, flower?" I asked, kissing her head.

She tipped her chin up, looking at me. "Happier than I've been in a long time."

Chapter Thirty Five

- Kiran

The door of Seth's office was closed, and I sat in his lap, pouting while he laughed. I just finished a phone call with Shah, who told me he would be staying with a friend tonight and that he had a date for prom. My flurry of questions had been met with single responses until he put the phone down.

"I can't believe he told you before me," I said.

"Flower, look at your reaction. That was what he was trying to avoid."

"I'm allowed to be excited that my son has a date for prom."

"There's a fine line between excited and psychotic where you are concerned, Kiran. You have your own brand of madness that not everyone follows."

I smacked him hard in the chest, hurting myself more than my boyfriend. Seth chuckled and pulled me in for a kiss.

Since our night together, crossing over the final physical barrier, things had yet to cool down. In every spare moment, his hands were on me, and I was just as bad. Sex was something I enjoyed immensely and after starving myself of intimacy for years, it was as if the floodgates had opened and Seth was only too happy to participate.

The guilt hadn't completely subsided. In silent moments during the early mornings, I ran my hands over Jamal's jumpers that were stored away on top of the wardrobe. After the first time with Seth, I came home and buried my face in one, his scent so faint I might have imagined it, and cried. I wanted to apologise to him for allowing someone else into my heart.

For moving on.

But the happiness that blossomed with Seth was impossible to ignore. The hope sprang up through the cracks in my heart, and I craved his presence in my life. Whether he was grumpy with stress or playful like this afternoon, I wanted every piece of him he was willing to give me.

Pulling back, I looked at his face. Something had changed in Seth from the first time I met him. He frowned a little less, and I heard his laughter more often. Small things, but it made me confident that I wasn't messing this up.

"What is going on in that mind?" he asked, tapping a finger against my temple.

"Seth," I said. "Can I ask you something?"

"Anything."

"What if... what if I wanted to tell people about us?"

Seth sat up straight and took a deep breath through his nose. "What's brought this on?"

"I've been thinking about it more. About telling the boys about you. Us."

It was impossible to keep the smile from my face, and neither of us was planning to run from what we had. The gala dinner had placed my boys in the middle of his family, and it was a stark reminder of what we could have if I was just brave enough to admit that I wanted them. And I wanted them with Seth.

"When?" he asked, eyes lighting up.

258

"After Shah's done with his exams. Three more weeks."

"Three more weeks of being your dirty little secret."

"Nothing about you is little," I said, shifting my ass and feeling him harden beneath me. Seth held my hips to stop me from moving, and I kissed his lips.

"You're a pain in the ass, Kiran," he gritted out. "How do you want to tell them?"

"You could come around for dinner," I suggested. "We can tell them together. I'm not sure what they're going to say."

"Whatever happens, I'll be there," Seth assured me. "And then you can come and meet my family properly."

I rested against him, lips finding his cheek, jaw, neck. "Tin Man."

"Hmm?" Seth hummed, eyes closed as I nipped on his earlobe.

"How many of your brothers know about us?"

He tensed underneath me and opened his eyes. "Noah."

"Mhm. And is it just Noah?" I asked, gripping his ear between my teeth and tugging gently.

He groaned, "No."

"Who else?"

"Aiden. Warren. Dad. I think Ethan and Mum figured it out."

I let go of his ear and sat up. "Your entire family knows?"

"That's not all of them, so no. Not the entire family."

"Seth," I groaned, dropping my head to his shoulder.

He wrapped his arms around me, hugging my body to his. "They haven't said a word. But they're excited to meet you properly." He nudged my face out and said, "You don't need to be nervous."

"What if they don't like me?"

It was a genuine fear, looking back at my track record. I didn't need to be liked, but it made life easier to know that your boyfriend's family wasn't unhappy with your relationship.

"Darling, I think two of my brothers are in love with you. Dad hired you. Mum won't stop talking about you."

I pressed my lips against his just to stop him from talking.

Maybe things would be different this time. Two families stitched together with love instead of crushing disapproval and isolation.

"Seth," I muttered against his lips, laughing. His hand moved under my skirt, bunching it around my thighs. "You have a meeting in ten minutes. Calm down."

"We could manage it in ten minutes," he replied earnestly.

"You'll be a mess."

"I don't care."

"You don't need rumours of an office fling," I said, running my hands through his hair. "It's not good for business."

"I'll tell them it's not a fling. My girlfriend is insatiable."

"I am not being blamed for this."

I held my breath as his fingers pushed the thong aside and dipped into me.

"And you said I needed to calm down. What's got you so wet, darling?" he asked, smirking at me.

"Don't," I squeaked as he flicked my clit and pinched it.

"Why not?"

"Because I have to do work this afternoon."

"Next time, you'll think twice before being a tease," he said, still playing with me and forcing a whimper from my lips.

"Later," I whispered.

He moved his hand from between my legs, both giving me relief and frustrating me. Seth's fingers hooked into the band of my underwear and tugged.

"What are you doing?" I said.

"Collateral."

"You can't be serious."

"I want these, and once you fulfil your promise, I'll give them back."

"I'm not giving you my underwear."

"You either give them, or I can take them," he said, shrugging as his grip tightened on the string like waistband.

"You rip these and you're being celibate until further notice."

"We both know that's a lie. So hand them over."

With a huff, I slapped his hands away and awkwardly wiggled out of my underwear. Seth held out an expectant hand, completely unfazed, and I deposited them into his palm.

"Good girl," he said, placing them into the inner pocket of his jacket. Seth stood, picking me up from his lap as he went. "Make sure you work hard this afternoon," he said, slapping my ass with a definite crack.

I yelped and pushed him away from me, but Seth caught my wrists and pulled me in for a kiss. Despite myself, I melted into it, letting him thread his fingers through my hair and tug tightly.

"You're going to be late," I panted, breaking the kiss.

"Fucking work," he muttered, letting me go and helping me straighten my skirt. He opened the door to his office and looked back at me. "Ladies first."

Taking in a deep breath and praying I looked the perfect professional, I walked out of Seth's office and across the corridor into mine.

It was going to be a long afternoon.

Chapter Thirty Six

- Seth

When you owned a business, nine to five was just a pretty phrase that was placed in a contract to keep HR happy. The truth was that if there was something that needed your attention, you answered the call. And so when the afternoon meeting continued to stretch on past five o'clock, I texted Kiran to go home because waiting around would be pointless.

Looks like I'll have to have all the fun by myself. I'll think of you.

That woman was more trouble than she looked. I was learning quickly that Kiran liked the physical aspect of the relationship just as much as spending time together watching documentaries. She could be filthy, but hated being told what to do. Hence her attitude while she handed her underwear to me earlier.

Things between us had continued running smoothly. She had taken me by surprise this afternoon when she said she wanted to tell the boys. Shah knew I planned to get to know his mother better, but

I hadn't exactly updated him on the progress. And Maaz remained clueless. If Kiran was willing to tell them, to officially let them know we were dating, then she had to see some longevity in the relationship.

The minute the meeting ended, I shot from the room, storming back to my office to grab my things. At the centre of my desk was a bright sticky note with Kiran's cursive across it.

You broke the contract, so that means celibacy for you x

Not a fucking chance.

I didn't make a habit of stopping at Kiran's home without warning. It was her domain, and it was a place for her family. Until things were out in the open, I would keep my distance. But not tonight. Kiran was alone and threatening to keep me celibate. If she wanted me to make good on our verbal contract, then I would do that.

When I pulled up outside the house, I jumped out of the car and walked up to the door. The sound of music was loud and drifted through the house. Kiran didn't do silence, and it came as no surprise that she had drowned it out with music until she went to bed. Her laughter sliced through the notes, and I knocked on the door. After a few moments of nothing, I balled my fist and pounded harder.

The music was cut short, and the door pulled open, but instead of Kiran, Mike stood in the doorway. He had a wineglass in his hand, hair dishevelled, and shirt untucked from his trousers. The sight of him made my stomach coil, and the contents climbed up my throat, burning my oesophagus.

"What the fuck?" I hissed, pushing past him into the house.

"Seth," he muttered, stumbling backwards.

"Kiran!"

Walking into the living room, I clapped eyes on her curled at one end of the sofa under a giant fluffy blanket. The coffee table was cluttered with junk food and the TV paused during a film.

"Seth?" Kiran asked when she saw me.

"This looks cosy," I said through gritted teeth.

She got up from the sofa, blanket falling to the floor to reveal she was in a set of pyjamas.

"It was a shit day at work," Mike said, coming into the room.

"Were you after some stress relief?" I spat.

"Seth!" Kiran said, eyes wide.

"Kiran invited me over," Mike told me, putting his glass down on the table.

"You told me you were alone," I said, looking at Kiran. "Because I couldn't make it, you found a replacement for me?"

"What the fuck is your problem?" Mike asked, forcing me to turn my attention to him.

"You!" I yelled. "You being here with *my* girlfriend. Always sniffing around her."

"Do you hear —"

"Mike, leave it," Kiran said, walking towards him. "I think it's best if you go."

"Are you going to be alright with him?" Mike asked.

The anger pulsed through me even stronger. "She's fine with me!"

"I'm fine," Kiran agreed. "I'll text you tomorrow."

He moved forward to kiss her cheek, and I grabbed her arm, pulling her back. "Try it."

"Just go." Kiran sighed.

Mike grabbed his phone from the table and left, throwing a glance over his shoulder as he went.

Kiran ripped her arm out of my hand when the front door closed and turned on me.

"What the fuck was that?" she asked, looking as angry as I felt.

"You tell me!"

She stood in front of me and sighed as she spoke. "Mike is a friend. He had a rough day at work. I caught him in the lift and told him to come over and watch musicals because you were busy so we didn't have plans."

"You're in pyjamas."

"I like being comfortable."

"He looked a mess."

"Mike's always a mess!"

"He's here late. You looked cosy," I said, gesturing around us.

Kiran rubbed her temples. "I'm not doing this. You know where the door is and you can see yourself out."

She pushed past me, turning off the TV and walking up the stairs. There was no way I was leaving her. Without a second thought, I followed her. Kiran went to slam the door to her room, but I caught it and walked in.

The space was painted peach and covered in a million sticky notes.

"Seth," she said, turning on her heel and spitting my name out through gritted teeth.

"I'm not leaving."

"Why are you here?"

"I came over to spend time with you."

"And then you pick a fight over nothing."

"It's not nothing!" I closed the gap between us, taking her face in my hands and walking her back until she hit the dresser. "Do you know how that looks to me? What would you have done if the roles were reversed?"

The fight flooded out of her instantly. I dropped my head against hers and took in a deep breath.

"I've been here before. Not picking up on signs and then being made a fool of," I told her.

Kiran's hands covered mine. "Seth, I swear to you nothing is happening between me and Mike. I'm sorry. I didn't think. I've known him since I was eighteen. This is just how we are, but I didn't think."

My thumbs ran along her cheekbones, trembling from the sudden burst of anger and unable to get rid of it entirely.

"You need to trust me," she whispered.

"I need to know you're mine."

"I am. Come here."

Kiran pulled my hands away from her face. Stripping me of my suit, my gaze remained on her as my mind pulsed with a million thoughts. I couldn't think of what would happen if Kiran ever betrayed me. We were inexplicably tangled together, and I had no desire to pull us apart.

She pulled me into bed, settling down beside me and running her hands through my hair. Her anger never lasted. Kiran was the logical one who could work beyond her red mist.

"Breathe," she said softly. Her face was so close I could feel the flutter of her eyelashes against my cheek. "I would never cheat on you."

"Never say never," I said bitterly.

She kissed me before biting hard on my bottom lip, and I hissed. "Kiran!"

But she had taken advantage of my shock, straddling my hips and pinning my arms above my head. Amusement swept away some of the anger.

"You listen to me, Seth Sinclair. You are enough. I would be insane to go looking for something else. But you have to trust me. Talk to me. You can't pick fights."

I took my hands away from her with ease and rubbed them along her thighs. "I am enough."

"Possibly too much at times, but I wouldn't want you any other way."

"Tell me when he comes over."

"You're not banning me from being friends with him?" she asked sarcastically.

"I'd lock you in a tower and throw away the key if I had it my way," I shot back. "But you'd find a way to break out. You're trouble."

Kiran leant down and kissed me, and my hands slid around her ass, pulling her close and deepening the embrace.

"I just want to know that you're mine," I said. "That you belong to me."

My possessive nature over Kiran had existed from the moment we met. Even when I believed she was someone else's, I kept her for myself at work. My slice of sunshine. My rainbow that cut through the gloom and monotony of my life.

"I'm yours for as long as you'll have me," she whispered.

For life, I wanted to tell her, but bit my tongue.

"I won't last long if you keep me celibate," I replied, flipping her over and pulling her t-shirt over her head.

"It's an empty threat. I enjoy sex too much," she admitted.

"I know you do."

I needed her. My hand went to her breast, rolling her nipple as I dipped down to lick the other. Kiran melted against my touch and let out a breathy moan.

"You can't get enough, can you?" I asked, kissing down her stomach.

"I don't hear you complaining."

I wasted no time in pulling her trousers and underwear off her body, leaving her naked on the bed.

"What would I complain about?" I asked, running my nose along her thigh. "That I have a filthy girl who can't control herself?" Sitting up, I instructed her, "Face down, ass up."

Kiran blinked at me a few times before shaking her head. That little glimmer of defiance was what she used daily in her work, but I didn't appreciate it here. Grabbing her hips, I forced her to turn over and she yelped in surprise.

"On your knees," I told her.

This time she listened, pushing herself up on her knees and pressing her face into the mattress. My index finger dragged down her centre, and Kiran groaned. She was already wet from anticipation.

"All I will ever need from you," I said, kneeling behind her and letting my tongue taste her. Sweet and sticky. Kiran had become my favourite meal. "Is honesty."

"I'm honest," she moaned.

My tongue darted in and out of her pussy while my fingers gently pinched her clit.

"Is to know you belong to me."

She nodded against the mattress, arching her back and pushing her ass back towards my face. I straightened up again, stripping myself of my boxers and looking down at her.

"I want to own you, Kiran. Mind, body and soul. I want them all," I told her.

"Selfish prick." She laughed.

My bare dick ghosted along her pussy and she pushed her hips back again, making me laugh.

"I might be a selfish prick, but you're the one who can't stay away," I reminded her.

"Fuck me or go home and I'll finish the job myse —" Her sentence was cut off with a yelp as I brought my palm down against her ass.

"You're always so polite until you don't get what you want," I said, rubbing the warm spot on her skin. "Ask nicely."

She pushed her face into the mattress and turned it to the side again. "Please, Seth."

"Please what, flower?"

"Show me how you want to own me," she whispered.

Words shouldn't have been enough to push me closer to the edge, but Kiran knew how to appeal to me in every way. Her body and her mind fell into step with mine. It was difficult to imagine a time where she wasn't a part of my life. Or maybe I no longer wanted to remember a time before she brought her personal brand of magic into the office and bewitched me.

I finally pushed myself into her, earning a satisfactory groan from both of us. Gentle wasn't something I could manage. My fist wrapped around her long raven hair and pulled while my other hand gripped her hip. Each thrust sent Kiran further into the bed as I sank in as deep as I could. Her hand snaked between her legs to play with herself and I smiled at the sight.

"Fuck! Seth!" She pushed her hips back towards me eagerly.

"That's it, darling. Keep saying my name."

When her knees gave out, I wasted no time pinning her body with my own and entering her again.

Kissing the side of her face, I spoke into her ear, "You can give everyone else the smiles. You can share that little spark you have."

She writhed beneath me, moaning my name as we moved as one.

"But this, the filthy girl you are underneath, that's all mine."

She nodded and turned her head to kiss me, biting at my bottom lip and tugging it. Reaching around her body, my hands cupped her breasts, pinching and rolling her nipples.

I needed this. The doubt that clouded my mind when Mike opened the door was remedied by the feel of her body underneath me. This woman was mine and no one would take her away. Nothing would come between us because I wouldn't let it.

Her body trembled under mine, tensing as she rose towards her climax.

"Wait," I told her sharply, and she whimpered.

"I can't."

"Wait, Kiran."

She squeezed her eyes shut and tried to slow down, but I wouldn't let her.

"Please, Seth," she pleaded.

But the tension coiled in my body with a few hard, deep thrusts, and I nipped at her ear. "Let go, baby."

Her pussy clenched around my dick, walls spasming as she finally gave into her orgasm, and I came deep inside her.

We laid like that in the silence for a few moments, both of us breathing heavily as we struggled to regain some composure. Peeling myself away from her body, evidence of our tryst running down her thighs, I carefully scooped her from the bed. A lazy grin spread across her face as she looked up at me with hooded eyes.

"So fucking beautiful," I said, kissing her gently before settling us back on the bed.

Kiran curled her body against mine, legs tangled together as she drew patterns across my chest. As I kissed the top of her head, the urge to make an admission bubbled up my chest and sat on the tip of my tongue, but I couldn't do it.

Not yet.

Chapter Thirty Seven

- Kiran

There was an unusual warmth wrapped around me, and I forced my eyes open, fighting with fatigue. I wriggled in my spot before hearing a chuckle. Opening my eyes properly, I was greeted with Seth, propped up on his arm and watching me.

"How long have you been awake?" I mumbled, stuffing my face into the pillow.

Seth brushed a hand through my hair. "Not long," he answered.

"You should have woken me up."

"You looked too peaceful."

Peaceful. That was the word to describe it. It had been so long since I'd fallen asleep beside someone and woken up in their arms.

Even wrapped up in his anger last night, Seth made me feel like I was his only priority. Being cared for and doted on again had filled me with a sensation I couldn't describe. It was as if liquid sunshine had been injected into my veins. I was warmed from my toes to my head and it made me weightless.

"I have a question for you," Seth said, and I unburied my face.

"What is it?" I squinted at him.

Seth turned away and pulled something from the bedside table. When he faced me again, there was a bright yellow sticky note between his fingers.

"Reasons Seth Sinclair cannot be interested in me," he said, reading the note.

I sat up so quickly the room spun. Seth pulled the note away from me when I made a grab for it.

"That's mine," I told him.

"Why does this note even exist?"

"Why were you pinching notes from my wall?"

"I needed to piss, and it fell."

"You've been tiptoeing through my home," I commented, but I wasn't mad at him.

"It's very colourful." He kissed my head. "Want to tell me about this note?"

Groaning, I rolled over onto my back and covered my face with my hands. "I wrote it a while ago. I forgot to take it down."

"So you don't believe any of this now?"

I didn't respond.

"Kiran, these are ridiculous reasons. Single mum, scars, stretch marks. *Damage*." He sounded offended by the last item on the list. "You aren't damaged."

"I am, but I've sort of stuck my pieces back together. It's not perfect, but I'm whole," I explained, turning onto my side so we could have the conversation properly. "But also because I worried I would damage you."

Seth slipped down the bed and pressed his nose against mine. "You're not going to damage me."

"You don't know that."

"I do," he said confidently. "You are the best thing that's happened to me, Kiran."

A small crease appeared in his brow but the eye contact remained steady, pinning me to the spot even though I felt like I should run.

"I'm not sure I truly realised how much my life was slipping into grey scale before I met you. I was tired of everything. Angry at the universe for what it put me through. And then you were delivered to me in a blindingly brilliant package, and I knew I wouldn't be able to give you up."

"Even when you thought I was married?" I choked out.

"Even then. I knew I needed you in my life, if only as a friend, because you made living so much easier. You taught me to soften again, if only for you," he said, brushing his knuckles against my cheek.

You made living so much easier.

Did he know just how much it meant to hear those words? That after years of carrying the heavy burden of guilt, I would cling to that sentence to help pull me out of the current when it became too much.

"Where are the sticky notes?" he asked.

I pointed to the vanity opposite the bed and replied, "Top drawer."

Kissing me softly, he threw off the blanket and walked over to it. Seth had regained his modesty, covered in a pair of boxers, and I watched as he stopped by the mirror. He reached out and plucked the photograph that was wedged in the top left corner between the glass and the wood.

"Seth," I said, sitting up quickly and holding the duvet to my chest.

The photograph he held was the last one we had taken with Jamal. Shah pulled a face at the camera — the last time I would see him as a carefree child. I stood next to my son with the same ridiculous expression, and Jamal was behind me, arms reaching around to cradle my bump.

"It's the only family photo with the four of us," I explained.

I gripped the duvet tightly, waiting for the wave of fury Seth would unleash. His jealousy had boiled over so easily when he caught Mike at the house last night that I expected him to shove the photo away. Instead, he carefully placed it back in its spot.

"It's a beautiful photo," Seth said, looking back at me with a small smile. "You should think about framing it. It'll get damaged if you keep it like that."

He turned back to the vanity and pulled open the drawer, and I let out a breath. I had worried that introducing Seth into my life meant pushing Jamal out permanently. But there was a balance, and Seth was helping me to find it in his own way.

When he returned to the bed with a pad of sticky notes and pen in hand, I hugged him.

"Not that I don't like my gorgeous woman all over me first thing in the morning, but what's this for?" he asked.

"For you to know that you are appreciated and valued, and that you will always, *always* be more than enough for me."

"Would this be a good time to tell you I told Maaz you wouldn't put him in a suit for a year?"

I released him from the bear hug. "I guess I could make good on that."

"And he wants a dog."

A laugh escaped my lips. "No way. Maaz is destructive enough on his own. He's part boy, part hurricane. I'm not about to give him a dog and see how well that goes down."

"He'll learn some responsibility with a pet," Seth argued.

"He's five and I'll end up with an extra responsibility."

"Shah would surely help."

"Not if he ends up with a girlfriend."

"I'll be able to help soon."

"You have time for a dog?" I asked, arching an eyebrow.

"Maybe."

"Sweetheart, I love that you want to make Maaz happy, but a dog is a big responsibility."

"Just think about it."

I sighed as my heart fluttered in my chest. "I'll think about it."

"I'll prepare a presentation for next week." He grinned, and I think my heart stopped in its tracks.

Seth leant back against the headboard and scrawled across the sticky note. My old list laid crumpled on the vanity. When he finished, I peered at the note and blushed.

Reasons Seth Sinclair is mad about Kiran:
Beautiful
Kind
Reminds me of sunshine
Puts up with my moody ass

I kissed his shoulder, letting my lips graze his bare skin.

"I have another question," he said, and I looked up at him. "What's with all the serial killer books?" He gestured behind us where the floating shelves held a range of true crime stories.

"I have a morbid fascination," I admitted sheepishly.

"Of course you do," he replied, cupping my face and kissing me. "You're my twisted sunshine."

I grinned at him. "And you're my miserable Tin Man."

"Always."

The sound of a door closing cut our kiss short.

"Shit," I whispered. "Shah must be home."

I pulled myself away from Seth and got out of bed. He let out a low whistle, and I hushed him aggressively, but still blushed.

"You need to go," I mumbled.

"What do you want me to do? Climb out the window and scale down the trellis?" he asked, amused.

"Can you do that?" I returned thoughtfully, and a pillow flew in my direction, nearly knocking me off balance.

"Seth," I hissed, trying not to laugh.

Heavy footsteps came up the stairs as I yanked on a t-shirt and some pyjama trousers. A knock sounded on my bedroom door, and I winced before opening it a crack.

"Are you okay?" Shah asked, looking concerned. "The living room is a mess and I don't think I've ever seen you sleep in past seven. Are you ill?"

"No," I said to him, stepping out of the room and closing the door behind me. "Mike came over last night and I was tired. I'll clean up this morning."

"I'll do it," Shah said. "Are you sure you're okay?"

"Mhm." I nodded.

"Okay," he said, relaxing slightly. "I'm going to grab a shower."

"Have you eaten? I'll make us some breakfast."

"Thanks, Ma."

He trudged off down the corridor with his bag in hand and I slipped back into the room to find Seth dressed.

"All clear?" he asked, shrugging his jacket on.

"Yes. You need to be quick."

He crossed the room and kissed me roughly, so I had to hold onto his lapels for balance.

"Go," I whined.

"A few more weeks and we don't have to hide anymore."

"A few more weeks," I repeated, a smile tugging at my lips. "But right now, you have to go."

Chapter Thirty Eight

- Seth

Aiden laid face down on my sofa for the third night in a row. The only sign he was alive was the gentle rise and fall of his chest. As much as Aiden loved his job, it occasionally took its toll when the bad news kept rolling in and he was left to deliver it.

"I think I'm going to New York," he said eventually, making me look up from the laptop.

His arm hung off the sofa, and he swung it lazily, brushing his fingers through the carpet.

"I thought you said you were happy here," I commented.

"I am, but Dr Rivera keeps emailing, and it's only six months. I feel like I need a change."

Partially closing the lid of my laptop, I leant back in the chair and took him in. "Might be for the best. Change of scenery. Learn some new skills."

"You sound like Dad," Aiden replied, laughing under his breath. "You practising your parenting skills for when Kiran decides you're not a complete liability?"

"She knows I'm not a complete liability. Not that you helped with using Maaz as your little wing man."

"Ladies loved his cute little face. It's a gift," he said, a lazy smile stretching his lips. "When do I get to tell him I'm his Uncle Aiden? Warren seemed to get on with her eldest."

"Give me the chance to get introduced properly before you paint yourself as family."

"And how long are we going to be waiting for that?"

"It's happening next week." I shut the laptop properly and laid it on the coffee table.

Aiden scrambled to sit up properly. "Things are getting serious between the pair of you?"

I shrugged and shifted in my seat, not wanting this conversation with Aiden. Outside of the hospital, he had the emotional capacity the size of a raindrop. Not that I was much better, but Kiran had helped to expand the boundaries.

"It's a dick move to meet her kids if you aren't serious," Aiden said, sitting up.

"For fuck's sake," I muttered. "She's my girlfriend."

"Do you *love* her?" He sounded like we were five years old, but when I didn't answer, the childish facade dropped. "You love her," Aiden stated.

"I haven't told her," I said.

"Why not?"

In case she didn't feel the same way. A small crumb of doubt still tainted my mind. She told me I was enough. That I would always be enough. But she never used the word love.

"Time hasn't been right," I lied.

Aiden blew out a breath. "The one thing I know from working in a hospital is life is short. No guarantee you're going to wake up tomorrow. If you love her, tell her."

"Because you're an expert?"

"Love is for suckers and you're the biggest one I know." He grinned at me, and I rolled my eyes. "But I'll support it because she wants me to fulfil my dreams and I'm ready to be an uncle."

I opened my mouth to reply, but my phone vibrated against the glass of the table, rattling noisily. Scooping it up, my brow furrowed to see Shah's name on the screen. It was almost midnight.

"Shah, is everything alright?" I asked, answering the call.

The last time he called with no warning was when Kiran was in hospital. My stomach tightened at the thought something might be wrong with her.

"Mr Sinclair?" a young female voice came down the line, and I sat up straight.

"Hello? Who is this? Where's Shah?"

"Hi. He's with me. I'm Roxy." Her voice shook as she spoke. "He's a little drunk. Very drunk," she corrected herself. "He said to call you. Could you come and take him home?"

"How drunk, Roxy?" I asked, but I was already getting out of the chair and searching for my keys.

"I'm a little scared," she admitted.

"Where are you?"

Roxy gave me the address, and I hung up the phone, walking out of the room, Aiden tailing me.

"Where are you going?" he asked.

"To grab Shah from a party. He's got himself in a state by the sounds of it."

"Want me to come along?"

I almost declined, but Aiden was a doctor, and God forbid something had happened, he could at least advise us on how to deal with it.

The entire drive through the city, my jaw was clenched tight. Shah was a sensible kid, and this seemed out of character for him.

"Are you going to put him up for the night?" Aiden asked.

"No. I'm going to call Kiran when we have him and take him home."

"He had a little fun. Don't ruin it."

283

"It's not my place, Aiden. She'll be worried sick if he doesn't get in by his curfew."

When I pulled up at the address, Shah was sitting on the ground against the outside wall of the house. A girl, who I assumed was Roxy, sat on her knees beside him. I jumped out of the car, feeling my heart hammering painfully in my chest.

"Is he okay?" I asked, coming towards them.

"Mr Sinclair?" Roxy asked, stumbling to her feet. "I think so. He's not making much sense."

"Seth!" Shah slurred from the ground, his head lolling to the side.

"Your mother is going to kill you," I grumbled, looking at the state of him. "And probably me."

"Let's get him to the car," Aiden said from behind me.

"I'm really sorry," Roxy said, wrapping her arms around herself.

"Don't apologise for him, sweetheart," Aiden told her. "He's a big boy. He got himself in that state. Check up on the idiot tomorrow."

"How much did he have to drink?" I asked her.

"I don't know," she said, bottom lip trembling. "A few beers, but there was a bottle of tequila going around."

I ran a hand down my face, trying to push down on the anger that was fighting to rise to the surface. They were teens, trying to blow off some steam after finishing their exams. Shah had obviously prescribed to the *go big or go home* mantra.

We hoisted Shah up from the ground and dragged him towards the car. His feet tripped over themselves and the words were garbled as he attempted to make conversation.

"Get in the back with him and keep an eye on him," I instructed Aiden. Once we got Shah into the car, I turned back to Roxy. "Are you good to get home?"

She nodded at me, and that was the only confirmation I needed before getting into the driver's seat and making my way to Kiran's.

"Is he alright?" I asked, glancing into the rear-view mirror.

"He's had a lot, but I don't think we have too much to worry about, aside from the usual vomiting and a killer hangover tomorrow," he replied.

Scrambling for my phone, I tossed it back to Aid. "Call Kiran and tell her we have him and the state he's in. She doesn't need the shock, and Maaz doesn't need to see him like this."

Maaz should have been in bed by now, but he was another one with his own ideas about the rules of life.

My heart constricted hearing Kiran clear as day on the other side of the line. High-pitched and panicked — Aiden tried to calm her down while monitoring her son. When she finally let him off the call, he pocketed the phone, and we drove in silence.

Kiran was waiting outside the door of her home when we arrived. I barely killed the engine when she flew at the car, opening the back door to see her Shah.

"What the hell happened to him?" she asked, sounding lost. "Shah."

"He's a little drunk," Aiden said.

"A little?" Kiran asked, fire in her voice. I got out of the car, standing behind her. "He's practically paralytic!"

Shah mumbled something from his seat and I grabbed Kiran by the waist, pulling her away, but she resisted.

"Kiran, let me get him out of the car and into the house," I said firmly.

"I can do it," she argued, steely nature coming to the forefront.

"Good luck with that," I replied. "It took me and Aiden to get him into the car. Move."

She did as I said, watching like a hawk and hovering as we extracted him from the car. Kiran walked ahead and opened the door to let us all into the house.

"We can try and get him upstairs," I said.

"No. Can you put him on the sofa?" she asked, shaking her head.

Unaccustomed to the layout of her house, Aiden bashed himself into the table and hissed before we managed to get Shah sitting up on the sofa.

"Ma?" Maaz's voice sounded, his footsteps thundering across the hallway upstairs.

Kiran's eyes grew, and she turned, but I grabbed her.

"I'll sort him. Stay with Shah," I said, slipping past her and walking up the stairs.

Maaz was halfway down them, rubbing his eyes when I met him.

"Seth? What are you doing here?" he asked, yawning.

"I needed to drop something off with your mum. She's looking at it now. What are you doing awake?"

"I heard a thump and woke up. I got scar…" He didn't finish the sentence.

"Scared?"

He nodded his head slowly.

"It was just me being clumsy. Walked into the table." I would kill Aiden later. "How about I tuck you in?"

That seemed to brighten his mood. Maaz turned around and led the way back to his room. The space was a complete mess, but he hopped back into bed, sitting up and watching me.

"Maaz, you need to lie down," I said.

"Okay," he said, sliding down the bed.

I crouched down beside him and pulled the blanket over his body. "Are you comfortable?"

"Mhm."

"Do you need anything else?"

"I don't think so," he yawned.

I ran a hand over his curls and he closed his eyes. "Get some sleep," I said softly. "You don't need to be scared of anything."

"Are you staying?" he muttered.

"I… I'll be downstairs with your mum for a little while."

"Okay," he said. "Night, Seth."

As I went to stand, Maaz stuck his hands out from under the blanket and held them out to me. It took a moment before I realised what he was after. Leaning in, I hugged him tight and kissed his head.

"Night, Maaz."

He cocooned himself back into the blanket and I left the room, walking back downstairs.

"Kiran, he's a teenage boy letting off some steam. Don't look so worried," Aiden said.

"He doesn't behave like this!" she hissed.

Ah, shit. I picked up the pace and entered the living room to see my girlfriend and my brother in a stand-off.

"Flower," I said.

She turned around to look at me.

"Maaz," she started.

"Is back in bed," I told her. Holding out my car keys to Aiden, I said to him, "Take the car and go home."

"You can go as well," Kiran said.

"Darling —"

"Thank you," she said, "for bringing Shah home, but I can deal with it from here."

"I can help."

"No." Kiran's tone was firm. "Please."

She was shutting me out again. The shock was forcing her to put up her walls and protect the unit she worked so hard for. She needed me to step back so she could gain some control again.

"If you need me, call me, and I'll come straight back."

She nodded, and I motioned for Aiden to leave. As I walked out of the room, I heard her words — quiet and resigned.

"You silly boy. What were you thinking?"

Chapter Thirty Nine

- Seth

I didn't hear a word from Kiran until Saturday night. Shah was alive and well. Well might have been an exaggeration. I was sure he had the worst hangover of his life, and Kiran had probably read him the riot act for being an idiot.

She accepted my offer for Sunday morning brunch, which was why my kitchen table was currently laden with crepes and waffles from Sugarworks. It was a little excessive, but Kiran needed to remember that I was in her corner. That she had me to turn to, and I wasn't running at the first sign of trouble. This was a small gesture to accompany three words that would solidify that I wanted everything she came with.

When I opened the door, Kiran stood on my doorstep, drowning in an old university hoodie and her hair twisted up in a bun. Her face was free from makeup, making it easy to identify the puffiness of her eyes.

She crossed the threshold when I stepped aside and walked into my arms. Her body trembled, and I closed the door with a hand before squeezing her close.

"I have a table of sugar waiting for you," I whispered into her hair. "Come into the kitchen."

Kiran refused to let go of me, and I lifted her up. She clung to me like a koala to a tree, arms around my neck and legs around my waist as I carried her through to the kitchen, pressing light kisses to her neck and the side of her head.

The sound of the chair scraping forced her to move her head from the crook of my neck, and I deposited my girlfriend in the seat.

"He's grounded for life," Kiran said, her voice hoarse.

"A harsh sentence but fair."

"He doesn't think so. He's pissed off at me. And you."

I cringed, taking a seat opposite her. Shah wouldn't thank me for taking him back to the house, but it was better for both of us to be honest because Kiran would have put us both in the firing line for trying to cover this up.

"Does the grounding include Massachusetts?" I asked, trying to lighten the mood.

Kiran planned to spend five of the six weeks of summer holidays out in Massachusetts working with the Professor on their new project. Maaz and Shah would shadow her over to the States, and I would be a miserable fuck waiting for them all to come home to me.

"He's coming to Massachusetts, but he's not stepping foot out of the apartment while we're there," she grumbled.

I couldn't see her making good on that threat, and I swallowed the offer of letting Shah stay with me over the summer if she was really that pissed off with him.

"Are you still letting him go to prom?" I asked.

"I'm not going to take that from him, but no afterparties. I was terrified," she whispered. "You hear horror stories about how people choke on their own vomit and die. I stayed up with him all night just to make sure he was okay."

"Darling, he's going to make some bad choices along the way. He's a kid," I said. "You should have seen what we were all like growing up."

"But that's not who he is," Kiran replied, looking up at me. Her eyes were glassy with tears and they hung on her lower lash line. "He's the sensible one."

"He was probably trying to impress Roxy. Do you want me to speak to him?" I offered. "I could pull him aside for a chat after dinner next weekend."

"He called you," Kiran stated. "He called you when he was in trouble."

"He did. I don't mind."

"He should have called me, Seth. I'm his mum."

My brow furrowed as I tried to figure out what she was saying. She didn't sound mad.

"Kiran, flower, I don't mind. I'm not mad at him for calling me."

"I know you aren't. But it shouldn't have happened," she said, looking down at her empty plate. "Seth, I feel like I've missed something. I missed a sign that he wasn't happy. Why else would he drink himself into oblivion like that?"

I leant across the table and shook my head. "He's been under a lot of stress with his exams."

"Exactly! And I'm splitting my time between the business and with you. I should have been there for him. He should have had my undivided attention."

A block of lead settled in the pit of my stomach. "Kiran."

"The next few years are really important for Shahzad, Seth. He needs to keep his head screwed on. I need to be there for him and make sure that he knows that he and Maaz are my priorities."

I saw it in her eyes before she said the words. Kiran had prepared herself before I even knew her intentions. She made her peace with the decision, and she was now ready to share it with me and shatter my world.

"And that means that I shouldn't date anyone." A tear rolled over onto her cheek. "No dinner next weekend. No more brunches or coming over. I just... They're my world, and I won't let anything happen to them."

The selfish and irrational part of me wanted to ask *what about me?* Wasn't I her world as well? Didn't I deserve to be made a priority?

But I knew when we started this that the boys would always win out. I respected that and still pursued her, but I never expected it to come to this.

"I understand," I told her flatly.

"I'm sorry —"

She wanted to be efficient, cutting to the chase rather than prolonging it over brunch. The way she clung to me wasn't because she needed support. It was her way of saying goodbye. The last piece of herself that she would spare me before she packed up her warmth and starved me of it.

"I understand."

What more was there to say? I couldn't convince her to stay with me. Her family came first. That was part of the reason I was attracted to her. She fought tooth and nail for her sons.

She wiped the tear away from her face and sniffed as she nodded. "I think it's best I go home to them."

"You should eat," I said, wanting to keep a hold of the sunshine for as long as I could.

"I don't really have an appetite," she replied, rising from her seat. Her shoulders were rounded, and I knew she took no joy from what she'd just done to us. "I'll see myself out."

Kiran walked out of the room, never once glancing back, and I sat at the kitchen table like a marble statue.

One second, I had everything I ever wanted in the palm of my hand; and the next, it was ripped away from me with no way to fight for it.

The sound of shattering filled the kitchen as the plates fell to the floor, food splattering across the kitchen tiles.

What the fuck was the point in even trying when karma always had the last laugh?

Chapter Forty
- Kiran

"I'll be working, so don't hesitate to email or call me if you have to," I said, pulling sticky notes from the wall of my office.

This was my last-minute attempt to tidy things before I left for the States for a few weeks. Handing over the reins to Mike meant compiling all the loose threads and tangled thoughts into something more coherent for him to follow.

"I know, Kiran," Mike said gently.

I threw the notes into a wastepaper bin and went to sit down in my chair. It wheeled away from me, and I landed on the floor with a thud, knocking my head against the seat as I went down.

"Shit," I hissed.

The tears pooled in my eyes, but it wasn't because of the physical pain. They sat at the surface most days, threatening to spill when I was on my own and stuck with only my thoughts.

Shah barely spoke to me. Maaz was in his own world, sulking about not spending the summer in London. And Seth and I avoided each other with all our might.

His office door remained firmly closed, and I barely saw him around the building. When I did, I slipped out of the room quickly before the torrent of heartbreak could swallow me whole.

Breaking up with him had ripped open the stitching of my heart. All the careful patchwork that had made me whole over the last few months was chaotically undone and left me in pain with every single beat.

But being a mum before all else meant that I couldn't be selfish. What I wanted didn't matter when it came to the cost of my children and their happiness. Although, it would have been easier if both of my sons would be receptive to my efforts instead of making me feel like the bad guy.

Mike was by my side in an instant, but I laid back on the floor of my office and let out a shuddering breath.

"Are you okay?" Mike asked, looking concerned.

"I don't know," I answered honestly.

"Did you hurt yourself?"

"Yes."

"Where?"

I tapped my chest, and Mike's expression softened before he laid down on the floor beside me. Instantly, I was transported back to years ago, laying on the sofa and sobbing while Mike laid on the floor, holding my hand.

"What's happened?" he asked, grabbing my hand and squeezing it.

"We broke up," I explained, and then corrected myself. "I broke up with him."

"But I thought you said you were going to tell the boys."

"Shah got blind drunk and called Seth to bring him home. I've never seen him in such a state, Mike. Not even after Jamal. I can't figure out what's going on with him."

"And that made you break up with Seth?"

"I can't risk anything happening to Shah and Maaz." The tears were hot as they coursed down my face. "I've missed something and I'm kicking myself. He'll barely talk to me at the moment and it's my fault."

"You didn't want to leave him, did you?"

I shake my head and squeeze my eyes shut tight. When I stepped out of Seth's house that morning, I had heard the shattering plates. I pulled his anger to the surface again. He was unhappy and the entire office knew about it if the whispers were anything to go by. But I was the reason behind it all. Everything I touched ended up in ruins, and that included Seth.

Mike squeezed my hand again tightly. "You have survived so much, Kiran. Sometimes I'm not even sure you're human."

That forced a strangled laugh from me.

"I don't know how to make this better for you, but I am always here," Mike told me.

He understood, just as Seth did, that there was no way around this. There was no choice. Just a lingering unfairness that I was accustomed to from life.

"Five weeks in Massachusetts, out in the sunshine, might be the remedy you need." Mike shrugged. "You might forget all about him by the time you come back."

The lump in my throat grew until it was painful to swallow. Seth was not designed to be forgotten. That was the problem. I didn't know how I would ever get over the intensity of his stare or the possessiveness of his touch. He wanted to own me, and I belonged to him after years of promising myself I wouldn't love anyone else. But it was over before it ever really started and I had to force myself to be okay with that fact.

Wiping the tears away from my face, I pushed myself back up and sat on the floor. Mike followed suit, keeping an eye on me.

"I think you have everything you need, but if you find something is missing, let me know," I told him, sinking back into business professional.

He sighed, and I thought he would keep poking at the matter, but Mike let me run and I was grateful.

"Do you need a lift to the airport?" he asked.

"I booked a car."

"You could cancel."

Shaking my head, I got to my feet. "It's okay. Gives me more time to spend with the boys."

He stood, collecting the files from the desk, and opened the door to the office. "I'm going to miss you while you're away."

"I'll be back before you know it."

Mike enveloped me in a hug and I crushed him with all my strength, desperate for the warmth and comfort it offered.

When I opened my eyes, they landed on Seth, who stood in his doorway, staring at us. His lip curled, jaw clenching and making the veins in his neck protrude. The next thing I knew, he disappeared back inside, slamming his office door shut violently.

Mike released me from the hug and looked over his shoulder. "Don't worry about him," he muttered. "Enjoy your trip."

That would be easier said than done.

Chapter Forty One

- Seth

A nger and sadness took their turns to rule my life. Anger took the lead when we had an audience, and sadness infiltrated when there was nothing but silence and darkness.

Kiran had been gone for three weeks. Twenty-one of the longest days of my life. Despite the fact we avoided each other, ignored one another after the breakup, at least I still saw her every day.

My silence and aggression weren't aimed at her. I didn't blame her for ending our relationship, but it hurt, and I couldn't slip back into friendship with ease. Not yet. Not until I healed myself and donned all my armour again.

The space was meant to help with that. Help purge her from my system and allow me to think clearly again, but all it had done was make the ache more prominent.

It didn't help that the last glimpse of her was hugging Mike like he was a lifeline. If I hadn't slammed the door shut on them, I would have ripped her away and thrown a fist straight into his face. She hadn't said a word to me, but she could keep him close. How was that fair?

I lost count of the times I opened our message thread, wanting to talk to her. I wanted to ask her if the boys were okay. If she was enjoying her trip. If she missed me.

"Fuck!" I choked out the word.

As I laid on the couch, lost in my thoughts, Aiden dropped his full weight on my stomach and sat on top of me.

"What the fuck is wrong with you?" I spluttered, trying to push him off.

"Mum wanted me to check on you. You've skipped out on family dinners and she's missing you." Aiden rolled his eyes. "Why anyone would miss your miserable face is beyond me."

"Get off me!" I shoved him, but Aiden didn't shift. Deep down, I always knew he would be the cause of my death.

"Tell me what's wrong. Are you missing Kiran?" he asked, tipping his head back and laughing.

Another rough shove and he tumbled onto the floor, groaning.

"We broke up," I told him bluntly. My silence was doing nothing to heal me and it was pointless prolonging the issue.

"Wait, what? What did you do?" Aiden sat on the floor, looking horrified.

"I didn't do anything," I hissed. "She needed to prioritise the boys, and I had to understand that."

He blew out a breath. "Still has to hurt like fuck."

I rubbed my temples, wondering why Mum couldn't send Warren or Zane instead of the man child.

"Tell Mum I will be at dinner on Sunday," I uttered. "And see yourself out."

When Aiden didn't move, I opened my eyes to see him staring back at me.

"Don't look at me like that," I snapped.

It was his doctor look. The one that was filled with sadness and concern, and I hated it.

"You know, it's alright to be something other than angry, Seth," Aiden said. "You're allowed to hurt and be upset."

"Why? It won't bring her back to me. Won't change her mind."

"But it's healthier."

"What do you want me to say?" I exploded, shaking. "She blindsided me in every sense of the word. She waltzed into my office with all this lavender and patchouli shit and smiled and laughed, and I fell so fucking hard. I wanted to tell her and she ripped my heart out and now I have to be okay with it." Something wet and warm fell from my eyes as I let out a strangled whisper of words. "I *have* to be okay with it."

For the first time since Aiden broke my fingers in the car door, I cried. Tears spilled and I let myself feel the anguish in its raw form rather than converting into anger and malice.

"Life's not fair," Aiden said, climbing onto the sofa and sitting next to me. "But you got a shit hand, bro."

"If this is how you console patients, you should be sacked."

"You're not a patient. You're my brother," he stated, wrapping an arm around my shoulder. "You spent most of your life making sure the rest of us were doing okay. We didn't do the same when Anna left, and that was on us. How about you let the family look after you this time?"

Aiden, for all his bravado, had certain things that were close to his heart. The first was family, and the second was mental health. Losing three of his colleagues over the years had left him aware of the way people managed their brains, and I knew he was worried about my sudden, severe dip.

"I'm fine," I assured him, wiping my face. "I'm better alone."

"No one is better alone," he argued. "Pack a bag and stay with Mum and Dad."

"How pathetic."

"I'll stay as well."

"You're not making it look any better."

"Shut up," he said, punching my arm and jumping to his feet.

"Where are you going?"

"I'm going to pack your bag."

"I never agreed."

"You never disagreed."

He had a point. I followed Aiden, dragging my feet as he stuffed things into a duffle bag.

Kiran once told me I needed to let people in, and I had made enough space for her, but maybe I needed to keep trying.

Maybe I needed to rely on more people than myself.

Chapter Forty Two

- Kiran

Five weeks didn't sound that long when I signed off on the plans and organised the trip. And it didn't feel long when the sun was high in the sky. Splitting my time between work and the boys kept me busy until I was tasting colours and seeing sounds. There wasn't a single minute of my day when the schedule wasn't packed.

Even at night, when the boys drifted to sleep, and it evaded me, I set up the laptop and worked through code the way I had during university. I let numbers and symbols soothe my soul and distract me from the pain.

But with three days left before we returned home, I was struggling to avoid the swirl of emotions that threatened to pull me under. Multiple times, my fingers hovered over the keyboard, tempted to send Seth a message, but I had no idea what I would say. The ease and familiarity were wiped away, and it felt awkward again, like when we first met.

Sitting on the couch in the apartment I rented, true crime played across the screen. The grizzly tales of murderers and their motives didn't capture my interest, and I wondered if I was slowly going insane.

A hand landed on my shoulder, and I let out a small scream, twisting my body and throwing a punch. Shah stepped out of the way in time, and we both stared at each other with wide eyes.

"Why are you awake?" I asked, trying to calm my heart. "And why are you trying to kill me?"

"Are you watching serial killer stuff again? Ma, this is really unhealthy."

He came around and sat on the sofa with me.

"Something on your mind?" I asked.

Shah had thawed a little while we were away. I ruined his prom night plans and made him look uncool for Roxy, but that didn't stop her from asking him for a date when he returned home. The prospect of the pretty Russian girl being his future girlfriend had put a bounce in his step and I'd caught them on the phone a few times during our trip.

"I was going to ask you the same thing," he said. "You don't seem okay lately."

"I'm fine, sweetheart. I'm just busy," I said, shooting him a smile.

"You look lost again, Ma. You're burying yourself in work the way you did when Dad died."

I swallowed back the nausea and shook my head. "It's a new project. We need to get it off the ground. Things will calm down soon."

Shah looked at me. "You're not sleeping. You're not eating properly."

The blush spread across my cheeks and down my neck.

"It's more than work, Ma. I know it is."

"When did you become so observant?"

"When Dad left us."

I reached across and took his hand in mine. "You don't need to worry about me."

"Did he break up with you?" Shah asked, brow furrowing.

"What?" I asked, feeling the room spin.

"Seth. Did he break up with you?"

"I don't know what you mean," I lied.

"Ma. I know that you've been seeing him. Dating him. Whatever."

"You know?" I whispered, trying to get my brain to play catch up. "Oh God." I dropped my face in my hands. "How long have you known? Is that why you got drunk?"

"What?"

"It's over now," I said, straightening up. "There's no more me and Seth, and I'm sorry I didn't tell you. It was stupid —"

"He broke up with you?" Shah's features warped into something familiar. It was the same look Jamal got when he was angry. Shah shot off the sofa. "I'm going to kill him."

"No! No. Seth didn't break up with me."

He sat back down on the sofa and said, "What happened?"

"I broke up with him."

"You didn't like him?"

"Shah, this conversation is a little awkward. I didn't expect to talk about my love life with my sixteen-year-old."

"You're going to ask all about Roxy."

"It's my job."

"And this is mine. What happened, Ma?"

I pulled my feet onto the sofa and hugged them to my chest. "Life happened, Shah. I don't have time for a... to see someone."

"Because of the job?" he pried, mirroring the way I sat.

"Yes. And you and Maaz."

"Maaz and I are fine."

"Seth and Aiden brought you home completely wasted. At least now I know why."

"No, you don't."

"I do. I never meant to upset you, Shah. I shouldn't have looked at another man. Not after your dad —"

"You think I got drunk because you were dating Seth?"

"Yes."

He dropped his head to his knees and then sat up straight. "Technically, you're not wrong."

I opened my mouth, but he shook his head.

"You're not right either," he continued. "Ma, I didn't get drunk at that party because I was mad about you dating Seth. Why would I be mad when I gave him permission?"

"I'm sorry. You, what?"

"When he came to the hospital, I asked him if he liked you. It was pretty obvious. He admitted it and asked if it was okay to get to know you better."

"He never said anything," I breathed.

"Plus, I saw his car on our street that morning I came back from Connor's. I don't even want to know, but you two aren't as secretive as you think."

There was a genuine prospect I would die of embarrassment. Shah had caught us more times than I cared to count when I thought we were being careful. And Seth knew. No wonder he worried less about the impact. He already had Shah's blessing.

"I got drunk because for the first time in years, I wasn't worried about you," Shah explained quietly. "I love you, Ma, but it's been tough sometimes. Being the man of the house."

A lump formed in my throat as he spoke. Shah had been forced to grow up so quickly.

"When you and Seth started seeing each other, you changed. You seemed happy. Proper happy, Ma. You were singing in the kitchen again and going out again. And I thought I could be a teenager. You had someone, so I could do something a little stupid."

I closed my eyes. Shah wasn't rebelling. He was living a life he always should have.

"You called Seth instead of me," I whispered, opening my eyes and feeling the burn of tears.

Shah rubbed the back of his neck. "I knew you were going to hit the roof. Seth was a safer bet."

"You never go to anyone for anything," I pointed out.

"I don't know. Seth's been alright. He treats Maaz really well apart from the Dad incident."

"What Dad incident?"

He cringed, and I waited for him to answer. With a sigh, he said, "Maaz called him Dad."

"When?" I asked, my voice raising an octave.

"When we got fitted for suits."

I had this all wrong. I broke up with Seth because I thought he wouldn't be able to fit into the boys' lives without some destructive consequences, but he had been working his magic behind the scenes.

"Ma, I didn't mean to ruin your happiness," Shah said.

"Oh no, sweetheart. Come here." I opened an arm and Shah scooted over, resting his head on my shoulder the way he used to when he was a young boy. "You didn't ruin anything."

"Sometimes I still get mad at Dad for leaving us," he admitted. "Because he left you to do it all — the business and us."

"It's an honour to be your mum."

"I'm not saying that you hate it. But you shouldn't have been left like that."

"He had his reasons, baby. We're never going to know why, but he felt that was his answer." I hugged him close and kissed the top of his head.

"But you deserve to be happy, Ma. You were happy with Seth, and I don't want you to lose that. Do you want me to talk to him?"

I laughed. "I think you lot have done more than enough talking."

"I'll explain it was my fault."

"It wasn't your fault," I told him firmly.

"Are you going to get back together with him?"

"I don't know if that's what he wants."

"You won't know if you don't ask him."

"That requires being exceptionally brave."

"And you're the bravest person I know." Shah looked up at me and rolled his eyes. "Don't cry, Ma. You're so soft." He wiped my cheek, and I pulled him in for another hug. "Talk to him when we get home. Start living your life again."

"You just want me to be busy so I don't ask you about Roxy."

He pushed away from me and got up from the sofa. "I'm going to bed now."

"We will be having the safe sex talk."

"Just as long as you practise what you preach," he called back before disappearing into his room.

Chapter Forty Three

- Kiran

he plan was to head into the office early. I would knock on Seth's door with all the courage I had mustered and demand for us to talk. I wanted him to hear me out and if, after that, he decided he didn't want to be with me, then I would learn to move on. Thank him for opening my heart again and live with the fact that maybe in the future, I could fall in love again.

But life never went according to my plans. My car battery was flat and by the time I made it into the office, it was closer to lunch.

"Boss lady!" Astra said, rushing over to me and pulling me into a bone-crushing hug. "We've missed you."

"Astra, we've chatted every day."

"Not the same as seeing you in the flesh. How do you like the new colour?"

Her teal blue locks had turned into a beautiful mixture of purples. Dark at the roots and lavender at the tips.

"It's beautiful," I said, catching the end of her bob in my fingertips.

She squealed and hugged me again before letting me go.

"Nice to have you back, Kiran," Kirsty said from her desk.

"Thank you," I replied with a smile. "Is Seth in his office?"

"Not this morning. He's with Molly."

Molly?

"I hope he brings her in this afternoon," Astra said, sitting behind her desk again. "She's bloody gorgeous."

My stomach dropped like I had taken the biggest dive on a rollercoaster.

"He doesn't like bringing her to the office," Kirsty argued.

Astra shrugged. "That hasn't stopped him before."

"I'll be in the office if anyone needs me," I said, trying to stop the unfamiliar sensation that was clawing at my chest.

"Kiran! The door!" Astra called.

But it was too late. I walked straight into the glass and hissed.

"Are you okay?" she asked.

I waved her off and pulled the door open before hurrying into my office. Closing the door for privacy, I dropped into my chair and started up my computer.

Molly.

Who the fuck was Molly?

I had no right to be hurt because Seth was... What was he doing? Flaunting his new girlfriend in the office. A new girlfriend who was gorgeous. So gorgeous that Seth didn't like bringing her in. He had a possessive streak, and probably didn't like anyone else looking at her.

Oh God. I told him the laws of the universe demanded he end up with some underwear model and the universe had delivered. I was sending a massive middle finger to the cosmos for listening to me. There was no way I was going to be able to compete with a model.

And if he was bringing her to the office, then they had to be serious. This wasn't a one-time thing.

A grand total of seven weeks was all it took for Seth to move on. The thought made me itch and the crushing weight of inadequacy made my shoulders slump.

He was happy, and that was what mattered. Seth craved stability and love. He wanted someone who would stick by him, and I had done the complete opposite. He deserved to find a woman who would give him everything he wanted and more.

Despite that thought, I pulled up Google and typed in 'Seth Sinclair and Molly'. It was against my better judgement, but I was a woman possessed. If I saw them together on the internet, maybe it would lessen the blow when he breezed through the office with his *bloody, gorgeous* girlfriend.

But there was nothing. Searching for Seth brought up old articles from before I went away. There was nothing new. If he was bringing Molly to the office, how had the press not got a hold of them yet? Unless he was being extra cautious after what had happened at the rugby game. He was being protective. Of course.

My day at work went from one disaster to another as I met with project students who were hitting brick walls in their research. By the end of the day, I was ready to type up my resignation, take a new name, and move to the other side of the world.

"No. You are not hiding," I muttered to myself as I packed up my things at the end of the day.

Getting up from my desk, I walked to the space in front of it and straightened out my dress. Taking in a deep breath through my nose, I pasted on a smile and stuck out my hand.

"Molly, right?" I said brightly. "Nice to meet you."

It sounded so fake that I sighed and tried again.

"Hi, Seth. Oh, *this* is Molly. So nice to meet you. Are you working here? Me? I have the office across from Seth so you'll probably see me a lot."

I was losing my mind.

"Hi, Molly. I'm Kiran. It's nice to meet y —"

"What are you doing?"

I squeaked in surprise and turned around to see Seth standing in the doorway of my office. The electronic buzz when it opened had been drowned out by my temporary madness.

He leant against the doorframe, ankles crossed and his arms folded across his chest. The designer shirt strained across his muscles and the trousers sat snug against his thighs. Seth sported a little stubble across his jaw and a glint of amusement in his eyes.

"Nothing," I said, wrapping my arms around myself.

"Sure," he said, sounding like he didn't believe me. "Good to have you back in the office, Jafri."

"It's good to be back. I missed this place."

I missed you.

"I was just leaving," I explained, grabbing my bag.

"Same. I stopped in to clear some things with the patents department. We can head out together."

He continued to stand in the doorway, forcing me to squeeze past him. The heat of his body so close to mine made my skin prickle.

"You weren't in the office today," I commented as we walked towards the lift.

"I was a little busy," he said, rubbing the back of his neck.

"With Molly?"

His head snapped towards me. "You know about Molly?"

"Astra and Kirsty were talking about her." The lift arrived, and we stepped inside as I continued. "Sounds like you found someone that everyone's taken a shine to."

Seth blinked a few times. "I guess I did," he said eventually.

"Where is she? I'd love to meet her."

"She's with Aiden in the foyer."

"You trusted Aiden with her?" I laughed. "She must be a keeper."

"Oh, she is," he said, shrugging his shoulders. "It was love at first sight."

My heart crumpled in my chest and the air rushed out of my lungs. "That's rare. You better keep hold of her."

"This is for life."

I stared forward, unable to say anything else.

"How was your trip?" Seth asked.

"Mhm. It was fine," I managed to answer.

The doors to the lift opened, and I was so grateful. The foyer was a bright open space and I could see the revolving door that would lead me to freedom.

"See you tomorrow," I said, feeling the lump in my throat.

As I went to bolt across the space, Seth caught my elbow and kept me by his side.

"What's wrong?" he asked, staring down at me.

"Nothing."

"Don't lie."

I shook my head, unable to tell him I was a ridiculous human being who was trying to piece my life together and made the biggest mistake when I let him go.

A shadow fell across us and I turned my head to see Aiden walking towards us with a huge grin on his face.

"Gorgeous!" he said, pulling me into his arms and hugging me. My feet left the ground and I couldn't help but laugh. "Broke my brother's heart and I can only hope that it's because you saw some sense and realised I am your one and only."

"Put her down," Seth said firmly.

"Two more seconds," Aiden replied, continuing to hug me.

"Now!"

He dropped me, and Seth grabbed my arm and pulled me to his side.

"What did I tell you?" he hissed at Aiden.

"She's technically not yours anymore," Aiden argued.

"Where's Molly?"

"Maaz and Shah are with her."

In my Molly-filled haze, I forgot my sons were meeting me tonight. And now they were with Miss Supermodel, and I looked like the frumpy mum who couldn't get her shit together.

"I don't appreciate you leaving my children with strange women," I snapped at Aiden. "I don't know anything about her."

"Strange women?" Aiden echoed, but I pushed past him, not wanting to listen to his reasoning.

As I strode across the foyer, I caught sight of my sons. Shah sat on one the chairs, but Maaz was on the polished floor playing with a large golden Labrador.

"Ma!" Maaz laughed, signing. "Seth got a dog! Come and meet Molly!"

My jaw dropped, and I turned back towards Seth, who stopped beside me while Aiden joined the boys.

Looking smug, he said, "I think we need to have a conversation, flower."

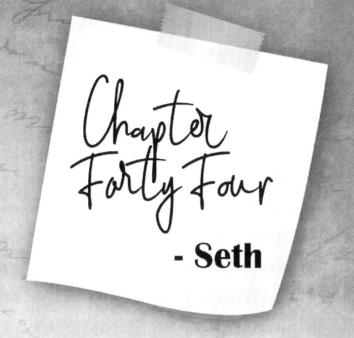

Chapter Forty Four

- Seth

I would never admit it out loud, but Aiden did the best thing for me by taking me to my parents' house. He stuck to my ass whenever he wasn't at the hospital and came to Battersea with me when I decided I wanted to put my efforts into a fluffy best friend. I owed him more than I would ever tell him for making sure I didn't get caught in my head.

That was fine until I realised Kiran was due back in the office. I avoided the building for the day, taking Molly to the groomers instead and sitting in the park where she ran around happily.

I'd done a lot of thinking over the past five weeks. There was a lot I wanted to say to Kiran, but I wasn't sure she would want to hear it.

At least, not until I saw her talking to herself in the office, introducing herself to an imaginary person.

Absence makes the heart grow fonder, was such a bullshit saying. It didn't make you fonder. It drove you to the brink of insanity until you finally had the cure in sight. Kiran dressed in that yellow dress was all I needed for the pounding thoughts to stop and the pain in my chest to ease.

And then came the flood of questions about Molly.

My flower, my ray of sunshine wouldn't admit that she was jealous. She pasted on a smile and told me what she thought she should. Covered up any speck of hurt to support my decisions. Kiran really believed that I would move on from her that quickly. If Aiden didn't already have the position, I would have crowned her the dumbest smart person in my life.

She didn't mutter a word as I drove us back to my house. Aiden had taken the boys and Molly to give us some privacy.

"Molly's the dog," Kiran said as we stepped into the house.

She walked through into the living room without invitation and my heart warmed at the familiarity. This was her sanctuary away from the rest of the world. I was glad she hadn't forgotten.

"Molly is my dog," I said, following her into the room.

"You have a dog. And you wanted me to believe she was your new…"

"I didn't want you to believe anything. You had an idea in your head and you ran with it. Would there be a problem if I had a new girlfriend?"

It was almost imperceptible, the way she crumpled for a nanosecond before pasting on the smile.

"No," she said. "If that's what you want."

My feet moved of their own accord, crossing the space between us. Kiran stood firm as my toes met hers.

"What do you want?" I asked.

"It doesn't matter," she replied, glancing away.

"Bullshit. It matters to me."

That forced her attention back to me, and I cupped her face in my hands.

"If you're ready to date," she said, covering my hands with her own. "You should."

"I'll be ready in another twelve to thirteen years."

Her nose scrunched up in that cute way it did when she was confused. "I don't understand."

"If I have to wait until Maaz is eighteen for you to give me your time, for us to try again, then I'll wait."

Kiran's red lips parted as she took in a breath. "You're not being serious," she whispered as colour flooded her cheeks.

"I am."

"Why would you do that?" she asked.

Gently, I brought my forehead against hers, staring into those dark eyes. It was stupid to think I could ever cleanse myself of her. Kiran was mine, and I would take her in whatever way she could offer herself to me. Right now, that meant friendship, but I needed her to know that the moment we could have more, I would take it without hesitation.

"Because," I said, resisting the urge to kiss her, "you are all that I want. I love you. I wanted to tell you that but…"

"But?"

"But you broke up with me."

She swallowed the lump in her throat. "Can we sit down, please?"

I took her hand and led her towards the sofa. The moment we sat down, she shifted, straddling my lap and locking her hands around the back of my neck. Her eyes were wet with tears and she took in a few shaky breaths.

"Shah knew about us," she said quietly. "But you knew that."

"I did," I replied, not embarrassed at being caught out.

"Why didn't you say anything? Why didn't you say that morning?"

"Flower, you have a family. I'm still trying to figure out how and if I fit into that. You needed to protect them, and I wasn't going to argue with you if that's what you felt was best."

"I thought there was a problem, and that's why he was drinking. I thought it was because of us but he said…" Her bottom lip trembled, and I couldn't help but lean forward and brush mine against them.

"What did he say, darling?" I asked.

"He said he was just being a teenager. Enjoying things the way he's supposed to."

The laugh that left my lips was bright and Kiran dropped her head on my shoulder. I rubbed her back gently.

"He's going to cause some trouble," I muttered into her hair. "Teamed with your little hurricane Maaz, I don't know how you're going to cope."

Kiran's body shook against my own, but only when she lifted her head did I realise it wasn't from laughter.

"I love you," she whispered, looking at me.

"I know you do."

The words lit me up like a Christmas tree. Deep down, I knew we had crossed the line from casual feelings into something more. The night I spent at her place would never have happened if she didn't love me. Kiran wouldn't allow me to keep her in my arms all night and wake up beside her if she didn't think we had something serious brewing between us.

"God, you have such a fucking ego." She tried to move off my lap, but I grabbed her waist and kept her seated.

"I love you too," I told her again.

"Are you sure?"

"Kiran." I laughed. "I've never been more certain of anything in my life."

"Seth, could we try again? I understand if you don't —"

I cut off her uncertainty with a kiss. She hesitated for a moment before letting herself melt into the embrace. Her fingers moved into my hair and my hands slipped down to her ass. There would never be a time where I let Kiran disappear across the globe for so long without me again.

"Is that a yes?" she asked against my lips.

"Yes. Are we hiding this time?" I teased.

"No," she said, kissing me again. "I want them to know we're together."

Aiden sat on the sofa at Kiran's home beside Shah and Maaz as if he was also one of her kids. Nothing we said could get him to leave, and it was a fruitless attempt when Maaz had attached himself to Molly. So news of our relationship was delivered to three people and a dog.

Kiran's hand trembled in mine and I pulled her into my side, wrapping an arm around her waist.

Shah nodded his head slowly. "I'm glad you guys worked it out." He stood from the sofa. "I'm going to call Roxy."

"Shah," I said as he walked to the stairs. He looked back at me. "Thanks."

He shrugged. "Don't expect me to call you Dad. And look after her. She's the best thing you'll ever have."

"Go," Kiran told him firmly, embarrassed.

Shah spared his mother a smile before racing up the stairs.

It was the most I could have hoped to get from him. He was still a closed book, still dealing with what life had given him. With everything out in the open, I hoped we could talk a little more so it could be less awkward, but I couldn't expect that overnight.

"Seth's your boyfriend?" Maaz asked, moving his hands as his brows pinched together.

Kiran moved from my side and sat on the coffee table in front of her youngest son. "Is that okay?"

"What happens now?"

"What do you mean?" Kiran asked.

"Are you getting married?"

Aiden tipped his head back and laughed, and I shot him a dirty look before sitting next to Kiran.

"Not yet," I said, ignoring the look she sent me.

"Maaz, buddy," Aiden cut in. "Seth might be here a little more because he wants to spend time with your mum. And you have more fam —"

"Aiden," Kiran said firmly. "No. Don't do that. I don't want his hopes up." She was still protective. Still planning for the worst when she didn't need to.

I thought Aiden would argue, but he just shrugged. "There's a lot of people that will want to meet you."

Maaz looked thoughtful. "Are you going to kiss?"

"Probably," I told him.

He pulled a face. "Can't you get another dog instead of a girlfriend?"

"Thanks, dippy," Kiran muttered.

"I think, for now, I'm going to keep your mum and Molly."

Maaz let out an exasperated sigh before sitting up straight. "Will you bring Molly over when you come to visit?"

"Sometimes."

"Can I visit her?"

"If your mum says it's okay."

"You two mean nothing," Aiden said. "He's besotted with the dog."

"I can tell," Kiran said, rolling her eyes. She leant forward and kissed Maaz's forehead. "I love you. Nothing is changing. Not really."

Part of me believed she was trying to convince herself. Kiran was tentative about thinking too far ahead when it came to her personal life. She needed to process things in her own time, but there would be plenty of changes around her. Plenty of time to adjust.

"Can we have fish fingers for dinner?" Maaz asked, apparently done with the conversation.

"Sure, sweetheart," Kiran said.

Maaz hopped off the sofa, with Molly dutifully following him out of the room.

"Second time!" Aiden wailed, collapsing across her sofa. "Fate gave you a second chance to pick me and you still went for the miserable git. How could you break my heart like that, gorgeous?"

My hands balled in my lap, but Kiran turned her head towards me with the genuine, blinding smile she possessed. "There was never any competition."

Epilogue

Six Months later

- Kiran

"What are you two whispering about?" I asked, catching Seth and Shah muttering to each other on the sofa.

"Nothing," they both answered.

I narrowed my eyes, but shook my head. "I don't trust either of you. I'm going up to bed to work on some emails."

"Kiran," Seth said, frowning.

"Two," I told him. "Two emails and I'll put work away for the night."

"I'll be up in five minutes to make sure that's true."

I poked my tongue out at him and left the room. Without question, Seth would follow me and make sure I switched off for the night. He understood the need to work, but he also wanted me to find some balance. It was a change.

Everything with Seth brought with it change.

Two months after getting back together, I moved with the boys into Seth's home. The attention from the press was enough to make me vomit, but Seth sent out a lengthy statement, backed by the threat of legal action, about privacy. It didn't completely stop the cameras, but it allowed us to breathe and it kept the boys away from column inches.

Seth had to adjust to changes too. His pristine house in its glorious show home state became an explosion of colour under my direction. We spent weekends as a family painting each room, which took longer than needed when paint fights broke out. The boys left a mess wherever they went, and I wasn't any better. But not once had Seth complained. I think he enjoyed the chaos of family life.

As I hit the top step, I stopped by Maaz's bedroom door and poked my head in. My little boy was tucked up under his covers, fast asleep, with Molly dozing at the end of the bed. She had taken a liking to Maaz from the moment they met, and nothing had torn them apart since.

Closing the door to his room, I walked into mine and Seth's bedroom. The walls had changed from beige to purple, and sticky notes hung around the room. Books on serial killers and ancient Egypt were stacked on the bedside tables.

My gaze landed on the framed photo on my bedside. The last family photo with Jamal. Seth had bought me the frame when I moved in, and I bawled, unable to thank him for a few minutes as I caught my breath.

Grabbing the tablet from the drawer, I opened my emails and replied to the two urgent ones that had come through over dinner. I was starting on a third when I looked up to see Seth walk into the room. He came towards me with a hand outstretched and I typed quicker before he hovered over me, pinching the tablet from my hand.

"Enough for tonight, flower," he said, kissing me.

"Fine." I sighed as he moved away to put the tablet in his drawer.

I plucked a pad of sticky notes from mine and started to scrawl reminders on them for the morning. Rolling out of bed, I went to the wall and placed them in a gap.

"Darling," Seth called. "Why don't you clean up the notes? It's been a while."

"I guess you're right," I said, jamming the pen behind my ear.

Methodically, I worked along the wall, tugging off notes that I already dealt with. Lists of books and shows I wanted to get through, Mike's annual leave dates, questions for Maaz's parents' evening.

I stopped at a note that had been taped to the wall. The list of reasons Seth wanted me. When we moved, I kept it in my purse, but Seth found it and taped it onto our bedroom wall so I could see it every morning. Three more notes had joined it since in his messy scribble, extending his list of reasons and making my heart completely unsteady every time I read them.

I heard Seth's footsteps behind me, one strong arm wrapping around my middle. Whether appropriate or not, Seth kept his hands on me whenever we were near each other. He didn't like space and I didn't argue. There was a sense of peace when I was with him. A sense of belonging that made everything feel like it would be alright. That nothing bad would happen.

With a smile on my face, I continued to clean up the wall until I came across another Seth-scribbled note. My brow furrowed as he released his grip on me, and I read the words.

I finally found my heart – Tin Man x

Plucking it from its spot on the wall, I laughed and turned around. The laughter died on my lips when I saw my boyfriend was no longer standing behind me.

Seth was down on one knee in the middle of our bedroom, looking up at me earnestly.

"What are you doing?" I whispered, unable to look away from his face.

"Kiran. Flower," Seth said, fiddling with the box in his hands. "When I met you, I told you I was still searching for my heart. I didn't realise that you had it all along. From the moment I saw you in the office, walking up to me like you owned the place, I knew I was completely powerless against you. You bled colour into my life, Kiran. You and the boys have become my world."

"And Molly," I interrupted, struggling to breathe.

"And Molly." He laughed. "Kiran, it would be the greatest honour of my existence if you became my wife. Will you make a miserable prick the happiest he can be? Would you marry me?"

Fat tears rolled down my face as I launched myself at Seth.

"Fuck!" he yelped as I took us both down to the floor.

"Yes! Yes!" I told him, still crying. "Yes, please."

He opened the box, slipping a solitaire diamond ring onto my finger. I might have tried to keep things modest and my family grounded as our fortune grew, but Seth had grown up in a luxurious lifestyle so modest wasn't in his vocabulary.

"It's beautiful," I told him, extending my hand out and looking at it.

"Still pales compared to you," he replied.

I bit my bottom lip. "We need to tell the boys."

Seth laughed. "They already know. That note has been stuck on the wall for two fucking weeks, sweetheart. You almost killed me."

"Two weeks! Why didn't you say anything?"

"And spoil the fun?"

"You still had to give me a gentle push."

"Because we probably would have waited a year otherwise."

I slapped his chest before he pulled me closer and kissed me deeply.

"I love you, Kiran. More than anything in this world."

"I love you too, Seth."

He sat us both up on the floor, him in his boxers and me in pyjama trousers that were covered in bats. It wasn't a fancy proposal, but it was perfectly us.

A little messy and full of a lot of love.

The End

Keep In Touch

If you want to keep up to date with all the news on my writing and releases you can follow me on:

Instagram:
@naaz_spencer

Facebook Group:
Happily Ever After Inc

Pinterest:
@naaz_spencer

Goodreads & Amazon

Acknowledgments

Alhumdulillah.

Mama and sis, you were both there when I almost fell of the sofa as the Sinclairs infiltrated my head. You pushed me to write this series and were as excited as I was to put these brothers into the world. I'm thankful for all your support. Also, Mama, thanks for answering every single question I had regarding children.

I may have written the words, but the sheer gorgeousness of this book comes down to two amazing humans. Val from Books and Moods, this cover is one of my favourites that you created. AJ, I'm so glad to have worked with you again for the interior. I'm so grateful to work with you both in making my books look the best they can.

I cannot write a book without my editor, Zainab. There is a deep gratitude to you that is difficult to express. You don't only polish my stories, but you keep my head on straight. Thank you for letting me cry my eyes out at you and dusting me off and telling me to keep going. You're an amazing human being.

My chaotic twin! Laura Sunday, you wonderful lady. Thank you for your infectious enthusiasm towards this story. You saw Seth and Kiran in their raw form and helped to shape them into what they are today.

Sarah, I don't know how you have put up with me. You were one of the first to hear about all seven brothers and the disastrous lives they lead. Thanks for listening to my half-baked ideas and helping form them into something more. I know you hate me saying thank you, but you can't yell at me here…

Every idea that ever pops into my head is sent directly to Ellie. Thank you for never doubting my madness. I was worried about stepping into a new genre, but you have been my biggest cheerleader. You inspired this story and I'm forever grateful to have you in my life.

Printed in Great Britain
by Amazon

76098373R00206